BATTLE CRY

By Rosie Jones

First Published in 2020 by Blossom Spring Publishing
Battle Cry © 2020 Rosie Jones
ISBN 978-1-8380188-1-8
E: admin@blossomspringpublishing.com
W: www.blossomspringpublishing.com
Published in the United Kingdom. All rights reserved

Chapter One

They were coming to the end of their tour, and there was a distinct buzz throughout the platoon. For six months they had endured what had, at times, felt like constant attacks, heavily restricted rations and a distinct lack of sanitary facilities. Now they were just days away from returning to the UK. In fact, it was their last day at the Forward Operating Base and this would be their last patrol.

They were all kitted up and ready to go, body armour and helmets on, psyching themselves up for what would be a very long day. The only light came from the glow of the moon; the base was vulnerable in the middle of the Sangin Desert, and artificial light would draw attention to it which they certainly did not need. Even when blacked out, the base had suffered numerous attacks which had only seemed to intensify in the last few weeks. The company had lost many soldiers to injury and several to death during the six months of the tour, and morale was low. But the thought of going home had given them a welcome boost. They just had to get through this last patrol.

"I can't wait to go out and get smashed," one of the privates, known as Melon, muttered to his best friend Jase, pulling on his fingerless gloves and rubbing his hands together as if preparing for battle.

"Roger that, mate," Jase grinned, fastening

the velcro on his own wrists. "And find a girl with massive…"

"Coulson. Perry. Shut your mouths," the voice of their section commander, Sergeant Mellor, cut him off.

"Sir," they stood to attention as their commanding officer, Lieutenant Swan, appeared at the front.

"Stand at ease," he barked, and the platoon relaxed.

While he ran through their mission, Lance Corporal Jess Fern scanned over the dozens of soldiers ready to go. She had served with these soldiers as their medic for six months, gone on patrol with them, eaten with them, slept with them and shared her very limited downtime with them. It was hard to believe that this time next week they would be back in the UK. It was a strange thing, returning home. She looked forward to it from the moment she first arrived on base in a war zone, and the thought of getting back kept her going even through the hardest of times. The thought of seeing her loved ones again, taking unlimited hot showers and eating proper home cooked food was enough to spur her on through any ambush. And yet when she arrived in the UK it was never what she had anticipated. Within a few days of leave, she was bored of the mundanity of civilian life; she ached for another challenge. Every time she found herself counting back down the days until she was back on base with the boys again. But, she reminded herself as she looked around, she couldn't take it as a given that they would all be returning home until the moment their aircraft touched down in the UK. Anything could happen.

Today, they were to offer support and security to Afghan soldiers searching nearby village compounds for weapons and IED components. It sounded straightforward enough, but it wasn't. Not at all. The area was rife with mines and IEDs and had to be scoured meticulously before they could pass through. That was Jase's job. As Vallon man, he would walk at the front with a military grade metal detector, scanning the ground carefully to provide a safe route of passage for the rest of the platoon.

Jess was proud of Jase. Six months ago, he had stepped out on his first patrol as Vallon man, the metal detector in his hand and a look of sheer terror in his eyes like a rabbit in the headlights of a car. But by the time he had led a few patrols, he walked taller, he was more confident and decisive. As the tour drew to a close, he alone had detected more than forty IEDs. Every member of the platoon trusted him with their lives. One wrong move or moment of distraction, and the whole section could be wiped out.

Jess scanned over the section for a final time. They were in full combat gear and ready to go. Private Callum North, or Cal as he was known to the rest of the section, was the youngest at just nineteen years old. It was his first tour and Jess had also enjoyed watching him grow from a bit of a loose cannon to a well disciplined soldier.

She caught the eye of Corporal Shane

Little, the company's lead medic, and nodded discretely. He smiled and nodded back, an exchange which spoke volumes but with no words. *Good luck.* They both knew that this patrol would be dangerous. They were both experienced enough to know that the last patrol was usually the most dangerous of the whole tour. Psychologically, the soldiers were almost home - and that often equalled complacency. Unfortunately, there was no room for that at all when at the mercy of the Taliban. The medics were optimistic but realistic; it was very unlikely that they would be bringing back a complete and uninjured platoon that evening. They would just have to do the best they could to support their soldiers and make sure that they received the very best medical treatment, should the need arise.

As the platoon prepared to move, Jess stood taller, straightening her helmet with one hand whilst maintaining her grip on her weapon with the other. Two heavily armed Afghan guards unbolted and opened the gate, and she felt a shot of adrenaline coursing through her veins. They began to move. Accompanied by a platoon of Afghan soldiers, 1 and 2 Sections were to leave in an easterly direction and start on the southern edge of the nearby village, and 3 Section were to leave in a westerly direction and approach the village from the north.

The sections split. Jase took the front of 1 and 2 Sections and they began to make their moonlit journey towards the village. Behind Jase, Colour Sergeant Merrett, 2 Section's commander, listened in his earpiece to control room intelligence from intercepted Taliban radio conversations. Whilst Jase continued the painstaking task of searching for IEDs, the rest of the section had their night vision goggle clad eyes on their surroundings at all times - any sign of movement and they would all drop down to cover while assessing the threat. The area was extremely hostile, and it was unlikely that any genuine villagers would stray this far from the village, especially this early in the morning. Even the village itself was a shell of its former self, abandoned compounds offering insurgents the perfect storage facilities for weapons and IED components.

The water-filled irrigation ditches, which they reached after walking through several poppy fields, were almost a relief as they dropped down into them. It was not even light yet, but the temperature was already in the low thirties, and the humidity stifling. Climbing back up the other side of the ditch, Jess thought about the cool, fresh air of England, her boots squelching with mud and beads of sweat already dripping from her forehead. Gunshot wounds and amputations were not the only things that they had to worry about in Helmand. Many of the soldiers were now becoming battle tired, suffering from exhaustion and other ailments.

Once the sun began to rise, they could see the shadow of the village in the distance, the first compound walls rising from the desert ominously. It felt like they had been walking for hours but they had only covered a couple of miles; their pace was painstakingly slow. Jess could see a few shades of colour starting to litter the black of the night sky; they began as a deep purple and then, once the blackness turned navy, she could see shoots of red, orange, yellow and a lighter shade of blue scattered across it. It seemed ironic, such a beautiful, peaceful sky sitting directly above one of the world's most dangerous kill zones.

Jess was almost at the back of the patrol, only trailed by Sergeant Mellor and a group of Afghan soldiers. She felt well enveloped by the group. Mellor was one of the most outstanding soldiers she had ever had the pleasure of working with, and she had really grown to respect him during the tour. She had not been sure when she had first met him; he'd had an air of arrogance about him, and the way he looked at her made her feel small, as though she was setting off for her very first mission as a brand new medic, straight out of training. But within a week she had clearly proven herself to him, as his attitude towards her had changed. Now he seemed to value her input a lot, and in turn she valued his. He had a very methodical approach, and that had clearly rubbed off on the young privates in the section - they were now efficient and well oiled platoon members.

As visibility increased, so too did the attention they drew to themselves. It had taken longer than expected to reach the village, partially due to the number of IEDs Jase had detected, and partly due to the number of times they had needed to stop when detecting movement around them and Afghan chatter on the radio. Approaching the village there was a very eerie atmosphere, and Jess instinctively felt on edge. It was difficult to describe why. It was just a feeling; after seven years of serving on the front line, she had a good sixth sense. They passed a couple of fighting age males who appeared to have no business being in the area. Mellor called it in, maintaining eyes on them as they passed the section.

Whilst passing Jess, one of them made eye contact with her. She narrowed her eyes and he looked right into her eyes as if he could see deep inside her soul. He narrowed his eyes back. Jess felt another shot of adrenaline course through her veins and she tightened her grip on her weapon, quietly relaying her gut feeling to Mellor who had noticed the same. But within a few minutes the men were out of sight again, and 1 and 2 Sections pressed on.

Two and a half hours had passed by the time they got to the edge of the village, and they were all tired. By now the temperature had climbed to the mid-forties and every member of the section needed to replenish the water they had lost through sweat. Dust swirled around in the air and coated Jess's skin; her lips felt dry and she licked them subconsciously, only to take a mouthful of sand.

They were only about ten meters from the first compound and the Afghan soldiers were about to initiate phase one of their search when it happened, so quickly that nobody had time to react. Jess was thrown backwards by the force of the blast. By the time she opened her eyes, she could barely see for the sand swirling around her and she had no idea where she was or where the rest of the section were. Her ears were ringing and the sounds from around her were distant and echoey as though she was at the end of a very long, dark tunnel. And then one voice emerged from the rest and she could hear him, loud and clear. *Medic! Man Down! Man Down!*

The dust began to clear. Jess leapt up off the floor and sprinted towards the casualties. The call for a medic was enough to break her out of the momentary bubble she had found herself in, and she rushed forwards to the bodies lying on the ground. Her ears were still ringing from the blast but she began to assess the casualties presented to her, ignoring the instinctive concern at the back of her mind that the insurgents were probably still around and ready to attack again.

Merrett, a group of Afghan soldiers, Shane and Melon had all been caught in the blast, as well as Corporal Gavin Jones. Silently she began to assess them, quietest first, her hands shaking and her heart thumping in her chest like a war drum. In the background she heard Mellor calling in for urgent assistance whilst the rest of 1 and 2 Sections jumped into defensive positions. Realising the true cost of the blast, she felt violently sick. Merrett and Shane had been killed instantly. Half of Merrett's face was missing, and the emptiness in Shane's wide, lifeless eyes brought tears to Jess's eyes. With trembling hands, she reached forwards and closed his eyelids gently, then forced herself to continue - it was of course what he would have wanted, and what he had spent many hours of his time training her for. They had also lost two Afghan soldiers to catastrophic blast injuries. It was heartbreaking having to effectively ignore those who were already dead, but she still had Gav and Melon to treat and she absolutely had to prioritise those who still had a chance.

Trying to stop just one of the injured soldiers from bleeding out would have been a job on its own, but here she was with four killed in action and two with category A injuries. On her own. In the middle of a kill zone. She no longer had Shane to lead her, and she knew it was time to step up.

"Four KIA, two Cat-A," she relayed as Mellor transmitted a nine liner over his radio.

"I'll be with you in a second, Melon," she reassured. He was screaming in agony, the lower half of both legs completely unrecognisable with blood and scrambled tissue. "Can someone get some pressure on those legs."

Whilst Raj, one of the other privates, did so she assessed Gav who was quietly clutching his right arm as it spurted blood rhythmically, the lower part of which had been completely annihilated by the blast. Quiet was never good. Once she was satisfied with his primary signs, she pulled the tourniquets out of her medical kit and pulled one tight around the stump of his arm. Then she covered the wound with a large gauze pad, administering a shot of pain relief in the hope that he wouldn't pass out from the pain.

"You're gonna be ok, Gav," she promised, once the bleeding was under control.

Turning back to Melon, Jess realised that both his legs had been completely obliterated. Her heart sank.

"Good job, Raj," she muttered, slipping a tourniquet onto each stump followed by a dressing. "Stay with me, Melon."

His eyes rolled back in his head and Jess shouted his name, trying to keep him awake. She was not about to let him go, not like this.

"Melon!" She patted his cheeks firmly with the palms of her hands. "Open your eyes! Stay with me!"

She looked up to find Jase standing there, wide eyed, his metal detector still in his hand. He looked completely spaced out, as though he was an unsuspecting civilian who had suddenly been dropped there. "Jase!" When he didn't respond Jess barked it again, louder, until he finally seemed to hear her. "Get down here and hold his hand. Keep him talking."

By now the section were looking to move to a less vulnerable position. They were like sitting ducks, and it was only a matter of time before the insurgents arrived to inflict further damage.

"The MERT is on its way," Mellor announced. "We need to move, Medic. I want the casualties behind that compound wall and then we've got clear sight over to the extraction point."

"Ok," she nodded. "Now is as good a time as any."

But time had run out. All of a sudden it started - the PUT-PUT-PUT of approaching gunfire.

"Incoming! Take cover!" Mellor commanded, and all the soldiers dropped to the floor as the first bullets began to rain down on them like a sudden burst of hailstones. Jess hated leaving the casualties exposed, but she knew that she had to do what she had been ordered or she risked the safety of the whole section. Still holding defensive positions and firing back at the insurgents, they began to follow Mellor's orders to move to cover. With the help of Cal, Jess lifted Melon and they moved as quickly as they could across the uneven dirt, towards the nearest compound wall. It wasn't ideal; they would still be exposed, but at least they would not be directly in the kill zone and they would be closer to the chinook when it landed.

They were almost at the wall when another shower of bullets came in their direction. Jess felt one bounce off her helmet and the force pushed it over her eyes; she pushed it back on with one hand while bearing Melon's weight with the rest of her body. Suddenly his weight doubled, and she saw Cal fall to the ground next to them, almost in slow motion.

"Cal!" She pleaded. "Cal! Get up!"

She knew that her first priority was to get Melon to safety and with all her strength, she managed to lift him across her back and carry him inside the relative safety of the compound, dodging bullets whilst crossing the last of the open ground.

By now the other section members were bringing in the other casualties, including the bodies of their fallen soldiers. She lay Melon on the dusty floor, propping what was left of his legs up on his bergen, in an attempt to reduce blood loss. Every bone in her body was screaming at her to get back out there to Cal, but she knew she had to stay. She was the only medic left; they already had two live soldiers with catastrophic injuries and every time she turned towards the compound entrance more casualties were being brought in. She wouldn't be any good to them if she became one too.

She could hear more approaching gunfire and was relieved to hear over her radio that Lieutenant Swan and 3 Section had arrived to provide further fire power. The chinook was expected to arrive in minutes and 3 Section were already valiantly at work, driving back the insurgents to leave a clear path for the extraction.

"Medic!" A frantic voice came through the deafening gun fire as two more casualties were carried in - Jess was relieved to see that one of them was Cal. By some miracle he was still very much alive, clutching his arm which was spewing blood like an erupting volcano.

"Get pressure on that wound," she ordered, rushing to assist with the second casualty who didn't look good. The soldiers who had brought him in slipped him carefully down onto the compound floor. There were no signs of life.

"His pulse is weak and thready," she announced, examining him as best she could through his uniform. It was hard to tell where the blood was coming from, given the copious amount of it which drenched his uniform. On further inspection, she found two entry wounds in his abdomen and one in his chest.

"Come on, Jay," she pleaded as his eyes rolled back in his head. "Stay with me!"

There was no response from him at all, and she knew that his chances were terrible. His abdomen was distended and with the ever increasing pool of blood saturating the dusty floor around him, she knew it wouldn't be very long until he bled to death.

She reached down to check his pulse again and couldn't find any trace. "Come on, Jay. Not like this."

She began CPR but she knew straight away that it would be fruitless. He was losing too much blood too quickly; clearly at least one of the bullets had pierced a major organ, and his abdomen was filling with blood. Not even the best medic in the world could save someone from that in a place like this.

As she tried and failed to resuscitate him, the casualties and small team of assisting soldiers around her looked on in devastated silence. She felt as though she might fall apart at any moment - he was only twenty one years old, a promising private with his whole career ahead of him. But then she looked around at everyone else who needed her help and she forced herself to compartmentalise - she was a medic, she would deal with her own grief later.

Once nothing more could be done and she had relayed an update for the MERT to Mellor she moved on to Cal, who was watching silently. His eyes were almost glazed over and he looked completely vacant. He and Jay had joined the platoon together and they were the youngest two members. He had a life threatening injury himself and had just watched one of his closest friends in the platoon die right in front of his eyes. Jess knew exactly what he would be thinking. It could have been me. It was nearly me.

"Cal," she lifted the gauze briefly to check the bleeding. The wound was still oozing blood. "I need to get a tourniquet on this, ok?"
Cal stared at Jay's lifeless body, unresponsive.

"I need you to keep this elevated," she directed to the nearest soldier, who obediently lifted Cal's arm above his head.

No sooner had she finished with Cal, she was back over to Melon. Jase had by now reappeared and was crouched next to Melon on the compound floor, his uniform soaked in his best friend's blood. Jess glanced at him briefly and then leant over Melon, forcing an optimistic smile.

"Melon. How are you doing?"

"I can't do this anymore," he choked, his voice weak and raspy. "I'm sorry. I'm going down."

"Yes, you can," she instructed, her smile

fading as she took his hand in hers firmly. "Hang in there, I can hear the chinook approaching. I promise you it isn't going to be long, Melon, you just need to keep fighting."

"I need you to do something for me," he rasped. Jess held two fingers under his chin. His pulse was growing weaker and his face was deathly pale, it looked as though all the blood had drained out of it.

"Tell me when we get back to Bastion," Jess smiled sympathetically.

Melon grabbed her by the elbow and held it tight, his fingers shaking with exertion.

"Tell Laura I love her. And make sure Millie always knows her dad. Tell her I'll always be there for her. Whenever she's missing me or she's upset…" he groaned as pain ripped through his body, but managed to compose himself one last time, so that he could finish his sentence, "look up to the stars. And I'll be there watching."

"Tell her yourself, mate. You'll be back in the UK by tomorrow," Jess ordered, but his eyes began to roll back in his head again and his grip on her elbow loosened.

"Melon! Keep your eyes open!" She ordered, as Jase watched frantically.

As she prepared to start CPR, the distant hum of vehicles approaching caught Jess's attention. A few seconds later, Lieutenant Swan strode in, together with 3 Section's medics.

"Three minutes until the MERT arrives. The armoured vehicles are approaching, they will be driving back the insurgents further so the

MERT can safely land, then they'll be evacuating us. Prepare the casualties to move."

Jess continued to pump on Melon's chest. "Yes, Sir."

She couldn't think too much about all the bodies around her. She couldn't risk being overcome by grief, everyone was relying on her to get the job done.

"Right, I need these casualties prepped and ready to go," she glanced up at one of the Afghan medics, checking he was listening before continuing her attempt to resuscitate Melon. "All walking wounded who need to go to the field hospital here and ready to board the aircraft. All uninjured soldiers are to help them onto the MERT. We have to be quick. The MERT will need to be out of here as soon as it touches down."

A further burst of gunfire rang out just the other side of the compound wall and she took a deep breath, momentarily pausing CPR to allow the soldier who was assisting her time to bag two breaths of air into Melon. She had no idea how the MERT was going to land and get back up again without being shot down, but she knew that she had to do everything in her power to make sure that happened. She could not lose any more soldiers.

Chapter Two

Once the last of the casualties were loaded onto the chinook, Jess ran back down the ramp past the machine gun which guarded it and took cover, sprinting back towards the compound with the rest of the soldiers who were to remain. Both 1 and 2 Sections had suffered heavy losses, as had the Afghan soldiers, with a handful of soldiers killed in action and several Cat-A injuries.

Jess's work was not done. Although the most seriously injured soldiers had been evacuated and were now in the safe hands of the Medical Emergency Response Team on their way to Camp Bastion, she still had several soldiers with minor injuries and she also needed to clear up the remaining kit. As soon as the area was secure enough, all three sections were to be extracted and return to the FOB. Once back in the relative safety of the compound, Jess looked down at her blood stained hands and arms and wondered how she would ever get them clean.

It took another ten minutes for the insurgents to fully retreat, leaving the town effectively deserted, and the platoon able to board the armoured vehicles.

"Exemplary work today, Medic," Sergeant Mellor complimented, with a glimpse of a smile. They began the painstaking drive back to the FOB. The vehicle only provided limited protection from IEDs so they had to move slowly, staying alert for anything suspicious. The alternative was for them to make their way back on foot, and the platoon was no longer strong enough to do that. Jess still had eight wounded soldiers in her charge and given the number of soldiers already extracted , they did not have enough man power to defend themselves on foot.

Jess couldn't find the words to respond. She busied herself with checking some superficial injuries sustained by the soldier next to her, all the while conscious of Mellor's gaze which was fixed on her. She couldn't talk about anything other than the job in hand because she knew that she would cry. Never in all her years of service had she lost as many soldiers in one go. She couldn't stop running it through her mind, what could she have done differently, was there anything that she had missed? She buried the thought deep in her mind for later; she had to stay strong for the rest of the platoon.

Looking up again, her eyes fell on Jase who was sitting opposite her, his head in his hands. He hadn't moved since they had boarded the vehicle.

"Jase," she frowned. "Are you ok?"

He nodded but didn't look up. Jess knew better than to push him. The whole platoon were shell shocked by what had just happened, and nobody more than Jase who had missed the IED.

"It wasn't your fault, mate," Raj clapped him on the shoulder supportively.

"Well nobody else missed the IED, did they," Jase muttered through gritted teeth. "If I hadn't have missed it then they'd still be alive."

Raj squeezed his shoulder. "Everyone makes mistakes. It's just one of those things."

"*One of those things*?" Jase reacted sharply, his eyes narrow.

"Alright, Private Coulson. That's enough. You did your best," Mellor diffused the situation instantly with a stern voice. Jase shut his mouth and stared back at the floor.

It took almost an hour for them to get back to the FOB. Reaching the base, the armoured vehicles slowed to a standstill. Nobody moved except for the soldier at the back who rose to open the rear doors. Eventually, Mellor stood up and addressed the soldiers within his vehicle.

"Alright. Those of you who don't need medical attention, get cleaned up and get some scoff. Then pack your things and get some rest, we'll be leaving at first light tomorrow. Debrief when we get back to Camp Bastion."

"Sir," they replied and then started to disembark, grateful to have made it back in one piece. Within 30 seconds the vehicle was empty except for Jess, who picked up her bergen and swung it over her shoulder. She hesitated. For some reason that she couldn't explain she felt unable to leave. Her legs suddenly felt weak and she leant on the side of the vehicle for support.

"You too, Jess," Mellor instructed softly. She glanced up at him. It was unusual for him to use her forename.

Jess opened her mouth to acknowledge him, but no words came out. Instead she felt tears prickling in the corners of her eyes and she cleared her throat, choking them back.

"I can't stop thinking about them, Sir," she whispered.

"I know. But you did your best, we all did. There was nothing more that could have been done for them. You did a brilliant job. You should be proud of that."

She gripped the handle of her bergen tightly as though it was the only thing holding her together. "I need to go to the medical centre. We still have dozens of superficial injuries to clear up…"

"No, you need to go and get cleaned up, eat and rest. The medics in the centre will manage."

"But Sir, they're already one medic down, I-"

"That's an Order, Medic," he warned sternly. "Do you understand?"

Jess paused for a moment, and then she gave in. There was no point in arguing, she knew that he wouldn't change his mind. "Yes, Sir."

"Good. Off you go."

She pulled her helmet off, then jumped out of the vehicle and began the solitary walk to 1 Section's tent. The mood on base was sombre. By now, everyone had heard about the doomed patrol. Jess knew that the rest of the team would want to know what had happened to Shane, and for a moment she contemplated turning around and walking to the medical centre against her orders. But she had little fight left in her, and she continued towards the tent.

When she got there, she dropped her bergen down on her cot and sat down next to it, her head in her hands. She was exhausted. Every inch of her skin and her uniform was covered in dried blood, it was so drenched that the pattern on her uniform was barely recognisable. She glanced at the empty cots which had been occupied by Gav, Cal, Melon and Jay the night before. In the corner of the room, Jase and Raj sat silently, having just gone through the same devastating trail of thought. Jess knew that she ought to say something to comfort Jase, but it was all she could do to hold herself together.

"We need to pack," she stated, matter of fact. She opened her bergen, pulling out anything that she wouldn't need now that their last patrol was over. "You heard the boss."

"When do you think we'll know?" Raj asked. "Whether they made it?"

Jess clenched her jaw and paused momentarily, staring at the small pile of relatively clean clothes next to her on the cot. She exhaled deeply and placed them inside the bergen.

"I don't know. As soon as I know, you'll know."

"Thanks, Jess," Raj turned back to Jase. "Melon will be fine, mate. He's a tough nut to crack."

Jase shook his head. "Nobody can withstand an IED though, can they? Not that close. If he dies, it's because of me. My *best* mate. Blown up because of me."

"It wasn't your fault, Jase," Jess dropped

the almost full bergen on to the floor. "Do you hear me? Stop it, right now. You did your best."

"I had *one* job," he narrowed his eyes. "One job, and I couldn't even do that right. It should have been me," he shook his head, tears now streaming down his face. "Why couldn't it have been me? Why am I even still alive? How am I going to live with myself?"

Jess got up off the cot and paced over to where Jase was sitting. She sat down and put her arm around him, pulling him close to her while he sobbed. It was all Jess could do to hold herself together whilst he finished his outpouring of pain. She imagined the families of the dead soldiers collapsing into tears as they were told that their loved ones hadn't made it. She cleared her throat and sniffed, looking up to the ceiling in an attempt to stop any loose tears from falling.

"It wasn't your fault," she said finally, once he stopped crying. "Now I'm going to get cleaned up. When I get back, we'll all go for scoff together, agreed?"

"Agreed," Raj replied, and Jase nodded. Jess got up and glanced at them again over her shoulder whilst leaving. Within a matter of hours, they had gone from two competent soldiers to two lost boys. War doesn't only leave physical scars, she thought to herself.

***

Sergeant Mellor left the command post completely forlorn. He stood outside for a few moments, watching the base around him. Life continued as normal. The sun was beginning to set behind the mountains in the distance, and even the odd bird continued to fly overhead. He had just lost five colleagues, three of them British soldiers, and yet you wouldn't know it looking at the base. That was the strange thing about war. There was no time to grieve for fallen colleagues because life had to go on. Tomorrow the next platoon would go out on patrol and risk their lives all over again.

He began to stride across the base towards one of the tents, the sound of his boots crunching through the sand ringing in his ears. He didn't feel like eating but he had to be there for the rest of the platoon, especially in the absence of Merrett. Passing by the shower tent, he took a deep breath and clenched his jaw. It was then that he heard it. He turned to look at the tent and then stepped forwards until he was within a foot of the thick camouflage material, and he knew exactly what it was. His stomach turned and without even realising that he was doing it, he reached out until his fingertips were just touching the tent.

Jess stood under the weak jet of water as it ran over her head and down her body. The lukewarm water she was standing in was red from the blood that was washing off her body, and she watched as trails of it ran down her limbs like a river of death. She could no longer control it; it was as though the blood was symbolic of the pain and guilt of the day breaking out of her and she gave in, succumbing to her grief in raw, angry sobs.

She thought again about the families of the fallen soldiers, answering the door only to be told that their loved ones hadn't made it. The thought was almost too much to bear. Tears streamed down her face and she continued to sob until she had nothing left. Afterwards, weak and exhausted, she turned the tap off and stepped out of the shower, then wrapped herself in a towel. It felt good to be clean. Tomorrow she would be at Camp Bastion and then on to Cyprus, where what was left of the platoon would spend a couple of days decompressing before returning back to the UK. The thought of seeing her family again and sleeping in her own bed seemed like the light at the end of the tunnel for Jess.

Once she was dry, she pulled on some fresh uniform and bagged up the bloodied clothes, ready to dispose of. They were tainted beyond recovery. In any event it just felt wrong to wear them again, somehow disrespectful to the soldiers they had touched while they slipped away. She stepped out of the shower cubicle and pulled her hair up in a quick ponytail, then slipped her boots on and walked out into the late afternoon sunlight yet again.

***

Sergeant Mellor approached the table where 1 and 2 Sections were sitting. They had trays of ration food but none of them were really in the mood to eat. It was bad enough having to eat ration food when they were hungry and in

24

good spirits, let alone when they were not.

"Alright guys, listen in. The casualties have arrived at Camp Bastion and Corporal Jones is still in surgery. Dickens and Brewer are out of surgery and stable."

Both sections breathed a sigh of relief to hear that two of their colleagues were out of danger.

"I'm sorry to have to tell you that Perry and North died on route."

The momentary sense of relief was gone and Jess watched as Jase stood up forcefully, knocking his chair on the floor with a clatter. Then he strode out of the tent. Jess started to get up out of her chair, but Mellor shook his head.

"Stay here, Medic. I've got this."

"But Sir," she started, but by that time he had already strode out of the tent behind Jase.

Jess sat back down at the table in silence and leant her elbows on it, running her fingertips through her hair. She was shaking. Cal had been alright when he got on the MERT - he had pretty much walked himself onto the chinook. How could things have gone downhill for him so quickly? What had she missed?

Outside, Mellor caught up with Jase.

"Private Coulson, you *stop* when I'm talking to you," he ordered, but it was as though Jase couldn't hear him. Eventually, he grabbed him by the shoulder and spun him around. Jase had tears in his eyes, and he looked completely broken. Mellor placed both hands firmly on his shoulders and gripped them tight.

"Now, you listen to me. How many IEDs have you detected on this tour?"

Jase's bottom lip wobbled, and he clenched his teeth together, desperately trying to stop himself from falling apart.

"Forty two, Sir."

"Right. Think how many lives you have saved on those forty two occasions."

"But I missed this one," Jase whispered, his bottom lip still trembling. "And seven men have died."

Mellor lifted his hands from Jase's shoulders. "Yes, seven men have died. But that isn't because of you. You did your best with the equipment you had available. If the Vallon missed the IED and there were no outward signs, how could you be expected to detect it?"

Jase said nothing. He knew that what Mellor was saying made sense, but he felt the weight of the dead soldiers heavily upon his own shoulders.

"I... I don't understand why it wasn't me," he faltered. "Why didn't I step on it? It should have been me who was killed."

"You got lucky," Mellor pointed up to the sky. "Someone up there is watching out for you. You got a second chance. Don't waste it."
Jase nodded and took a deep breath, standing taller.

"Good. Now, go back to the section."

"I'm not hungry, Sir. I just want to be on my own," Jase replied.

"Alright. But don't shut them out, ok?

Nobody thinks this is your fault, Jase. We work as a team."

Jase nodded and walked away. Mellor watched him disappear through the door of the tent. He felt like a hypocrite. There he was telling Jase not to blame himself, when all he had done since arriving back at the FOB was the same thing. All he had thought about was what he could have done differently, whether lives could have been saved if he had reacted more efficiently. There was no denying that the explosion had taken them all by surprise, and the loss of Merrett had unsettled him. For the first time in his military career he began to question whether he really was good enough. He had been in command of the section on what should have been a routine patrol and seven men had died, and more than a dozen had been injured. He shook his head and began to walk back towards the command room.

***

Jess finished packing her bergen and then slung it on the floor by her cot. She lay back and stared at the ceiling of the tent. It was unsettlingly quiet. Only three of them now occupied the tent and nobody had anything to say. On one hand the silence was welcome; her ears were still ringing from the explosion and she was exhausted. But she also liked being distracted. When there were no distractions, her mind slipped back to the events of the day and she struggled again.

She closed her eyes and forced herself to

think about home instead. She couldn't wait to get back and spend two weeks with her mum and her brother, Liam. After that she would be back on base for a bit until her next deployment. She pictured her bedroom with her comfortable double bed, and the big squishy sofa in the living room where she would sit with a glass of wine and watch rubbish on the television. She thought about the framed picture of her dad on the mantlepiece, which sat in pride of place. It was the last photograph they had of him. Jess stood next to him holding his hand and looking up at him proudly, and he held Liam gently in a blanket in the crook of his other arm. His army beret was perched on Jess's head; it was so big that it was slipping over her eyes, but she didn't care. She still remembered that photograph being taken and feeling like the coolest kid in the world, wearing a real army beret. It was at that moment that Jess had decided she wanted to follow in her dad's footsteps and join the army as soon as she could.

She felt tears in her eyes as her mind continued to wander, and she let them fall. One of the things she found hardest when she lost a soldier was the thought of their family receiving that fateful visit, just like she had when her dad had been killed. It was a cold winters day, just a week before Christmas, and Jess had been helping her mum make gingerbread men to take round to the neighbours while Liam slept in his crib. The smell of gingerbread lit up the house like a real life Christmas grotto and once the biscuits were ready, Jess had sprinkled icing sugar on them like a soft dusting of snow.

"Go and get the bags and ribbons then, Jessie," her mum smiled, and Jess skipped happily off to the living room where she knew they were waiting on the table next to the Christmas tree.

Whilst picking them up, she caught sight of two people walking up the driveway. She heard the crunch of their boots in the frost and scurried to the door, calling her mum's name. She got to the door first and opened it wide. "Hello."
The two people, a man and a woman, shifted awkwardly on the front step.

"Is your mother in?" The woman asked.

Jess's mum appeared behind her wearing her apron, which was still covered in flour. "Can I help you?"

The man folded his hands in front of him and looked down solemnly. "Mrs Fern. I'm afraid to tell you that your husband has been killed."

Her mum said nothing at first, and when the woman asked if she understood what they had said, she looked up with a strange smile on her face and told them she was very busy making gingerbread right now, and didn't have time for visitors. It wasn't until she had closed the door on them and leant against it that she began to sob, huge devastated sobs, and Jess stood there rooted to the spot, unsure of what she should do.

"Mummy?" Jess whispered, taking a few steps forward and taking one of her mum's hands. Jane sank to the floor in a heap and Jess sat down next to her, wrapping her little arms around her neck and holding her until she had no tears left to cry.

The thought of that day still made Jess cry now, but she knew better than to sob loudly. She pulled her thin pillow over her head and let the tears run out of her eyes, all over the sheet covering the mattress. She wondered whether her dad was proud of her now, watching down. Maybe he would be disappointed in her. Seven soldiers dead, and she hadn't been able to save them. Just like his medic hadn't been able to save him.

Chapter Three

As the chinook touched down at Camp Bastion and the ramp opened, D Platoon began to disembark. Laden with their bergens and helmets, they jumped down and crouched low, running through the downdraft of the aircraft. Jess felt a sense of relief at being within the Camp's hesco walls. Being extremely large and well manned, it felt a lot safer than the much smaller Forward Operating Base in which they had been based for the past six months.

They were shown to the tent where they would be sleeping for the night. It was larger than the one they had become used to sleeping in at the FOB and contained a row of bunk beds on each side. There were two tents to be shared between the whole platoon, and Jess breathed a sigh of relief that they would have more company that night. The fact that they were half a section down didn't seem so glaringly obvious when they had half of 2 and 3 Sections sharing with them as well.

Before leaving the base that morning they had been told that Gav had come out of surgery and was being flown back to the UK, together with Dickens and Brewer. The news had been very welcome and provided a well needed pick up for the whole platoon. Most of the soldiers had struggled to sleep that night, tossing and turning while running through the events of the day. Lieutenant Swan was well aware of the fact that a close eye would need to be kept on the soldiers

31

over the coming weeks. It had been a very difficult day, one of the worst in the company's history. It was only to be expected that some of the soldiers may struggle more than others.

Raj tossed Jase's bergen on the floor. "I'm having the top bunk. There's no way I'm sleeping under you with your stinky-"

"Sleep where you like, mate," Jase interrupted him flatly.

Sitting on her bunk, Jess watched him out of the corner of her eye. He was still struggling massively, and she was growing more and more concerned about his mental state. Last night she had woken at least eight times; on every occasion he was awake too. Sitting up on his cot, or pacing around the tent, or thrashing around under his sheets. She wasn't sure that he had actually slept at all. Judging by the black rings around his eyes, probably not. She knew that she had to tell Mellor. She had tried to address it with Jase herself, but he had just shut her out.

"Pizza?" Raj tried to lighten the mood.
Jess shrugged. "Yeah, if you want."

She glanced around at the other soldiers buzzing around the room, making plans and exchanging banter as if nothing had happened. The other sections had not been as heavily hit with casualties. She heard footsteps crunching through the gravel outside, and then Mellor appeared in the doorway.

"Listen in, guys," he announced, a small cardboard box in his arms. "Tomorrow evening before we head out, we'll hold a memorial service for the guys we lost yesterday. I know you're all struggling, and I just want to say how proud I am of you all for stepping up and getting on with it. It's what they would have wanted."

He made eye contact with Jess for a few seconds and then he looked down momentarily, clearing his throat. Then he handed the box to the soldier nearest the door.

"This is a bit of a morale boost. It's not much but there will be more when we get to Cyprus."

Then, he turned on his heel and was gone. Jess stood and watched as a couple of the privates pulled the box open and cheered, then handed out bars of chocolate. She couldn't watch them any longer, it just felt wrong to celebrate the fact that they were on their way back to the UK when half of the section were not going with them. Before she knew what she was doing, she followed Mellor out of the tent and across the dusty tarmac.

He had moved quickly and she had to almost run to catch him up. He was almost back at the operations room when she caught up with him.

"Sir, can I have a word?"

They came to a standstill a few metres from the operations room.

"What can I do for you, Medic?"

Jess looked around her. Although they were quite far from the tent there were still soldiers walking around near to where they were standing, and she didn't feel comfortable discussing it out in the open where anybody could hear.

"Can we go somewhere quieter?"

"Yeah," he nodded curiously. "Yeah, of course. This way."

He led her back to his tent, brewing with anticipation about what she wanted to discuss. He didn't know whether to be optimistic or not. Her eyes had lost their usual spark and were instead full of sadness. After hearing her in the shower yesterday he had been hoping to catch her alone at some point, but with all the preparations in respect of their evacuation from the FOB and meetings with senior officers about yesterday's events it hadn't happened. Nevertheless, she seemed much better today and he knew that he probably didn't need to worry.

"Come in here," he pulled back the fabric and entered his tent.

Jess looked around and then followed him, surprised at the space inside. "Perks of being the boss, hey?" She smiled weakly and he nodded, smiling hesitantly back.

They held eye contact for a few seconds, neither of them able to break the other's gaze. And then Mellor cleared his throat and stepped back, raising his eyebrows.

"So, what was it that you wanted to talk to me about?"

Jess felt her heart thumping in her chest. There were so many things that she wanted to say but she didn't know whether she should. Her head had been all over the place since yesterday.

"It's Jase," she answered finally. "He's not doing great, Sir. I'm worried about him."

He nodded. "Yeah. I know. I'm keeping a close eye on him, he'll definitely need some extra support when we get back. He just doesn't seem to acknowledge that he isn't to blame for what happened."

Jess pushed her hands into her pockets. Suddenly she felt a little uneasy, but she didn't know why. "Yeah. He really needs to see someone, quite urgently. Every time I try to talk to him about it, he just shuts down."

Mellor nodded. "Well thank you, Medic. It's all in hand but please do come back to me if the situation escalates or you have other concerns."

Jess nodded but she didn't move. It was as though an invisible force she couldn't see was pulling her towards him like a magnet, and she couldn't leave.

"Was there something else?" He shuffled some papers on his desk.

Jess shook her head and looked at the floor. He stopped what he was doing and took a few steps towards her.

"Jess?" He asked, more softly now. "Is everything alright?"

Jess looked up at him and her eyes watered. She swallowed hard in an attempt to force back the tears and shook her head.

"Yes. No... Not really, Sir."

He was standing just inches away from her; she could almost feel the heat radiating from his body and his breath on hers.

"What's wrong?"

She looked up, into his deep brown eyes and felt an instant connection that she couldn't explain. They shared something that tied them together now, losing such a vast number of their section members in just one patrol. Grief that would now bind them forever no matter how hard they tried to fight it.

"I um...' her voice wobbled. It was exhausting trying to be strong. As she often did, she wished that she could just skip the decompression and return home right now. "I can't stop thinking about them, Sir. I just keep thinking... what if I'd done this... did I miss that? What if there was something else I could have done to keep even one of them alive?"

Mellor reached for her and placed both hands on her shoulders. The weight of his arms made Jess feel safe, and she relaxed slightly in his grip.

"Listen to me," he squeezed gently in an attempt to reassure her. "You're an exceptional medic, Jess, and you have a brilliant career ahead of you. You did everything that you could have done for them, do you hear me? Absolutely everything. There was one of you, and five critical casualties for you to deal with, right in the middle of a fire fight. To be quite honest it's a miracle that we managed to get any of them out alive, let alone three. And that is down to you. Thank you."

Jess looked up at him again and smiled, but the smile didn't reach her eyes. He could tell that she wasn't convinced and he sighed, then removed his hands from her shoulders.

"I don't really know what else I can say to make you realise just how fantastic you are, Jess. Just know that you are."

She suddenly had an overwhelming and unexpected urge to reach forwards and fling her arms around him, but instead she cleared her throat and stuffed her hands back in the pockets of her trousers.

"Thanks, Sir," she pulled a tissue out of her pocket and dabbed at her eyes which were again threatening to overspill. "And sorry for being a sap."

"You are many things, Lance Corporal Fern, but a sap isn't one of them."

They both laughed then, and he tapped her firmly on the forearm.

"Go on. Get some rest. Team bonding exercises tomorrow."

She rolled her eyes and smiled, then left the tent. He watched her go and let out a deep breath, then sat back down at his desk, pen in hand, trying to continue with the eulogy he had been working on since they arrived. He jotted down a few words but then crossed through them and started again. He tried again but it just sounded wrong. Frustrated, he scrunched up the paper in his fist and threw it at the waste paper bin, before running his hands through his hair. He was running out of time.

***

Mellor was up early, before sunrise. He

was used to being up all hours of the night, and after recent events he felt even less able to rest. After a few hours of tossing and turning he gave up, glancing at the watch on his wrist before rolling out of bed at 3.30am. He stretched, pulled on some shorts and a vest and sat back down at his desk in front of the half written eulogy.

Afghanistan was one of the most hostile places on earth, and occasionally losing platoon members was inevitable. He had lost colleagues before, even seen them blown up right in front of his eyes. So why was this time different? It had never affected him like this.

He put the pen down again and rubbed his eyes wearily. He just couldn't focus. All he could think about was the boom of the explosion and the sight of his stricken soldiers on the floor through the clearing dust. It had happened almost in slow motion; the frantic calls of *Medic! Medic! Man Down! Man Down!* as Jess had scrambled up off the floor and rushed over to them. He could still feel the ringing in his ears as he had fought to get a hold of the situation. The adrenaline rush he felt as the gun fire started and he ordered his team to hold defensive positions. The pride he felt when watching the platoon move the injured and dead soldiers out of harm's way, and Jess working her magic on them as best she could. The pressure he felt as they tried to press the Taliban back while waiting for back up, and the relief he felt once the casualties were airlifted to Bastion and their back up arrived to take them back to the base.

He couldn't sleep because he kept

replaying the whole sequence of events over and over in his mind, constantly questioning himself - had he missed something? Was there an indication of what was to come that they could have picked up, and therefore avoided such a terrible loss of life? And then there were the what ifs, what if things had been worse? What if he had lost both his medics? What if he had been shot and not Merrett, would Merrett have handled the situation better? Truth be told, he had never been happier to see Lieutenant Swan than he had been on that patrol. It had been a long time since he felt such inadequacy. What if Swan hadn't have arrived when he had?

He scraped the chair back and pulled his boots on, then stepped out into the darkness. The base was quiet except for the few personnel who were already up and going about their business. He jogged towards the air strip, where aircraft were already taking off and landing. Except for the faint glow of the air strip lights in the distance, the base was dark but for the light of the moon which cast ghostly shadows across the sandy tarmac. He concentrated on the rhythmic crunch of his boots on the sand and managed to block out all other thoughts. It was a welcome relief for his brain, which had been on overdrive for more than twenty four hours now.

Continuing across the tarmac, he thought of nothing else but the steady crunch, crunch, crunch of his boots. Before long, his body got used to the speed he was running; his breathing and heart rate levelled and it became easier. He ran and he ran until he had lost count of how many minutes he had been running and he reached the field hospital, his thighs burning from exertion. There he stopped and doubled over, his hands on his knees, breathing deeply until the pain subsided.

As Mellor looked up at the canopy covering the casualty reception area, his heart began to thump harder in his chest as his imagination ran wild. He could see them now, being wheeled in on trolleys straight off the helicopter. Some dead, some alive, just hanging on by the skin of their teeth. He could see them in the mortuary, still and blue like wax works. He shook his head and carried on running, faster now, back in the direction he had come. Every time he looked back at the hospital they were all he could see, their eyes wide open, staring straight at him, their lips tinged with blue and their skin covered in blood.

He turned back towards the tents in the distance and ran faster and faster, until he could feel his pulse raging in his head. Still he pushed harder, now sprinting past the platoon tents. He was completely engrossed in running and he almost collided with Jess, who was just coming out of the tent.

"Whoa," she stepped backwards just in time as he skidded to a stop right where she had been standing. "Are you alright, Sir?"

Suddenly, she saw something she had never seen in him - for a few moments his eyes looked wild and desperate like a caged animal.

40

His chest was heaving heavily up and down while he caught his breath, and being drenched in sweat he looked as though he had been swimming. Then he stood tall with his hands on his hips, breathing more steadily as his heart rate began to slow.

"Yep. Just having an early morning run. What are you doing?"

She studied him curiously. "Couldn't sleep. So I thought I'd make myself useful."

"Right. I er… I'd better go take a shower."

She nodded with a curious smile and then watched him jog off in the direction of his tent. For a minute she stood, staring into space, thinking about what she had just seen. He had looked so different to the strong, methodical commander she was familiar with. With a sigh, she started to walk in the opposite direction.

***

They stood around the Second Cairn, as the setting sun cast an orange glow over the barbed wire surrounding the camp. Higher in the sky, the clouds were an ominous shade of dark grey, reflecting the mood of the soldiers who stood beneath them.

The platoon stood to attention in three lines in front of the memorial, with Lieutenant Swan and Sergeant Mellor before them. Jess, Jase and Raj stood at the front, flanked by a couple of the other medics who had returned from the FOB and a few members of 2 Section. The remaining members of 1, 2 and 3 Sections stood in the rows behind. A single poppy wreath lay on the stones at the bottom of the memorial, surrounded by five helmets. Just the sight of the helmets was almost enough to break Jess. She blinked away the tears in her eyes, still standing to attention, waiting for the service to begin.

She clenched her fists down by her sides as Lieutenant Swan began the service. His voice boomed over the silence of the troops, instructing them to stand at ease. Jess glanced at Jase. His eyes were fixed on the helmets at the front, his face emotionless. She willed him to look at her but he didn't. Then she looked back to the front, just as Mellor began his piece. He stepped forward to address the platoon, a single piece of paper held firmly in his left hand.

"As the sun sets today over this camp, we remember our fellow soldiers who fell yesterday in Sangin."

He cleared his throat and glanced down at his paper, then looked up to address the platoon once again. "We lost some of the finest soldiers in our platoon. I was proud to serve with each and every one of them, and their loss has sent a shock wave throughout the entire company."

Jess saw movement out of the corner of her eye, and she glanced again at Jase, who now had tears streaming down his face. She wanted to put her arms around him, but she knew better than to move. Instead, she swallowed hard to knock back the tears which were now threatening to fall from her own eyes.

"Colour Sergeant Merrett was a highly

experienced soldier, and a well respected commander to 2 Section. 2 Section is an exceptionally well trained section, and that is testament to the hard work he spent training each and every one of you. I know that he will be present in all of your future missions, as you continue to serve in his memory."

"Corporal Shane Little was the lead CMT within the company. He was again, an exceptional medic who saved many lives throughout the six months he served with us in Sangin. I will be forever grateful to him for what he achieved, and he lives on in the high calibre team of medics who he believed in and trained up to the best of their ability. I have absolutely no doubt that he would be very proud of what you achieved yesterday, Lance Corporal Fern."

Again, he paused, looking straight at her. Jess managed a weak smile and then, as her eyes fell on Shane's helmet lying empty on the floor, she looked down at the desert floor, blinking back fresh tears.

"And Privates Perry, North and Fox, three determined soldiers destined for great things. It is tragic that their lives were cut short so soon, before they had really had a chance to achieve what they were capable of. Throughout the last six months their skills have improved immeasurably and each of them had grown into a very capable soldier. They died heroically, saving the lives of their fellow comrades, and we will forever be proud of them."

Lieutenant Swan bowed his head as

Mellor continued. He looked up at the sky which was now turning darker. There were still splashes of colour scattered across the sky, oranges, purples and reds.

"As those of us who are staying continue with our mission here in Helmand, they will be with us. They will be the moon lighting up the base at night, the voices in our heads telling us not to give up when things are tough. As we hold their loved ones in our thoughts tonight, we celebrate the remarkable men that they were and their endless achievements. And each and every one of us will hold on to the memories we have of them."

Silence ensued, the whole platoon lost in their memories. Jess closed her eyes, recalling the banter that 1 Section had exchanged the night before the patrol in their tent, the stories they had told, all the plans they had for their leave. Plans that would never now materialise, because they would never be going back to their families. Not alive anyway. She remembered the last look she had exchanged with Shane, the last time he had nodded at her, how well they had worked together just the day before he died. And finally, moments of banter between Merrett and Mellor when their sections trained together at the base.

When she opened her eyes again, she saw Jase creeping forwards towards the memorial, almost in slow motion. The whole platoon watched silently. He walked to the foot of the memorial and looked up at the cross which adorned it, made from empty shell cases. Slowly he fell to his knees, picking up the helmet which had once sat on Melon's head and clutching it to his stomach. He bent over, the helmet still clutched tightly to his body and began to sob, his heart broken at the loss of his best friend.

* * *

The first thing that Jess noticed when she stepped off the plane in Cyprus was how cold it was. She had become acclimatised to the stifling heat of Afghanistan, and now it was in the low twenties it almost felt like winter. Once she got to the hotel where they would be staying for the next twenty four hours, she replaced her fatigues with a zip up hoodie and jeans, then headed down to the beach where the rest of the platoon were winding down.

Mellor was standing by the barbecue wearing a ridiculous pink apron. It reminded Jess of one of her mum's, and she couldn't help but laugh as she approached him. Laughing was a relief. Now that the air was fresh and she could breathe again, she had started to feel better. The memorial service last night had been really hard; it was devastating to watch Jase break down in front of the memorial with Melon's helmet in his hands.

Jess stood next to Mellor, who was turning the sausages on the barbecue, and glanced over at half the platoon who were engrossed in a volleyball match.

"You don't fancy a swim then, Medic?" He grinned.

Jess raised one eyebrow playfully. "It's freezing. I wouldn't get in that water if you paid me."

He laughed and went back to turning the sausages. Jess looked around. She couldn't see Jase anywhere. The smile faded from her face. "It's laughable. They think a few packs of cheap sausages and a box of beer on the beach will sort out all our troubles. I think it's going to take a bit more than that for Jase."

"Yeah. I haven't seen him since we arrived."

"Maybe I'll go and find him," Jess suggested. "I don't want him to be on his own."

"Just give him some time by himself. He'll come back to us when he's ready."

Jess watched as one of the soldiers tripped over his own feet while trying to bat the ball over the makeshift net they had fashioned from some old washed up fishing nets. She shook her head as one of the others shouted in jest, *Medic! Man down!*

She yelled back at them, her hair blowing around her face in the wind. "I'm off duty!"

Mellor snatched a glance at her but she caught him, and for a moment their eyes locked together again just as they had done in his tent at Camp Bastion. Then they were interrupted by one of the platoon's young privates, who ran over.

"Are those sausages not done yet, Sir? What are you doing, cremating them?"

"Hilarious," he replied flatly. "I bet you've never cooked a sausage in your life, Private Nicholas."

"I'll have you know I'm very good with a bratwurst."

Mellor shook his head and rolled his eyes. "Go on, sling your hook."

Nicholas ran back off to the game with a grin on his face.

Jess's smile faded. She breathed in a deep breath of fresh sea air and looked out to sea. It was windy and the waves sparkled in the afternoon sun before they broke on the beach in a cascade of bubbles. She was glad to be here now. The whole platoon had been devastated by the service last night, but now here they were running around playing volleyball. Later, when the beers and sausages had gone down nicely, she was sure that there would be time for some fireside banter on the beach and probably some heart to hearts. Hopefully, talking about their experiences would mean that they would go home at least in the process of coming to terms with what had happened.

"What are you thinking about, Medic?"

His voice broke her out of her daydream and she looked up at him vacantly.

"Not much. Just how weird this feels, being on a beach having a barbecue two days after being shot at by the Taliban."

Mellor took a long sip of his beer. "Yeah. It is a bit. I still can't believe they're not going to come around the corner and join us. But there you go. Life goes on."

"Yeah," Jess narrowed her eyes and looked back out to the horizon. "Life goes on."

***

By the time it was dark, they had sunk most of the beers and they sat around a makeshift campfire, the only light from the fire itself and the distant lights on the side of the hotel. Jase had finally joined them, and everyone had made sure that he had caught up on his fair share of beers. It had gone straight to his head and he was half way through a ridiculous story about what he had got up to on a night out during his last period of leave.

"I think I'll pretend I didn't hear that, Private Coulson," Mellor stood up, throwing his empty beer bottle into the bucket they had been filling steadily throughout the afternoon. "I'm going to turn in for the night anyway. Behave yourselves."

"Night, Sir," Jess said, her voice mixed up with the dozens of others who answered at the same time.

She watched him walk up the beach towards the hotel. He was putting on a brave face, but instinct was telling Jess that he wasn't coping quite as well as he appeared to be. It was the subtle things; his voice wasn't quite as booming as normal, his face was softer when he looked at her. When he walked his posture was different; he no longer stood quite as straight. She knew that, like the rest of the platoon, he needed his leave desperately. She wondered how lonely it was to be at the top. Of course he had Lieutenant Swan to talk to, but it wasn't the same - he hadn't actually been there, at the time of the explosion. In front of

Swan he had to put on a brave face, a stiff upper lip, and lead his section. And 2 Section too, at the moment, since their section commander had been killed.

Once he had disappeared in the direction of the building, she let out a long breath and then turned back to the fire, pulling her knees to her chest and wrapping her arms around her body tightly.

"What about you, Jess?" Raj asked, taking another swig of his beer.

Jess looked up. "Hmm?" She had been so lost in thought that she hadn't kept up with the conversation.

"What's the craziest thing you've ever done?"
She pulled a face and then shrugged. "Oh... not much really. My life isn't that exciting."

"Oh, come on," he pressed. "There must be something."

Jess was keen to deflect the conversation away from her. "Not really."

Luckily it worked, and one of the other privates started telling a story about a drunken encounter they'd had on a night out on holiday. She zoned out again and began to look around the platoon, analysing each and every soldier. She was trained to spot the signs of PTSD, and she knew that she wouldn't be doing her job if she didn't keep an eye on them. For that reason she had only had two beers that night, with the rest of the platoon well onto their fourth and fifth. They were only supposed to have four, but for some reason they had ended up with a surplus; presumably they had Lieutenant Swan to thank for that. After six months without alcohol there had been no complaints from the rest of the platoon on that count, of course.

Hearing Jase start up another one of his stories, Jess felt slightly relieved. He had been very quiet earlier, when he finally emerged from his hotel room. But just as they lit up the camp fire he had joined them, and after a few beers he had loosened up a lot. Now he looked physically better - less wound up, more relaxed, just like he usually did after a few beers with friends. But she knew that she still had to keep a close eye on him. Alcohol was an easy mask. The problem was that in the morning, when he woke up and it had worn off, it would probably hit him twice as hard.

Chapter Four

Mellor breathed a sigh of relief, turning the key in the lock and stepping inside his flat. The door clicked shut behind him and he leant against it, sinking to the floor as wave after wave of guilt hit him. Guilt for being alive when three of the privates in his charge were dead. Guilt for not having dealt with the ambush as well as Merrett would have done if he were alive. Guilt for the thoughts he'd had about Jess, when she was in his charge. He put his head in his hands. What had he become? He had dreamed of being at the very top of the army for as long as he could remember. He had never felt this way. Now he wasn't even sure whether he was fit to command a section on his next tour.

Eventually he stood up and kicked his boots off, flicking the hallway light on and then walking through to the kitchen. Everything was uncomfortably quiet. Usually, he enjoyed the peace and quiet of having his own space when he returned from a tour, but this time he felt on edge. He opened the fridge, which was empty apart from a couple of bottles of beer. He pulled one out and flicked the top off with a bottle opener, then sunk into the sofa by the patio doors. He only sat for a couple of minutes before he got up and started pacing around the flat. He wanted something to keep him busy - anything to keep him busy. But the flat was spotless, having been cleaned the week before he got home. When he was on tour, he let the flat on short term tenancies and it was always spotlessly clean when he got back. Usually that was a relief; he could come home, sleep for a couple of days and then enjoy the rest of his leave without having to worry about housework. But tonight he would happily have spent a couple of hours cleaning, if it kept his mind off all the things that he didn't want to think about.

He pulled open the patio doors and stepped onto the balcony, the cool night breeze hitting his face. He took a deep swig of his beer and looked out across the parkland which surrounded the block to the twinkling lights of the town centre, then pulled his mobile out of his pocket and stared at the blank screen. What was she doing right now?

***

The taxi slowed to a standstill, stirring Jess from her sleep. She opened her eyes and rubbed them wearily.

The taxi driver flicked the interior lights on. "That's forty three pounds, please."

"Sorry," she fumbled around in her bergen for her purse. "I must have dropped off."

"No problem, love," he waited patiently while she found a bundle of notes and then thrust them at him.

She opened the door. "Don't worry about the change."

"Oh, thanks very much love. You have a

good evening."

"You too," she nodded and closed the door behind her, turning to look at her house.

She stood there for a minute or two, staring up at the house in front of her. The porch light was on, just as it always was when she got back from a tour. No matter what time of the day or night, her mum would be waiting for her, lights on, ready to guide her home. Swinging her bergen back over one shoulder she smiled with relief, then walked up the path to the front door.

As it always did, before she even reached the door it swung open and she was greeted by Jane's smiling face.

"Jess!" She flung her arms around her and held her tight. "Thank God you're home! I've been so worried!"

"Sorry, Mum. The flight was delayed. I did text."

Jane released her daughter from her grip. "Yes, I know. But I was worried something might have gone wrong."

Jess followed Jane through the front door and closed it softly behind her. "It was just a mechanical issue. Happens all the time."

Jess set her bergen down at the bottom of the stairs and then followed her through to the living room. She relaxed into the sofa and closed her eyes, breathing in the familiar scent of washing powder and her mum's favourite air freshener.

"Feels good to be home," she breathed.

"Hot chocolate?"

Jess smiled weakly. "Yeah. Thanks."

It had become a bit of a tradition, her mum making her hot chocolate when she returned from deployment. It hadn't been intentional - she had come home the first time in the middle of winter, and it was freezing outside. Jane had offered her a hot chocolate. Then she had done it again the next time, and the next - and now it was just what they did, even when she returned in the middle of summer. Jess closed her eyes again and relaxed, the soft hum of the television in the background lulling her back to sleep.

"Here you are," Jane interrupted, walking back in with the mug. "Are you hungry? Do you want something to eat?"

Jess's eyes snapped open. "No, I'm fine thanks, I had something before we took off. Once I've drunk this I'll be off to bed. I have about six months of sleep to catch up on!"

Jane sat down next to her and stroked her hair gently, just like when she was a little girl. "I'll bet. Oh, I've missed you very much, Jessie."

"I've missed you too, Mum," Jess took the warm mug and held it with both hands. "Mmm. And I've missed this."

Jane smiled weakly and then leant against the arm of the sofa, watching her daughter out of the corner of her eye. How she wished that Jess could have chosen a different path. She had known ever since she was a little girl that she wanted to be a soldier, but after Ken had died she had hoped that she would see sense. Unfortunately, the loss of her dad had only seemed to spur Jess on with her dream. Jane's eyes wandered to the photograph on the mantlepiece of the three people she loved most in the world.

They were interrupted by the news reel from the ten o'clock news, and the photograph which flashed on screen caught Jess's attention. Jane watched Jess visibly freeze, her body tense, listening to the story. *"There have been fresh calls on the Government to fund additional resources for soldiers in Afghanistan as five British soldiers are killed in one day in Sangin,"* the newsreader announced.

"Did you know them?"

Jess nodded and looked down at her mug. Suddenly the milky contents seemed too difficult to stomach.

"Do you want to talk about it?" Jane pressed.

Jess did want to talk about it - she needed to. But she had never really told her mum about the things she had encountered whilst on tour. Knowing that Jane already battled with anxiety when she was away, Jess played down what she had experienced. *I'm a medic Mum, not a soldier. I don't get involved in much action, I just pick up the pieces,* she had told her many times.

Jess set the mug down on the coffee table with a clunk. It hit the table harder than she meant it to and a splash of the contents splashed over the top. "No, Mum. Not tonight. Actually, if you don't mind I'm going to head up to bed. I'm exhausted. I'll see you in the morning."

Jane nodded and watched her go, the barely touched mug of hot chocolate still steaming on the coffee table. It could have been her. So easily. She clasped her hands together and began to rub one of her thumb nails against the skin around her other thumb, which was already red raw from her habit. It was hard enough watching her leave every time she went on deployment, worrying on a daily basis about whether she was dead or alive. Every time there was an unexpected knock on the door she froze, expecting the worst. She had resolved never to tell Jess just how much she hated her leaving, because it was her life and she had no right to stop her doing what she loved.

The sound of the front door closing made her jump off the sofa, and she took a deep breath, painted on a smile and turned to face her son as he walked through the living room door.

"Hi, love. You'll never guess who's just got home!"

***

Jase stepped through the front door and held his breath, waiting to be knocked over by an incoming bundle of fur and muscle. He had been looking forward to seeing Monty, his golden retriever, ever since he had left Afghanistan. The thought of being home and seeing him had been the only thing that had held him together throughout the flight home.

"Hello? Monty? Come here, boy!"

He frowned, closing the door behind him.

The house was never this quiet. Perhaps his parents had taken Monty out for a badly timed walk. He kicked his boots off and headed through to the kitchen, where he was surprised to see them both sat at the table. "Hi."

His mum stood up and flung her arms around him so hard that she almost knocked him off his feet. "Oh, Jason! I've missed you!"

His dad reached past her and patted Jase on the back. "Hi, son."

"What are you doing in here? Where's Monty?" Jase looked around him. His bed, which sat in the corner of the room, was empty.

George and Elena exchanged worried glances, and then George put one hand on Jase's shoulder, squeezing it tight. "There's something we need to tell you. I'm sorry, lad."

Jase's chest felt tight. "About what?"

They glanced at each other again and then George turned back to Jase. "I'm afraid… Monty is no longer with us."

Jase said nothing. He looked at his dad in disbelief, his eyes wide.

"He was eighteen, Jase. He had a lovely life. But it was his time to go. And we had to let him. It wouldn't have been fair."

"Go where?" Jase asked, although he already knew what they meant.

"Jason." Elena took his hands in hers and squeezed them gently, her eyes filling with tears. "Monty died."

Jase stared at her. Both his parents were watching him, waiting for him to break down in tears. But Jase had cried enough tears in the last few days, his eyes were dry. Instead, he just nodded.

"I'm sorry we didn't tell you before, love. But we knew how busy you were out there... and it wouldn't have changed anything, even if we did tell you. We didn't want you to be distracted from your job."

"In case I missed a device?"

"Well.... yes," George confirmed. "We decided it would be best to tell you in person, when you were home."

Jase felt a bubble of anger rising up in his stomach. He had put his life on the line for his country, and these were the cards he had been dealt. First, he had lost his best friend, watched him being blown apart right in front of his eyes, and now he had lost his loyal dog who he'd had since he was five years old. And he hadn't even had a chance to say goodbye. When Jase had joined the army and left for his initial training, it was Monty who he had missed the most. At the thought of Monty's delighted face and wagging tail every time he had walked through the door when returning on leave, Jase felt a pang in his chest. That dog had waited for him every single time without fail and given him the warmest of welcomes. Now he was no longer here, the house felt different. It felt empty, like all the love had been sucked out of it. He looked again at Monty's empty bed in the corner and pulled his hands away from Elena's grip.

"Yeah. You're right. It was for the best."

Elena and George watched him cross the kitchen and scoop up Monty's bed, before storming through the house to the front door.

George followed him down the hallway, a look of concern etched across his features. "What are you doing, lad?"

Jase didn't respond, he was too angry. When he got to the green wheelie bin by the path to the front door, he swung it open and dumped the dog's bed in it, squashing it down until the lid would close.

"Jase!" Elena protested.

"He's gone," Jase stated flatly, walking back through the front door. "Keeping his bed isn't going to bring him back. It's time to move on."

Chapter Five

Ironically, the sun was shining as the cortege crept down the high street in Wootton Bassett. Together with the rest of the platoon, Jess, Jase, Raj and Mellor stood to attention on the kerb, surrounded by hundreds of civilians and a handful of veterans who had come to pay their respects to the five fallen heroes on their final journey to Oxfordshire.

Jess watched the families and close friends of the soldiers throw roses on top of the approaching quintet. Each coffin was draped with the Union Flag and adorned with flowers. She watched Laura, Melon's partner, throw a single rose on top of the third hearse, and her eyes filled with tears. Laura placed her hand flat on the glass window and broke down. It took two family members to pull her away from cortege, which continued its journey. Next to her, one of her other family members held their daughter, Millie, who was not even a year old. It was devastatingly unfair that she would grow up not even knowing her dad. Jess had been eight years old when her own dad died, and that was bad enough.

The funeral director passed their position and Jess raised her hand to salute the soldiers one last time. It felt surreal to think that each coffin contained one of their friends and comrades; they had become like family members to Jess by the end of the tour. Just a week ago they had all sat around in the evening Afghan sun, talking about what they would do when they returned to the UK. It just didn't feel real. She kept her breathing steady and choked back tears, staring at the dozens of roses that covered the top of each hearse like a blanket.

Beside her, Mellor watched as Merrett's widow stood in silence, her eyes fixed on the hearse containing her husband of a year. She looked spaced out, as though she didn't really know where she was. Recalling the moment that Merrett had told him of his plans to propose when he returned from tour, two years ago, Mellor's gut wrenched. He had attended their wedding, and later listened as Merrett had confided in him about their fertility troubles. It struck him that they would never get the chance to have their own child now. His widow looked broken. He wondered if she would ever recover.

The wind whistled through the trees which lined the packed high street, and Jess looked up at the sky. Despite the sheer volume of people who had turned up for the repatriation, the street was eerily silent, the only sounds being the engine noise from the vehicles, the cries of the soldiers' devastated loved ones as they watched them pass through, and the occasional baby or toddler who didn't know any better. The bell from the nearby church began to ring eerily as the hearses passed through. Within half a minute or so, the last hearse had passed their position. Jess glanced over to Jase who was stood very still, his eyes on the floor. She could see the occasional rise and fall of his shoulders and she knew that he was crying.

Nobody moved until the procession was well out of sight, and then the crowd began to disband. Most of the platoon headed to a nearby pub to have a drink in their colleagues' memory but Jess stood still, watching Jase walk forwards and pick up a stray rose which had fallen off the top of one the hearses and into the road. For a moment he crouched down, holding the rose in his hands as if it was the most precious thing he had ever seen.

Suddenly, the sound of hysterical crying caught her attention and she turned to see Laura collapse into a relative's arms. Unexpectedly, Jess felt like she was back there again. The fresh breeze which teased its way down the high street became dusty and hot, and she could see Melon slipping out of consciousness for the last time right in front of her, his mind firmly on Laura and their daughter.

"I never got to say goodbye!" Laura sobbed in the arms of the older man, who Jess presumed to be her dad. "I don't even know what his last words were! What if he was all alone and scared?"

But I do, thought Jess. She hesitated momentarily, wondering what to do for the best, and then made her decision. It was the last thing he had asked her to do, that meant it was the right thing to do. Approaching the devastated family, she took her beret carefully off her head and held it gingerly in her hands. "Excuse me. Laura?"

Laura broke out of the man's grip momentarily and turned to Jess, her mascara smudged face hot with tears. "Yes," she managed.

"I'm Jess. I'm the medic who was with the platoon when Nick died."

Jess felt all the eyes in the group turn on her, weighing up what she had just said. She knew that each and every one of them would be wondering why she didn't do more. It was human nature to try to find blame when trying to process a loss. She couldn't blame them.

"I'm really sorry for your loss."

Everyone stared at her in stunned silence, and Laura looked as though she was going to be sick.

"I just wanted to let you know that he wasn't alone. And he wasn't scared. He was really, really brave. He was thinking of you, and that comforted him. And he asked me to tell you that he loves you, and if ever Millie is missing her dad, tell her to look up to the stars. And…" her voice wobbled and she cleared her throat. "And he'll be there."

The group stood in silence for a moment, and Laura turned to face Millie who was held safely in her grandmother's arms, completely oblivious to what was going on. At the sight of her daughter, Laura's eyes softened and she smiled briefly, holding a hand to her mouth as if she was trying to stop her sobs from escaping.

She turned back to Jess. "Did he say that?"

"Yeah," Jess nodded. "It was really important to him that I told you that. It was the last thing he said."

Much to her surprise, Laura suddenly

flung her arms around her and Jess staggered backwards, regaining her balance just in time. She put her arms around Laura and held her. Jess felt Laura's whole body relax as if the weight of the world had just been removed from her shoulders, and she knew that she had made the right decision to tell her.

"Thank you," Laura breathed. "It helps to know that he wasn't alone. And that he was thinking of us. We barely heard from him when he was out in Afghanistan."

"That wasn't his choice, the base was really remote. But he always talked about you both. He was so proud to be a dad."

Over Laura's shoulder, Jess watched in silence as Mellor approached Shane's grieving wife and put his arm around her shoulders gently. She looked at him with a dazed expression on her face and then all of a sudden, it appeared that she realised who he was; she grabbed him in a tight embrace and cried out, releasing devastated sobs while he struggled to keep her standing on her feet. Suddenly Laura released her grip and Jess took a couple of steps backwards.

"I'm so sorry for your loss. Take care of yourself," she nodded solemnly, turning back towards Shane's wife, who was now being led away by a couple of family members.

Then her eyes fell on the solitary rose which was now lying back in the middle of the road, and she looked around for Jase. By now the crowd had mostly dispersed and cars were beginning to crawl back down the high street as everyday life for most of the town's residents resumed. There was no sign at all of Jase and she turned back to the road just in time to see the rose being crushed under the wheel of a passing car, its driver seemingly oblivious. Jess felt tears in her eyes as the thought of being too late to save it hit her yet again. The guilt erupted from her as a fresh torrent of tears and she turned at the sound of Mellor's voice calling her name.

Turning to face him, she had no strength left to hold herself together anymore and she relaxed, allowing her grief to pour out. They were alone now; Jase was long gone and the rest of the platoon had gone to the pub.

"I can't forgive myself, Sir," she choked through her tears.

To her surprise, he walked forwards and wrapped his arms around her, pulling her into a tight embrace. An unexpected wave of relief washed over Jess as she breathed in his scent; she finally felt as though she could relax and let it all out.

"Neither can I. But as I've said before, you're an amazing medic, Jess," he let go and stepped back, but his hands still held her upper arms securely. "Don't ever blame yourself for what happened, because none of this was your fault. Do you understand?"

She nodded. "Yes, Sir." But then she looked at the memorial which was now covered in flowers and her eyes filled with fresh tears.

"Come on. Let's go and get a drink."

Jess wiped at her eyes furiously. "I don't

think I can face them. I don't want them to see me like this."

"Then let's go somewhere quieter? We can have a chat properly and then join them later?"

"Yeah, ok."

**

They found themselves in a quiet little pub some way from the high street, and after a few glasses of wine which had gone straight to her head, Jess finally felt comfortable enough to open up. It had been hard coming home. One day of decompression was never enough to readjust to life off the front line, and coming back home was even harder for Jess because she had nobody to confide in away from the army.

She probably would have felt a lot better if she could have talked to her family or friends about the things she had seen, but she couldn't. Her mum and Liam worried about her as it was, and she didn't like to burden them with how she was feeling. She barely kept in touch with her school friends these days; she had learnt pretty quickly once she had joined the army that whilst she had moved on and grown up a lot, they hadn't. It wasn't their fault, but it seemed as though the things they talked and worried about were trivial in comparison. Naturally, they had drifted apart.

Returning from the bar, Mellor set a new pint down on the table. "So, you lost your dad when you were young?"

Jess ran her nails lightly along the base of her wine glass. "Yeah. I was eight. He died in Bosnia. Land mine."

He nodded and bowed his head slightly. "I'm sorry."

"It was a long time ago," she mumbled, taking a sip of her wine. Now that she was on her fourth glass it was slipping down quickly. The fuzziness in her head was a relief; she could only really concentrate on doing one thing at a time, and that meant that she couldn't think about Afghanistan.

"What made you want to join up? Was it losing your dad?"

Jess shrugged. "Not really. I always wanted to be in the army, I really looked up to him, you know. Losing him didn't change that. When he died... I felt like a piece of me was missing. I guess it did make me want to do it even more, I thought I might feel closer to him you know... experience the things he had experienced."

"Yeah. That makes sense."

They sat in silence for a few moments, each of them drinking more of their drinks. They had only intended to stay in the pub for a short time and then return to the others, but it hadn't happened. One conversation had led to another and they both found it a massive relief to be able to open up properly to one another.

"What about your parents?" Jess changed the subject. "Are they still around?"

He puffed his cheeks, letting out a deep breath. "Yep. Still very much alive and kicking."

Jess raised an eyebrow. "You say that like it's not such a good thing."

"Oh, don't get me wrong. I love them and that, of course I do. They're my parents. But... well let's just say I don't enjoy their company much."

"What's wrong with them?" Jess asked curiously.

"What's *right* with them?" He answered, and then he shook his head. "I'm not the golden boy they always wanted me to be."

Jess watched him bow his head and take another sip of his pint, this one longer than his last. He put his glass down a bit more forcefully than he had before, and when he looked up she was sure that she saw a momentary trace of resentment flash across his eyes. "What do they do?"

"Dad has his own company. My mum's been nagging him to retire for ages... all he seems to do when he's not working is play golf, he's like your stereotypical middle class balding business man."

Jess laughed, and then he raised his eyebrows. "You think I'm exaggerating. Here, look."

He fumbled through his phone and found a recent photograph of his dad, then held it out for Jess to see.

"Oh, wow. Yeah, you weren't kidding."

"No," he smirked. "No, I wasn't kidding."

Jess blinked at him across the table, willing him to say more. He looked deep in thought for a few seconds, and then he looked up at her again. "You know, all I ever wanted was for them to be proud of me. But I was never good enough for them."

"In what way?"

"When I was fourteen, I got kicked out of the jumped up, poncey school they insisted that I go to. All I wanted was to go to the local comp with my friends. But Dad's business had really taken off and they made their decision based on a load of rubbish drivelled at them by their new middle class 'friends'. They wouldn't listen, and I didn't want to be there. I stopped trying."

"I'm sure they did what they thought was best," Jess reasoned. When she saw his expression, she put her hands up as if in defence. "I'm sorry, I shouldn't have said that. I know nothing about them. I'm sorry."

He shrugged and then went back to drinking his beer. He looked troubled and Jess wanted him to go on. His background was a world away from what she had expected.

"What made you join the army? Was that their idea?"

He laughed incredulously. "Yeah, right. No, it was literally the opposite of what they wanted for me. Dad wanted me to join the family business and kept banging on that it would 'all be mine' one day. But it was the last thing I wanted, to be stuck there, tied to them forever. As soon as I was old enough, I signed up. Mum pretty much disowned me for a while after that. Imagine having to explain that to all their stuck up friends. A squaddie, not even an officer. I think she pretty much died of shame."

"It's hardly a shameful career, is it?" Jess raised an eyebrow. "Fighting for your Queen and country?"

"No, but she didn't see it that way. She said I'd thrown away every chance they had ever given me. Why would I want to be cannon fodder when I could be at any university I wanted, with the money they had? Well, I made it my life's mission to prove them wrong and get as high up in the army as I could."

"You've done well," Jess glanced at his uniform. "Twelve years and three chevrons already."

He looked down and smiled weakly. Jess realised that he looked visibly relieved to have got that off his chest.

"As have you, Lance Corporal," he complimented, and their eyes locked together for a few seconds before he downed the rest of his pint and then stood up to get another one. "Another glass?"

"No, I'm fine thanks. I'd better be heading back soon. Mum wants to go out on some day trip tomorrow, I don't think she will appreciate it if I'm in bed all day chucking up."

He smiled and headed off to the bar to buy yet another pint.

Jess looked out of the window. The evening sun had disappeared now, replaced by oppressive, dark clouds. It almost seemed surreal that just a few hours previously, they had been stood outside watching the cortege pass down the high street. She had been in the pub for ages with Mellor, drinking away their angst, and she felt as though a massive weight had been lifted. Whether she would feel the same in the morning when the alcohol wore off, she didn't know; all she did know was that she was grateful to have him here to talk to. They both had their own internal battles to face and it was nice that they were both able to get things off their chests.

"Sir..." she started, as he reached the table.

He put his pint down on the table and sat down on the chair again, shaking his head with a small smile on his face. "You're not in my charge today, Jess. You can call me Rix."

"Rix?" She repeated, a little surprised. "That's your name?"

"Yes. Well, no. Richard's my name. But I hate it, it reminds me of my mum going off on one when I'd not conformed to her expected standards. So, it's Rix. For short."

Jess drank the last of her wine. "Ok."

"What were you going to ask me?"
She hesitated for a moment. "Do you ever think you could have done more that day?"

He took a few gulps of his drink again and then sat back in the chair, running his hands through his hair. "Honestly? Yes. Every day. But thinking about it isn't going to change anything. We have a split second to make a decision, Jess, and we don't always get that 100% right. All we can do is make the best decision we can and take responsibility for that."

Jess contemplated what he had said, and then she nodded. "You're right."

"Why do you ask? Look, we've been through this, you did a stellar job. I couldn't have asked for more from my medic."

"I've never lost as many soldiers," she stated quietly, her voice almost a whisper. The dynamic had suddenly changed, and she felt as though she was back there again, choking the dust from the explosion out of her lungs. Using what strength she had to get up off the floor and get over to the casualties to do her job.

Rix watched her carefully. She was tense again - on edge. He leant across the table and placed a hand on her shoulder, squeezing it gently. "Hey. You have to stop this. You saved lives that day Jess, just like you did every other day we were on tour. You cannot save them all."

"I know," she whispered. "But that doesn't mean it hurts any less."

***

Much later than she had planned to leave, Jess almost stumbled down the front steps of the pub when the door swung open a lot faster than she had expected.

Rix grinned, holding his arm out to steady her. "Careful, Medic."

She batted his arm away jovially and

managed to steady herself, coming to a standstill outside the pub.

"We should have joined the others," she glanced down at her watch. "Do you think they'll still be there now?"

"No. I think they'll have left ages ago. And to be honest, we're probably not really in the best state to join them. If Swan's still in there I'll be in for it. And you will too."

"Yeah, true," she agreed, and they continued to walk down the street.

The fresh night air whipped through Jess's hair, and collided with the alcohol in her bloodstream which went straight to her head. She blinked hard. The streetlights around her were fuzzy. She never drank this much. She never got drunk at all, especially not in her uniform. Suddenly she felt stupid and she stopped, placing a hand on Rix's upper arm.

"I'm going to call it a night," she stopped and looked up at him. His eyes were bloodshot and his pupils dilated, and she could see that he was just as inebriated as she was.

"Yeah. Me too. Shall we get a cab back to the station?"

She wanted desperately to get away and sober up before she made an even bigger fool of herself than she already had. But truth be told she didn't really know where she was going, and her brain wasn't working well enough for her to work it out. It would be much easier to get home if she just went along with him.

"Ok," she agreed.

Discretely, she took some deep breaths as they walked back towards the high street, where Rix hailed a cab. She felt her mind wandering as the streetlights lit up his chiseled features, and she felt herself blush. What was she doing, thinking about him in this way?! She cleared her throat as though that would clear all thoughts from her mind, and climbed through the door of the taxi behind him.

"Swindon Station, please," Rix requested, and the taxi pulled away.

Jess concentrated on keeping her stomach contents safely down, watching out of the window as the taxi passed down the high street and then out of the little town, down a field lined road. She was exhausted. It had been a long, very emotional day, and she was looking forward to collapsing in her own bed. She snatched a glance at Rix who was sitting in the other passenger seat, seemingly engrossed in the night time scene outside the window. His eyes were narrowed and he looked like he had the weight of the world on his shoulders. She wondered what he was thinking about.

The journey only took fifteen minutes, and when they arrived at the station Rix paid the taxi driver and they both climbed out. Jess followed him silently into the station, and they came to a standstill at the departures board.

"Which platform are you?"

"Um… two." Jess replied.

"Ah, I'm one. We both need to go this way."

Jess followed him, quietly glad that she didn't have to navigate the station with a head as groggy as hers was. She tried her best to pull herself together and followed him down the stairs, then across to the platform. Platforms one and two were right next to each other, and they both had a while to wait. They sat down on a bench which was positioned between the two and sat in silence for a few minutes. Eventually, Rix broke it. His voice was uncharacteristically soft - almost vulnerable. "Thank you."

Jess turned to him. "For what?"

"Being there. Listening."

Jess paused and thought about what to say, her mind churning away like an old clock. "Well, it's important that we're all there for each other. That's how a section works, isn't it? We all rely on each other."

Rix looked away again and stared into space. There were numerous things that he wanted to say but couldn't.

"I think about them every day," he confessed eventually. "I see their faces. Their injuries. It's the last thing I think about before I go to sleep and the first thing I think about when I get up."

"You need to talk to someone."

He glanced at her evasively. "I'm talking to you."

"Yeah, I know but… someone who's trained properly."

"I'll be alright," he dismissed, turning away from her again.

Jess took his hand in hers and squeezed it. Perhaps she was crossing a line - but at that moment she didn't care. "Listen. There's no shame in admitting that you're struggling. Ask to speak to the psych and they'll help you, before it becomes a bigger issue. But bottling it up won't help. You know that. It'll just make it a hundred times worse."

Rix looked down at his hand enveloped in hers. He knew she was right, but for his entire career he had been taught to keep his chin up, his upper lip stiff, and get on with it. Admitting that he was struggling was like admitting defeat. If he couldn't keep himself together then how could he expect the rest of his section to?

"Please. Listen to your medic?"

Even though he knew that it shouldn't, the warmth of her hand on his felt comforting, and Rix managed a small smile. "Alright. I'll speak to him when I'm back at base next week."

"Good," Jess squeezed his hand and then released it, tucking her hands back under her legs awkwardly.

Suddenly an announcement came over the speakers, and Rix stood up, looking up at the board on platform two.

"That's you," he announced. "Two minutes."

The lights from the front of train lit up the track in the distance, and Jess stood up and began to walk over to the platform beside him. As the train drew nearer, she heard the hiss of electricity coursing through the tracks and then felt the plume of air hit her as the train reached the platform and slowed to a standstill.

"Well, that's me," she muttered, glancing at the nearest train doors which were conveniently positioned right next to them. Rix leant over and pressed the button, causing a loud bleep as the doors opened.

She stepped inside and stood just inside the doors. She felt strange. It was like something was pulling her back towards him, telling her to get off the train. She knew she was being ridiculous, and she forced a smile. "Bye."

"Bye," he echoed, his voice unsure.

Around them, a handful of other people began to board and she heard the whistle on the platform, announcing the train's imminent departure. Her eyes locked with his and her heart began to pound in her chest, and before she knew it, he had stepped forward and pressed his lips to hers, his hand pulling her towards him by the small of her back. As their lips crushed together, she felt as though she was melting against him and she closed her eyes, losing herself in the softness of his lips and his musky scent. Suddenly, the whistle blew its warning again. He pulled away from her and stepped back onto the platform. The doors closed between them with a definitive clunk.

Chapter Six

The sound of his phone ringing woke Rix with a start, and he jabbed at the screen trying to turn off his alarm, still disorientated from sleep. Then as his brain began to function, he realised it wasn't an alarm at all - someone was calling him.

"Hello?" He croaked groggily, lifting the phone to his ear.

"Hello, Richard."

He rolled his eyes at the sound of her voice.

"Are you still in bed? Did I wake you?"

"Yeah... don't worry. I would have been getting up soon anyway."

He heard her tut. "Well, I should hope so. It is half past eleven!"

He glanced at the digital alarm clock on the bedside table and realised that she was right - it was in fact nearly lunch time.

"Yeah, well. Being on tour in a desert hellhole getting shot at by the Taliban for six months does get *quite* exhausting." He instantly regretted his choice of words.

"Language, Richard," she replied, as usual more bothered about the language he had used than the thought of her son in mortal danger. "Anyway, your father and I were wondering if you'd like to come over for dinner this evening? I was expecting you to have got in contact by now, I thought you got back last week?"

He rubbed one hand over his forehead exasperatedly. "Yeah I did. Sorry, I've just been a bit... preoccupied. It was the repatriation yesterday."

"Yes, I saw on the television. Absolutely frightful, isn't it? All those young lives wasted, some of them barely out of school, the poor-"

"I'll see you at about five then?" He interrupted, cutting her off. His head was throbbing, and he wasn't in the mood to listen to her bleat on.

"Yes. Five o'clock would be fine. I'll see you then," she replied curtly, and without saying anything further he hung up.

Rix dropped the phone down on the bedside table and let out a huge sigh, mentally preparing himself for dinner at his parents. He couldn't really think of anything much worse to endure after a night of heavy drinking. His mind wandered to last night and suddenly he remembered that moment at the train station.

His eyes widened with shock. "Oh, God."

What had he done? He groaned and pulled the pillow over his head, wondering what on earth he had been thinking. His life was turning into a car crash right in front of his eyes and he felt out of control, as if he could do nothing to stop it. Ever since that day his judgment had seemingly been shot to bits, she had been on his mind more and more but he couldn't believe that he had actually done something about it. And in his *uniform*. Anyone could have seen them.

Eventually he pulled the pillow off his head and threw it on the floor, staring up at the ceiling. Could this day get any worse?

***

Jase screamed, opening his eyes and shooting upright in his bed, his fists clenched around his sheets so tightly that his knuckles were white. His heart was beating faster than it did when he was in close combat, and it felt like it might burst out of his chest. Struggling for breath, Jase felt like he couldn't get enough oxygen no matter how hard he tried.

"Jason?!" Elena burst through the door and rushed across the room to take him in her arms, as though he was a little boy again. "Shh. It's ok. I'm here."

His chest was heaving against her, and within a few seconds his sweat was soaking through her clothes. She held him tightly until his breathing levelled and he relaxed, and then let go of him, sitting back to inspect him.

He was not the same young man she had waved off at the station six months ago. He had gone off full of life, optimistic and brimming with pride as he straightened his beret and strode off towards the platform with his bergen on his back. He had come back an empty shell of a man, his eyes vacant half the time and full of anger the rest. At first, she had thought it was the shock of losing Monty, but within a couple of days she had realised it was a lot more than that. The things he had seen on tour had broken him. She had tried so hard to get him to open up, but he was completely closed, barely able to talk to her about anything, let alone what he had experienced out in

Afghanistan. He had only been back for a week and he seemed to be getting worse by the day.

Jase shrugged her off and she stood up, trying to make eye contact with him. But he wouldn't even look at her. He wrapped his sheets around him and she heard the creak of her husband's footsteps in the hallway behind her. She turned around and he gave her a small nod - she knew what he was saying to her.

"I'll be downstairs if you need me," she patted Jase's leg gently through the covers and then stood up to leave. She passed George and he smiled reassuringly, then entered the room and closed the door behind him.

Even George, one of the most laid back men you could meet, was gravely worried about his son. He had hardly eaten since he had returned, and George knew that he had been restless in the night. Every other morning he seemed to be waking up drenched in sweat after a nightmare; in the past four days alone he had seen his bed sheets blowing on the washing line three times.

"Nightmare?" George asked, pacing across the room and slowly lowering himself into the chair in the corner of the room.

Jase barely looked at him but nodded, turning his head to look out of the window.

"You know you can talk to me about anything, son. Whatever it is. Me and your mum, we just want to support you."

Jase glanced over at him. For a moment he was tempted, and he opened his mouth as if ready to speak, but then he closed it again promptly. He didn't even know how to find the words, and worrying his parents was the last thing he wanted. It was bad enough replaying the moment over and over again in his mind, he didn't want to burden them with it too. And once they knew it was all his fault, what would they think of him? Surely, they couldn't support their son knowing that his actions had killed all of those innocent soldiers.

"I'm fine. Thanks, Dad."

George eyed him suspiciously. "It's not good to keep things bottled up."

What would you know, thought Jase, a ripple of anger running through him. But he clenched his fists under the bedsheets and suppressed it, a wave of guilt then washing over him. It wasn't his old man's fault.

Jase cleared his throat. "Honestly. I'll be fine. Now I'm going to take a shower."

George reluctantly rose from the chair and padded over towards the door in his slippers.

"Alright. But I'm always here, son. You know that?"

"Yeah. Of course."

Jase waited until George had left the room and closed the door behind him, then he sank back against his pillows, his eyes closed, wondering when this was all going to end.

***

Jess wandered around the garden centre with her mum sedately. She had barely been able to drag herself out of bed that morning, but she knew that Jane was looking forward to spending time with her and to be honest, she just wanted to forget about her hangover and get on with it. Despite the amount of alcohol she had consumed the night before, she had managed to get a full six hours sleep, which hadn't happened since before she had left for Afghanistan many months previously. The alcohol seemed to have done its job and she had been out like a light, only waking in the morning at the sound of Liam leaving for work.

As Jane leant over to examine a tray of dahlias, Jess pulled her mobile out of her pocket and glanced at the screen hopefully. No missed calls. No messages. She slipped it back inside her pocket and leant against the wooden display table with a sigh.

Jane lifted two polystyrene boxes full of plants. "What do you think? Dahlias or marigolds?"

Jess shrugged. "I don't know. Both?"

"Mmm," Jane mumbled, looking back and forth between the two. "I don't know. I'm not sure if they go together... I was thinking about getting some lobelia as well..."

"Get them too," Jess snapped decisively.

It seemed like such a ridiculous thing to agonise over. She was used to making life and death decisions in a matter of seconds, and here her mum was taking minutes to decide between a few trays of bedding plants.

Jane looked up at her and Jess could see

that she was a bit disappointed. She felt a sudden stab of guilt in her stomach and she looked down at the floor. "Sorry, Mum. I am interested. I'm just knackered."

"I know you are. I thought you liked pottering around."

Jess glanced up at her. "I do. I just… I've still got yesterday on my mind, you know."

Jane nodded and put the trays back down on the display table. "We can come back another day."

"No!" Jess protested. "No, let's get them today. I'll help you dig them in later, I need something to take my mind off everything else. Get all three, I'll treat you."

Jane was touched and it shone through in a smile. "You don't have to do that."

"I want to," Jess picked up the trays that Jane had put down and placed them in the trolley. "Get some more too. You said you wanted a fruit tree?"

"Oh, fruit trees are expensive. These will be lovely for now. Come on, I'll get us a cake from the café."

Jess took the trolley. "Choose a fruit tree. Just choose one."

They wandered over to the fruit trees, and whilst her mum was busy agonising over which variety to choose, Jess slipped her phone out of her pocket again. Still nothing. She felt completely confused, in a way she was glad that he hadn't been in contact because she didn't really know what she would say… but on the other hand she just wanted him to call or text or something. It was all she had really thought about all morning, and she just didn't know what to do.

Jane's voice broke Jess out of her little bubble. "This one. Definitely this one."

Jess read the label. "Pears. Are you sure?"

"Yes. It will look lovely on the patio."

Jess picked it up with one hand on the pot and the other on the trunk, and moved it into the trolley. Jane watched quietly, a strange expression on her face.

"Are you alright, Mum?" Jess questioned.

"Yes. Yes, perfectly fine thank you. I was just thinking, that's all."

"What about?" Jess asked, pushing the trolley in the direction of the check outs.

Jane looked at her sadly. "How you aren't a little girl anymore. It only seems five minutes since I was pushing you around in a trolley and now... well, here we are."

***

The gravel crunched under the weight of the tyres as Rix drove slowly up his parents' driveway. The track was long and winding, and bordered on each side by perfectly mown lawns and well cut hedges. Despite the fact that his mum had barely worked a day in her life, they had a gardener and groundsman - she didn't even have to lift a finger. It seemed ironic to Rix that one could become so well off simply by running a business in something as trivial, yet there were soldiers on the front line who were giving their lives for their country in exchange for a pittance.

When he got to the front of the house he slowed to a standstill and pulled the hand brake on, turning the key to switch off the engine. The engine stopped and for a few seconds he sat in silence, enjoying the peace and quiet of hearing nothing much at all. Before he got out of the car, he leant over and picked up the semi-decent bottle of wine he had picked up from the petrol station on route, together with a bunch of pale coloured flowers. He wasn't even sure that his mum would like them, but at least she couldn't say that he hadn't made any effort.

Hopefully, he glanced at his phone. He had been checking it all day waiting for Jess to call him, but she hadn't. He had considered calling her several times but then he hadn't known what to say. His mind was buzzing with thoughts but he could barely get them to make sense in there, let alone out loud. He stuffed the phone in his pocket and mentally prepared himself for his mum's verbal assault, opening the car door and stepping out onto the gravel with a crunch.

Rix pressed the doorbell and he heard the loud chime inside, followed by Lynne's shrill voice calling her husband down from upstairs. Rix clenched his jaw and took a deep breath, the bottle of wine in one hand and the flowers in the other. Within a couple of seconds the door swung open and she was there, dressed up to the nines in yet another dress he had never seen her wear.

"Richard!" She flounced out and put her

arms around him in a false show of affection. "It's so good to see you. Come in!"

She stepped back, and he held the flowers and wine out stiffly to her. "Mum."

"Oh, thank you!" She clenched her teeth, forcing an over the top smile. "Aren't they lovely. Come in, I'll grab a vase."

He followed her towards the kitchen as she strutted through the doorway and out of sight. When passing the stairs he saw his dad walking down, his bald head shining under the light of the chandelier. Rix smirked to himself, his mind wandering back to his conversation with Jess the night before.

"Welcome home, Richard."

"Thanks," Rix replied, although it didn't feel at all like home to him, and it never had.

"I'm glad you came, your mother has been fussing all week about when you're going to come over. Doing my head in, she was! That's why I told her just to phone you. And here you are."

"Here I am," Rix plastered on a fake smile.

Inside he felt exasperated already and he had only just walked through the door. Just being here reminded him of all the reasons he had been desperate to leave, years earlier.

"Shall I take your jacket?" Gerald asked.

Rix slipped it down off his shoulders and over one arm, before handing it over and walking through to the kitchen. "Thanks."

Suddenly he felt underdressed. Gerald was wearing a freshly pressed shirt and trousers, together with a tan coloured waistcoat which made him look even older than he was.

"We have a visitor coming this evening," Lynne announced.

Rix looked down at his jeans and casual shirt. "Oh? You never said. I'd have worn something a bit… smarter."

"Never mind," Lynne's voice was uncharacteristically breezily. "She'll still be impressed by all your… battle stories, I'm sure."

Rix cringed at her choice of words. He was incredibly suspicious. His mum barely liked to talk about his choice of career most of the time, let alone share it with someone else.

"She?" Rix watched her take a sparkling clean wine glass from the cabinet and fill it almost to the top.

"Yes, she. You remember Charlotte, Louisa and Maurice's daughter? From the Bowles Club?"

Rix took the glass from her and immediately drank a long sip. "Yes."

Lynne said nothing else and he took another gulp of wine, then set the glass down on the marble counter.

"What about her?"

"Well, I thought it would be nice to have some company this evening…" she filled his glass again and then her voice trailed off. "Oh, don't be cross, darling. It's just, you're not getting any younger and I'd hate to see you grow old on your own."

Rix almost laughed at the ridiculousness

of it. "I'm 30 years old. And anyway, I don't really have time for a relationship right now. I'm busy with work. You know that."

Lynne narrowed her eyes in frustration. "Even captains have wives, Richard. And it doesn't hurt to give it a go, does it? Meet someone new? Especially someone of her calibre. She's a London lawyer, you know."

Rix raised his eyebrows and picked up his glass before necking another two large gulps. Lynne eyed him beadily but even she knew not to say anything. Someone of her *calibre*. That word in particular got stuck in his throat, and he had to swallow hard to get rid of it.

"Whatever. But don't be expecting me to suddenly get down on one knee, because I'm really not interested in that right now."

She raised her eyebrows as if she didn't believe him. "Hmm. Well, we'll see. She's a very pretty girl."

***

Rix tried to look interested as Charlotte bleated on about her latest corporate client and how she had won them over, but he couldn't help his mind drifting. He couldn't help but wish that it was Jess he was sat next to. He had never spoken to anyone else as openly. It had felt so good to get it off his chest, to find someone he could speak to completely honestly. But then he'd had to ruin it all at the end with that dangerous drunken kiss at the train station. He still had no idea what he was going to do. It was now against army regulations for them to serve together, but the thought of not seeing her again was almost too much to bear. She was like the glue that stuck the section together, the one medic he trusted with his life and the lives of all the others. But if it was spread around the platoon he would lose the respect of the whole company, and probably his job too.

"Richard?" His mother's sharp voice broke him out of his day dream and he looked up, staring at her blankly. "Well? What do you think?"

"Uh…" he hesitated, looking around at the three faces who were staring at him.

He had no idea who had even asked the question, let alone what it was. To be honest, he didn't care, and he pulled his napkin up from his lap, crushed it and dropped it onto his plate.

"I'm sorry - I'll be back in a moment. I just need some fresh air."

He stood up and strode out of the room towards the front door, where he left the house and closed the door behind him. He walked up the gravel drive and across the lawn, the evening breeze blowing through his hair. It was a relief to get out of that claustrophobic environment. Coming here had been even worse than he had expected. Charlotte was dull. He wondered what his mum was thinking, inviting her here - she wasn't his type. Most of the time he felt like his mum didn't even know him at all.

When he was far enough from the house that they would no longer be able to see him, he sat down on a bench and pulled his phone out of his pocket again. He just needed to hear her voice, clear the air - he couldn't bear to think about it any longer, it was consuming him. He scrolled through his contacts and found her number, and before he had a chance to change his mind he pressed call.

"Hey," she answered, after just a few rings. He instantly relaxed at the sound of her voice. She sounded happy, and that made him feel better.

"Hi," he replied, and then found himself tongue tied. He hesitated, finding himself in an awkward silence. "I um… I'm sorry to call you at this time."

"It's only eight. Don't be silly. Are you ok?"

"Yeah. Well… no. Not really."

"What's up?"

Rix told her about the dinner at his mum's and how she had decided to mark the occasion of his homecoming by trying to set him up with one of her friend's suitable daughters. He hadn't realised how angry he felt about it until he said it all out loud. When he got to the end he sighed, leaning back against the bench wearily.

Jess was astounded. "Wow. You weren't lying when you said your mum was mad."

Rix snorted. "No, I wasn't. She is, 100%."

Another silence ensued and Rix pictured her lying on her bed, winding her hair around her fingers as she talked to him. He felt his pulse quicken slightly at the thought.

"Everything alright with you? Sorry for going on."

"Yeah, yeah I'm fine. Did a spot of gardening with Mum today - don't laugh. Her choice not mine. But I don't mind it, it's good to have something to take my mind off... well. You know."

"Yeah. Listen, Jess... about last night."

He heard her shuffle around a bit on the end of the phone. "Yeah..."

He was tongue tied again, like a stupid teenager. He shook his head as if to sort his head out and then leant against the back of the bench.

"I shouldn't have done what I did, I'm sorry for putting you in an awkward position."

"Oh, no, it's fine. It was a hard day, we'd both had too much to drink. Forget about it."

"No, it's not fine. You're in my charge and I shouldn't have abused my power like that. It won't happen again, I promise. I don't know what I was thinking."

"Well, it takes two, doesn't it?" She said quietly. "It wasn't just your fault."

They were both silent for a few seconds and, contemplating what to say next, Rix pinched the bridge of his nose with his spare hand. His heart and his head were telling him to say completely different things.

"You know... nobody can know about what happened... we need to be discrete... if it got out... there would be repercussions for both of us."

"Oh, of course. Let's just... forget it ever

92

happened?"

"Thanks. And I am sorry. Really. And it won't ever happen again."

She was quiet on the end of the phone and he wondered what she was thinking.

"Well, I'll see you next week then, back at base?" She muttered eventually.

"Yeah. Thanks for listening. Again."

"Any time."

Once she was gone Rix sat silently on the bench, the phone still in his hand as if it was stuck there with glue. He clenched his jaw, frustrated with himself. What was happening to him? In the twelve years he had served in the army he had never allowed his feelings to get in the way of his job. He couldn't understand why he felt like this, why he was unable to get Jess off his mind. For his entire adult life he had devoted every aspect of his life to the army. He had not been interested in relationships and he had thrown himself into absolutely every opportunity the army had given him. And now here he was, sat on a bench in the garden at his parents' house, pining after a woman after a drunken kiss who just happened to be his medic.

Chapter Seven

"You're a day early, Lance Corporal Fern," Lieutenant Swan said as Jess marched across his office and then stood to attention. "At ease."

"Thank you, Sir. I know. I wanted to talk to you in person, before the rest of the guys come back tomorrow."

Swan's features folded into a concerned frown. "Everything alright?"

"Yeah. Everything's fine. Thank you."

Jess pulled the letter she had typed up last night from her pocket. She had agonised over writing it for the past week since her conversation with Rix. She couldn't stop thinking about him, and the thought of not seeing him again was excruciating. But she knew that she couldn't have both. She wasn't even sure that he felt the same way, and she had come to the conclusion that this was the only way.

She handed the letter to him. "My transfer request, Sir,"

"Oh?" He raised an eyebrow, taking it from her hesitantly. "May I ask why?"

"I want to get some more experience in the field hospital in Camp Bastion."

It wasn't strictly a lie. She had spent a couple of days in the field hospital before transferring to the FOB and had been almost mesmerised by some of the life saving work the team had done.

"When I was there last I got talking to some of the medics who are based in the hospital, and I got back in contact with them this week. They're keen for me to join them, as am I."

Lieutenant Swan opened the envelope and skimmed through the letter, then nodded and placed it down on his desk. "Ok. But I'm sure the platoon will be sad to see you go. They all think a lot of you."

Jess nodded regretfully. "And I will miss them. But with everything that happened last time... I just feel like it's a good time for something new."

"I understand," he replied, although Jess knew that he didn't - he couldn't because he knew nothing about what had happened on the day of the repatriation. "Well, if you're sure, I'll set this in motion."

She nodded, more certainly than she felt. "Thanks, Sir. I'm sure."

***

Jase woke to the sound of the front door slamming as one of his sisters left the house for school. He stumbled out of bed and stretched, glancing at the alarm clock on his bedside table. Then, rubbing his eyes, he made his way to the bathroom.

Once in the bathroom he locked the door and filled the sink with water, staring at his face in the mirror. He hardly recognised himself. His face was covered in thick stubble and the skin around his eyes was sunken and bruised from lack of sleep. For the past two weeks he had stayed up late, distracting himself with video games until the early hours and then falling asleep awkwardly in his chair, half the time intoxicated and still in his clothes. He woke late whenever something disturbed him, and then tried to busy himself with long runs around the local area. The only problem was, the adrenaline coursing through his veins brought it all back, and he had to run faster and faster in an attempt to block it out. Just yesterday he had returned from a run and barricaded himself in his bedroom, convinced that he was outnumbered and someone was about to blast through his door with a rocket propelled grenade. And it wasn't just during day time hours that he suffered, he had been experiencing night terrors too. Every time he closed his eyes he could see their charred, lifeless faces, lying on the sandy floor of the Afghan desert while he stood there transfixed, his metal detector still in his hand.

But tomorrow was the day. He couldn't wait to get back to base and find out what his next mission would be. He always struggled when he got home from tour, and this time had been even harder than normal. He just couldn't be around his family at the moment, they seemed to say all the wrong things and were forever getting at him. Getting through everyday life on civvy street was impossible when all he could think about was that day in Afghanistan. He hoped that if he could get stuck back into something else at the barracks, the memories would fade and he could start to get over it. He really, really hoped so because he felt as though he was going mad. The only person he wanted to speak to about it was Jess, and he knew he couldn't because if she reported it then he might be stuck here even longer, forced to sit down with a shrink who hadn't even left Europe, let alone travelled to a war-zone like Afghanistan. The thought made him want to jump off a cliff there and then.

He opened the bathroom cabinet and pulled out his razor, before rubbing shaving foam over his thick stubble. Staring at his reflection in the bathroom mirror, Jase pulled the razor over his skin in long strokes and took a deep breath, straightening his posture. It was time to stop wallowing now and get on with it. He knew that Melon and the other guys would want him to.

Once his face was shaven he splashed it with cold water and patted his skin dry. Then he ran his hands through his tousled hair and wondered what to do about it. He really needed to go to the barber shop but he didn't have the time. He had far too much to prepare today. Instead he pulled his dad's clippers out of the cabinet and flicked them on, running them over his scalp until it was grade one all over. He smirked a satisfied smile. He looked like a proper soldier again already.

***

As Mellor passed through the security gates which protected the garrison, he took a deep breath and straightened himself up. He didn't really know how he felt about returning to base. As much as civilian life made him restless and he missed the routine that the army gave him, he felt differently this time. He couldn't really explain it, but it was like there was a voice nagging in the back of his head telling him not to go.

Marching across the tarmac towards the building, he nodded at some of the soldiers who recognised him. He knew that Swan would be waiting for him, and within just a few hours what was left of his section would also be arriving, together with the rest of the platoon. No doubt there would be a mix up now that they had less than a handful of soldiers left. His heart began to race at the thought of seeing Jess, and he consciously pushed all thoughts to the back of his mind. He had a job to do, and he had to do it. He promised himself not to be that stupid again.

Mellor swiped himself into the building and began to climb the stairs towards the command room, where he knew Swan would be waiting for him. Just outside the door, he straightened his beret and then glanced at his watch - he was right on time. He cleared his throat and knocked on the door loudly. He heard Swan call him in and he opened the door, marched in and stood to attention.

"Sir."

"Sergeant Mellor," Lieutenant Swan greeted him with a smile. "Stand at ease."

"Sir."

Swan pushed some papers to one side.

"Take a seat. How was your leave?"

"Good thanks, Sir. You?"

"Yes, it was… eventful."

Mellor raised an eyebrow as if to encourage him to continue, but he didn't. He knew better than to ask. Swan clasped his hands tightly together on the desk in front of him.

"Right. Let's cut to the chase. You have two privates left, Coulson and Siddiq. Corporal Jones is recovering well but obviously he isn't medically fit to rejoin the platoon, and won't be for some months. I can't send you out anywhere as a section of three, so I'll be moving over a couple of the more experienced guys from 3 Section and you'll have a few new recruits too. I want you all on base training together for the next few months until you have them all up to speed. Keep a special eye on Coulson, the psychiatrist is happy for now, but he does need ongoing monitoring."

Mellor frowned in confusion. "Yes, Sir. But there are four of us, including Lance Corporal Fern."

Swan shook his head. "Lance Corporal Fern is transferring."

Mellor's stomach dropped as if he had just driven over a hump back bridge at considerable speed. "She's… what?"

"Transferring. She put her request in yesterday. You didn't know?"

"No," Mellor choked, trying not to show that he was shocked at the news.

"She wants to get more experience in the

field hospital in Bastion, apparently. The timing isn't great, obviously, but I can't deny that she will be brilliant there. Anyway, I've a new medic in mind and I'll introduce you to him in the next few days."

Mellor clenched his fists in his lap, trying to keep his face straight and his voice level. "Sir."

The conversation was over and he stood up, saluted and marched out of the room. Once the door was closed behind him he picked up his bergen, which he had dropped in the hallway, and swung it over his shoulder so violently that it almost knocked one of the framed certificates off the wall next to him. Before anyone could see his obvious anger, he marched down the stairs of the building and pushed his way through the double doors, marching across the path towards the barracks furiously.

How could she just do that, without even speaking to him? He had trusted her with information he had never shared with anyone, and she was just going to disappear without even telling him? He tightened his grip on the strap of his bergen as his hands began to shake with rage. This was all his fault. If he hadn't have done what he had at the station then none of this would have happened. She would still be serving with them, and his soldiers would be safe in the hands of the best medic he knew.

Once he arrived at his room, he opened the door and then slammed it shut behind him with a thump, tossing his bergen down on the floor. He breathed deeply and paced the room, running his hands through his hair. Catching sight of himself in the mirror, he felt another stab of regret. He had to calm down. What was he becoming? He was so far away from the calm, collected sergeant he had been at the beginning of their last tour that he didn't even recognise himself. He laughed. What a hypocrite. How could he expect Jess to trust him when he didn't even trust himself? It seemed that he destroyed everything he touched - it was just as well that she had got herself out when she could. A lucky escape.

Chapter Eight
Six months later

Jess pulled off her latex gloves with a satisfying snap and threw them inside the clinical waste bin in the corner of the room. "All done. You'll need to keep it clean and dry, and come back in a couple of days. I'll re-dress it for you."

Sitting on the edge of the bed, the young private glanced down to admire the fresh bandage which was now wrapped around his forearm. "Thanks, Medic. My first battle wound."

Jess smiled knowingly. "And hopefully your last. You've been lucky. Shrapnel injuries aren't always this minor."

"Yeah, I know." He jumped down from the bed.

"Take care of yourself."

Once he had left, Jess picked up the clipboard with one hand and used the back of her other hand to brush away some loose strands of hair from her forehead. It had been a long, busy day - she had seen dozens of soldiers already, mostly for minor injuries and complaints and a couple with virus-like symptoms. She had been at Camp Bastion for two months now and it felt like home. She had learnt an incredible amount already and had worked with some of the best medical professionals she had ever come across. Every day was different - one day she was triaging, the next she was dealing with minor injuries and complaints, the next she was in the operating theatre assisting with major traumas.

Despite that, she couldn't deny that she missed life on what she considered to be the real front line. There was something about it that drew her back; her mind seemed to have forgotten all the bad parts and remembered only the good; the surge of adrenaline as she loaded the casualties she had managed to keep alive onto a chinook, and the rush of relief when she heard that they had made it or they returned to the FOB with everyone intact. She also missed her platoon and the rest of the company. She had tried to keep in touch with them, especially those in 1 Section - she knew that Raj was going for special forces selection, but she had struggled to contact Jase. She supposed that it was because of his recovery, he had been more traumatised than anyone else in that last patrol. She wondered if speaking to her brought back memories that he would rather forget. Last time she had spoken to him, more than five months ago, he was back with the platoon at the UK base and working with a psychiatrist with a view to getting back on tour. He had seemed quite positive about the future but also a little distant - and the next time she called, he hadn't answered. She had tried a few more times but she had been busy, and life had got in the way.

She also missed Sergeant Mellor. It had been almost unbearable at first, saying goodbye to him. She had only seen him briefly, the day after he returned to the base, and he had barely spoken to her. She was sure that she could see actual resentment in his eyes when she tried to explain why she hadn't told him sooner. But she knew that she had to be strong. It was for both of their sakes. He had tried to call her a few times since, but she had ignored his calls. She didn't know what to say, and every time she spoke to him it brought all those feelings she had back to the front of her mind. It was much easier to bury them if she just tried to forget it had ever happened. So instead, she immersed herself in her new team and worked hard, forcing distance between them.

And it had worked very well - it was becoming a lot easier with time. She barely had time to think about anything other than her current work, anyway; she worked long days, often going over and above what was required, and by the time she got cleaned up and had some scoff it was time to fall into bed for a few hours until her next shift began.

She tucked the clipboard under her arm and walked in the direction of the minor injuries waiting area. Reaching the cluster of chairs of which half were occupied by various soldiers, she opened her mouth to read the next name on her clipboard when her eyes caught on someone standing in the corridor in the distance. She did a double take. He was right there, his arms crossed against his body and his eyes fixed on one of the resuscitation bays. She stopped immediately as though she was rooted to the spot, her eyes wide with surprise. What was he *doing* here?

It was as though he sensed her there because he immediately turned to face her, his eyes fixed on her helplessly as though they were both opposite poles of a magnet. Her heart began to pound in her chest and she gripped the clipboard hard as though she was trying to stop her heart from bursting out of her. For a few moments they both stood staring, neither of them knowing what to do. The sight of him standing in his blood stained fatigues with his helmet down by his side brought it all back - the rush of emotion she felt when they got back to the FOB, a stricken platoon with half of their members killed or injured, and the admiration she had for him when she watched him stand in front of the company at the remembrance ceremony, talking about the brave soldiers they had lost.

Suddenly she realised that he was walking towards her, and she swallowed hard and cleared her throat, her airways tight.

"Corporal Fern," Mellor nodded at the two chevrons which now emblazoned her uniform.

"Sir," she managed, her eyes still wide. For a moment it was as though they were the only two people in the hospital; medics and soldiers rushed around them, but they didn't even notice.

"Congratulations. Well deserved."

She swallowed and managed to force some more words out. "You too, Sir," her eyes fell on the Crown and three chevrons on the arm of his uniform.

"Colour Sergeant Mellor, eh," he grinned awkwardly. "Bet you never thought you'd see the day. As you can imagine, my mother is thrilled."

She laughed nervously and then loosened her grip on the clipboard slightly, realising that her fingers were white with pressure. "What are you doing here? I didn't know you were back in Afghan."

"Yeah. We came out here last month."

They both stood silently again, tongue tied. Finally, he looked back over in the direction of the resuscitation area. "My medic. It's not looking good."

"I'm sorry," she glanced down at his helmet which was sporting a bullet shaped indent. "What happened?"

"Sniper," he replied solemnly. "I didn't think he was going to survive the journey but he's still hanging on. Just got him in the MERT in time. He arrested twice on the way here."

"I'm sorry, Sir. Are you ok?"

"Yeah, I'm fine. Just in a bit of a predicament now. I need a new medic."

His hopeful gaze returned to her and she felt her cheeks flush slightly. Her brain was telling her to say no but her heart was thumping in her chest and willing her to say yes. She missed the company and she missed him.

"Fancy a change?"

She shrugged. "I don't know... they kind of need me here."

"Not as much as we do," he suggested hopefully.

Her eyes widened and he quickly added, "on a strictly professional basis of course. There's a line drawn firmly under what happened before. But, anyway... think about it. No pressure, obviously. But we'd love to have you back. I need someone we can trust, with lots of experience as to what we're up against here. I can't have someone fresh out of training. I expect Lieutenant Swan will be in contact, speak to your superiors and let him know what you think."

"Ok, I will."

"I'd better get going," he clapped her on the shoulder gently with the palm of one gloved hand. "Good to see you again, Corporal Fern."

"You too, Sir."

The steady thud of his boots on the hospital floor, leaving her again, matched that of her heart. Even once he had turned the corner and was out of sight she watched after him, as if he was going to reappear at any moment. Eventually she let out a huge breath that she didn't even know she had been holding and shook her head, glancing down at the clipboard in front of her. Decision or not, she had a job to do right now, and she was going to get it done.

***

Mellor was drinking his coffee under the canopy when he heard the armoured patrol vehicle approaching the base. He heard the chatter of the Afghan soldiers guarding the gates, and he looked up just as they opened them to allow it safe passage. He took another sip of coffee and kept his eyes on the vehicle expectantly. She was due to arrive any time.

He took another big gulp of coffee, watching as the rear doors opened and the troops started to jump down from the vehicle with their bergens, into the rain. He was beginning to wonder whether she had changed her mind when he caught sight of one final soldier leaving the vehicle. Watching her from a distance, he couldn't help but smile. Slinging her bergen over her shoulder casually, she ducked her head against the rain to protect her face and started to jog towards the corrugated metal cover. She couldn't see him, but within a couple of seconds she was spotted by a couple of the other soldiers from the platoon and they leapt on top of her with a jovial welcome. He heard her laugh as she greeted them. The sound of her laugh lit him up, and for the first time in months he felt as though perhaps, everything might be alright.

So far, the tour had been difficult. The base was very remote and there was no safe route for air support, which meant everything had to come in via road. Due to this, they were all on very basic rations and not just with food - even water had to be conserved carefully. A couple of times the local insurgents had almost managed to cut off their road access, and they had to be extra stringent when out on patrol in relation to IEDs. It was quite obvious to the Taliban where they would be heading - and that meant it was all too easy for them to cause maximum damage. They had already faced several ambushes when out on patrol, the worst of which had been when their own medic was shot by a sniper the previous week. They had been scraping by with minimum equipment and not enough medics to really keep the company safe. Despite Lieutenant Swan's best efforts, they didn't even have enough radios for everyone which made their job all the more dangerous. And worst of all, even when they were within the boundaries of the FOB they still weren't safe - it had faced several night time attacks from RPGs within the last couple of weeks. So far they had been lucky but Mellor couldn't shake the feeling that something big was about to go off.

Jess's arrival calmed him somewhat. She was an extremely competent medic - in fact, perhaps the best he had ever worked with, with the exception of Corporal Little - and she had brought with her a raft of medical supplies. She had, as always, been meticulous, if the number of crates being off loaded from the vehicle by the Afghan soldiers was anything to go by. He heard her voice drifting back across the base, directing them to the makeshift medical centre they had fashioned on base. He grinned to himself. She had been there five minutes and already she had her sights set on the medical centre. He tipped his flask right up and downed the last mouthful of coffee, then descended the stairs towards her. It was time to make himself known.

"All of these to the medical centre please," she instructed the young Afghan soldiers who were lifting the crates from the vehicle. "As quickly as you can."

"I see you're making yourself at home, Corporal Fern."

At the sound of his voice, she turned

around with a smile. "Of course. Would you expect anything less of me?"

"No," he answered, honestly.

He looked up and down at her neat and tidy appearance and pulled a face. "Sorry, the facilities aren't great here. The shower took a bullet last week and it isn't fixed yet. I'm afraid you'll have to put up with the smell from the rest of us for a few days."

"I heard. Never mind. I made the most of unlimited showers while I was at Bastion. What's this about ration packs though, funny you never mentioned that when you asked me to come!"

He grimaced. "Yeah, sorry. Pate and crackers and biscuits fruit for the foreseeable. But you do get the best company, it's not all bad."

"Quite," she grinned, and then she stepped forward to pick up the last crate which had been left by the side of the truck. "Well, I'd better get on. Work to do."

He nodded. "Don't let me keep you."

She walked off in the direction of the medical tent, and he watched after her. Her boots squelched in the wet sand and she carried the crate effortlessly, as though it was empty.

"Fern," he called after her.

She turned around. "Yeah?"

"Thanks for this."

She nodded. "Any time, Sir."

***

It wasn't long before Jess was in the swing

of things, and the cupboards of the medical tent were well stocked with fresh supplies. She stood back with her arms folded, proudly admiring her handiwork. The rustle of the tent door caught her attention, and she turned.

"Ah brilliant, more supplies," another medic grinned, walking into the tent. "I'm Lance Corporal Smith. But you can call me Jenny."

Jess held out her hand. "Hi, Jenny. I'm Corporal Fern - Jess."

Jenny shook her hand and then placed her bergen down in the corner of the room. "Nice to meet you. I've heard a lot about you."

"All good, I hope," Jess raised an eyebrow comically.

"Of course. The boss hasn't stopped singing your praises since he said you were coming. Anyway, I'm sure I'll learn a lot from you."

"Well, we can all learn from each other."

Jenny looked young and optimistic. She also looked like she could do with a good shower and her uniform was dusty, but other than that she didn't look too battle worn.

"It's my first time in Afghan," Jenny volunteered, admiring the neatly stacked shelves of equipment. "The boss said it's your second?"

"Yeah. I've been a medic for seven years though. Although I've done mainly humanitarian missions up until now."

Jenny looked impressed. "Wow. This is only my third deployment."

"You learn quickly out here," Jess said,

111

coolly. "Before long it feels like you've been here forever."

Jenny nodded thoughtfully and then grinned. Jess noticed that her smile lit up her whole face.

"Do you know what I miss the most?"

"What?"

Jenny sighed theatrically. "Chocolate! I'm addicted to chocolate, I've never been without it for this long!"

Jess gestured to her bergen in the corner of the room, which was much lighter now that it was not stuffed full of every piece of medical equipment she could fit inside it. "Look in the top pocket."

Jenny's eyes widened and she walked over to the bergen to unzip the pocket. "Oh my god! No way! You guys have it good at Bastion!"

Jess nodded. "Go on. It's yours. Luckily it's winter here or it would be chocolate sauce by now."

The packet rustled as Jenny opened it, broke off a few squares of chocolate and then savoured the smell, her eyes closed. "I have missed that smell *so* much!" She took her first bite and savoured it with a sigh, then reached into the packet and snapped off the next line. "Here."

Jess shook her head. "You're alright. Your need is greater than mine."

"No. I *insist*. We're a team now! I've got your back, you've got mine."

Jess couldn't argue with that. She reached forward to take the line of chocolate from Jenny.

"Alright then. Sounds good to me."

They stood in silence for a couple of minutes, working their way through the bar of chocolate. Jess was really pleased that the ice was well and truly broken with Jenny, not that she needed to worry. She knew that they were going to make a good team, and that she would be great to work with.

Jess finished her last square of chocolate. "Who else have you got here? Medic wise, I mean?"

"It's just me! There were two of us, but Archie got airlifted to Bastion a week ago."

Jess's eyes widened and her mouth almost dropped open. "You've been on your own for a week? But that's ridiculous! What would you have done if there was a major incident?"

"There are a few Afghan medics who've been working alongside me. We've managed. Luckily without incident."

Jess folded her arms crossly. "They shouldn't have put you in that position. We're stretched just the two of us. It was just the three of us last time and that didn't exactly end well."

"What happened?"

Jess blinked and the sight of Corporal Little's burnt, lifeless face flashed before her eyes momentarily. She took a deep breath and forced her eyes open. "We were out on a routine patrol. We'd almost reached the compound when we set off a daisy chain IED. The Vallon missed it. We lost four soldiers in the blast including the lead CMT and one of the section commanders. As we were getting them to safety, they started firing at us. Another soldier was shot dead and I had dozens more injured, five Cat-A. We lost five from the company in total, plus some of the Afghan soldiers. In one day."

"Jesus," Jenny breathed. "And you coped with that all by yourself?"

"I had to. There was no plan B. Not until the backup arrived."

Jenny shook her head and they both stood in silence for a couple of minutes, both deep in thought. Jess relived the whole thing in her head; she could smell the explosives, feel the thick desert sand in her throat and the rumble of the shots being fired in her chest. Immersed in thought, she jumped slightly when Jenny opened her mouth and spoke again.

"They weren't lying when they said you're an amazing medic. The best."

Jess shrugged nonchalantly. "I was just lucky. I did my best, patched them up, got them on the MERT. There's nothing else we can do except cross our fingers and hope for the best."

"I think you're doing yourself a disservice playing it down. You ought to be very proud of yourself. You saved dozens of soldiers that day!"

Jess knew that she was right, but she couldn't let herself be proud of her actions that day, not ever. She had still lost seven soldiers. Maybe there was nothing she could have done to change things for most of them, but not Melon. She had run through events more than a hundred times in her head and thought of a list of things she could have done differently. If only she could have stemmed the bleeding more quickly, if only she could have kept him talking for a bit longer. She wasn't sure if she would ever forget the petrified look on his face when he realised that it was too late for him. The look of longing in his eyes when he knew that he would never see his partner and daughter again. Some nights when she fell into bed exhausted and shut her eyes, it was all she could see.

Chapter Nine

Jess had just finished treating her first patient in the Forward Operating Base, a young private named Ryan, who was suffering with blisters caused by his boots. She cleaned them up and covered them with dressings, before handing his boots back to him.

"Keep them dry, as much as possible. And come back tomorrow so I can check on these again, ok?"

He jumped down from the bed. "Ok. Thanks, Medic."

He was extremely young. He was only just eighteen, and in the short time that she had spent with him she had learnt that not only was it the first time he had been abroad, but it was also the first time he had ever left his parents for longer than a night. Something about him reminded her of Liam, and that troubled her. He was someone's son and someone's brother, too. There was a very real possibility that he might not make it home at all, let alone in one piece. Cleaning up the treatment bay, Jess tried to put those thoughts to the back of her mind and then snapped off her gloves, dropping them inside the bin in the corner of the room.

Turning around, Jess almost knocked straight into someone who was standing right behind her in the doorway. She took a step back but then immediately realised who it was.

"Jase. Everything alright?"

"Yeah, fine. The guys said you were back. I just wanted to know if it was true."

She smiled, genuinely pleased to see him. "Well, it is. It's good to see you."

"You too," he shuffled awkwardly in the doorway with his hands in his pockets, holding back.

Jess eyed him suspiciously. She couldn't help but feel uneasy. There was something about him that she didn't recognise, although she couldn't quite put her finger on what it was. Eventually she decided that it was his eyes. They had changed. He had come to the section full of optimism, his eyes sparkling with excitement and determination that he would do a good job. Now they just looked dull and tired, they had lost their sparkle.

She knew that she had to tread carefully. The last thing she wanted to do was push him away. She had tried to contact him a few times since leaving the platoon, but he had ignored her calls. "How have you been?"

He ignored her question. "Why did you leave?"

Jess bit her lip and felt her pulse quicken slightly. What on earth should she say? Eventually she gulped and managed to string a few words together to respond.

"I told you. I wanted to get some more experience in the field hospital. They had an opening there… and it just felt like a good time to transfer over."

"Why?" He glared at her, his eyes

piercing.

"I don't know. I guess... after what happened... I just wanted a fresh start."

"But what about us?" His cheeks flushed pink as his voice raised slightly. "We needed you. *I* needed you. You were the only ones who understood, you and Raj. And then Raj went for special forces selection and I was stuck here with Mellor. You know he doesn't trust me, now? I can see it in his eyes every time I pick up the Vallon."

"That's not true," Jess reached forward to place a hand on his upper arm, but he stepped back and shrugged her off. "If he didn't trust you, you wouldn't be here. He does trust you, Jase. I know he does."

Jase's eyes narrowed to slits. "How could you possibly know? You don't even know him, and you haven't even been here. We've all struggled. How do you think it felt for us when you left us, after we lost everyone else? There were only three of us left! It's not the same."

Jess blinked at him. He was almost shaking with anger now and she took a step back, allowing him space to cool down. She understood how he felt. She couldn't deny that she would have felt the same if it had been the other way around. But he didn't know the full story, and he never could. It was hard trying to justify her actions when he didn't know everything.

"I'm sorry," she folded her arms across her stomach defensively. "I shouldn't have run away. I know that now, I made a mistake. I should have stayed with you guys, we could have worked through all this together."

Jase eyed her across the room for a few seconds and then shook his head, running his hands through his dusty hair in frustration.

"I'm sorry. I can't blame you for wanting to get away. But it was hard, you know? I lost three people who were like brothers to me, and then I was just getting my head back together and then I lost you. And then Raj left. And all I had left was Mellor. And most of the time it was like… he wasn't even here anymore either. And I was all alone. The outsider. It's just not the same with them."

Jess's ears pricked up. "What do you mean? About Mellor?"

"He hasn't been the same since we came back from leave. Most of the time… it's like he can't even look at me. He's distant. There's no banter with him anymore, you know… it's almost like a part of him died with them."

Jess turned over what he had just said over and over in her mind. Suddenly the guilt she had felt about leaving him so suddenly hit her again, and her mind started to run away with her. She had left because she thought it was the best thing for both of them, and the thought of him being negatively affected by her decision horrified her.

"He's not the same boss he was," Jase continued. "Even when he got promoted… it was like he didn't even want it. He just shuts himself away."

"Maybe he's just trying to keep his distance. Show his authority to the new platoon members."

"No, it's more than that. There's something going on with him. I almost mentioned it to Swan a couple of times, but… I don't know. If there's something wrong with him then it's on me, isn't it? I don't want to make things any worse for him than they already are."

Jess shook her head. "Listen to me, alright? Whatever is going on with him, it's not your fault. What happened was awful, Jase, but it wasn't your fault. It was nobody's fault, except for the guy who buried the device in the ground. You have to stop blaming yourself."

Jase said nothing but continued to look at the floor, his face utterly miserable. Jess took his hands and squeezed them reassuringly.

"I'm back now. And if you ever need to talk, about anything… you come and see me, ok? I won't let you down again, I promise. And I'll speak to Mellor. I'm glad you told me, because we all need someone to talk to when things get tough. Just because he's the boss doesn't mean he's immune from feeling the way we do."

Jase nodded. Jess let go of his hands and they dropped down by his sides.

"Promise me, no matter how small it might seem, if something is bothering you or… or you're just having a hard day, you come and talk to me about it, alright?"

He cleared his throat, folding his arms across his chest. "I will. I promise."

***

There was no such thing as breaking in gently in Afghanistan. Within a couple of days, Jess was filthy enough to look as though she had been with the platoon for the entire tour, thanks to the absent shower. Every morning she made do with a bucket wash, which was quite torturous due to the freezing weather. The tents were poorly heated and she was almost glad to get up and go for a jog with the rest of the section every morning, just to warm herself through.

Thankfully, they seemed to be going through a quiet period - there had been a couple of minor attacks by insurgents overnight, but nothing they couldn't easily handle. Their day time patrols had also been very tame, there had been no need to engage at any point and they seemed to be making a lot of progress with the local villagers. Local relations were vital because the locals were able to provide invaluable information about insurgent activity within nearby compounds. With ground support from the platoon, the Afghan army had managed to seize a significant amount of weapons, ammunition and IED components within the last week, and the situation locally appeared to be quite stable. When they were able to, most of the section took the opportunity to have some down time. They had been running on empty for several weeks, and even just a couple of hours extra sleep made a huge difference.

Jess had tried to find a good time to speak to Mellor about what Jase had said, but she hadn't managed to find one. Quite quickly, she realised that Jase was right - Mellor just wasn't available to the section like he had been on their last tour. He kept himself to himself, and although he still seemed to have a good sense of authority over the other platoon members, he wasn't the same. There was no banter with him, and he seemed to spend a lot of the time shut away in the command room with Lieutenant Swan and the other section commanders. Part of Jess wondered whether he was actively trying to avoid her. She knew that she should be glad - they both had a job to do, and she had promised herself when she made the decision to come back that she wouldn't do anything to compromise her career or his. But the reality of seeing him every day and feeling the distance that had grown between them was hard.

One Monday, 1 Section were out on a foot patrol to one of the nearby villages that they had visited many times. Led by Jase with his metal detector, closely flanked by Mellor, they trudged through almost freezing ditches, across fields and along the dirt track approaching the village. When they got to the village, everything seemed quite normal - or as normal as was possible in the middle of a war zone. The villagers were going about their daily lives, children were playing in the sandy passages between the compounds and women were carrying infants on their backs, running errands. Still, they knew better than to be complacent. They had almost been at the village last time, and that was when they had suffered their biggest loss. There was no way anyone wanted that to happen again. Mellor had brought six soldiers out on patrol, and he would be taking six back again.

Once in the village they began to chat to the locals, keeping their eyes on their surroundings at all times. Jess looked at the children around her; they were running around in sandy puddles, half of them partially covered with ice. It was cold enough to make steam with your breath, yet some of them were out in shorts and sandals because they were the only clothes they had. Despite that, they didn't seem to notice and happily ran around, screeching with laughter. It was humbling to see them making the best of such an awful situation. They hadn't chosen to be caught up in war.

"Coulson, on me," Mellor barked, striding over towards the Afghan soldiers who were scouring nearby compounds for any suspicious activity. "The rest of you, stay alert. If you see anything suspicious you inform me immediately, understood?"

"Yes, Sir."

Jess watched from a distance as Jase followed Mellor across the track, his hands on his weapon. She heard her name and turned her head to see one of the youngest privates in the group next to her. "What's up, Harris?"

"It might be nothing..." he hesitated, his eyes sliding away from her. "But that kid doesn't look right."

She followed his gaze over towards a young girl, perhaps eight or nine years old, who was inching along a nearby compound wall, one hand skimming over its walls with the other arm shielding her stomach protectively. Jess's senses heightened instantly and she realised the girl was trying (and failing) to keep her eyes off them.

"Go and tell Mellor," Jess ordered quietly, and Harris jogged off towards him.

Jess narrowed her eyes and started to walk towards the girl, slowly so as not to frighten her. She noticed the girl clock her out of the corner of her eye and she began to walk faster, but just as Jess was about to reach her, she stumbled and fell against the wall with a cry.

"Salaam Alaikum," Jess greeted softly. The girl looked looked up and Jess noticed that her eyes were full of tears. "Do you speak English?"

The girl hesitated for a moment and then nodded very slightly.

"It's ok. I'm here to help."

The girl kept her arm tightly wrapped around her stomach and Jess glanced down, immediately searching for any sign of an explosive vest. "I'm Jess. What's your name?"

"Apana," the girl replied hesitantly, her eyes widening with fright at the sight of Mellor and Jase marching over.

Jess glanced behind her and put a hand out towards them. "It's alright. Just a moment."

"Be careful, Corporal Fern," Mellor warned sternly.

Jess turned back to the girl. "Apana, can you lift your top for me please sweetheart? Very slowly?"

Apana was petrified, she was shaking. She shook her head, tears leaking from the corners of her eyes.

"Is it ok if I take a look?" Jess asked.

She could feel the heightened sense of alert all around her - the whole of the section were watching, waiting for command from Mellor. Apana nodded slowly and closed her eyes, as Jess reached forwards and very carefully lifted the thick fabric of her top.

"Clear," she announced with relief when she saw that there was no vest. But then she gasped, her eyes fixed on the angry purple and red bruises that covered half of the little girl's torso.

"How did you get these, Apana?" She asked, her finger tips skimming over them.

Apana trembled as fresh tears spilled from her eyes. "I... can't..."

Jess glanced back at Mellor, who shook his head. Clearly the little girl had been beaten; it was abhorrent. Before they had a chance to do anything, they heard heavy footsteps behind them and they turned to see a furious Afghan man striding towards them.

"Apana!" As his voice boomed, the girl ripped her shirt back over her stomach and began to limp away from the soldiers. "Apana!"

Jess watched the man grab her by the collar of her shirt and drag her away; the girl cried out in pain.

"Hey!" Jess cried, unable to stop herself.

"Corporal Fern!" Mellor's voice boomed over hers, but she didn't stop. She couldn't just stand by and watch that bully take the little girl away.

"Hey!" She shouted again, this time louder, and she managed to catch them up.

The man turned around and squared up to her, shouting something in pashto that she didn't understand. Jess stood proud in front of him and narrowed her eyes at him.

"Don't!" Apana pleaded, cowering against the compound wall.

"Did he do this to you?" Jess demanded. Apana shook her head furiously. "No."

Jess could tell that she was lying. She narrowed her eyes, adrenaline coursing through her veins. More than anything she wished that she could take the little girl to safety, but she knew that she wouldn't be able to. "How could you do that to her?"

"*Corporal* Fern." Mellor emphasised her title to show his authority. "Stand down immediately. This is a local issue, it is not for us to get involved."

"But Sir," she protested, turning back to him just as the man spat a huge glob of spit in her direction. It landed on the lapel of her uniform.

Suddenly, all hell broke loose. Next to her, Jase jumped forward and lifted his rifle right up to the man's face. Jess's stomach flipped as Mellor's voice boomed over them.

"Lower your weapon, Private Coulson. Immediately."

Jase showed no sign of listening. Jess noticed that his eyes were wild; he seemed to be in some sort of trance. He looked almost blood thirsty, out of control. That scared her. She had never seen that in him before.

"Lower your weapon *immediately,* Private Coulson. You're putting the entire section in danger."

Jase narrowed his eyes and shook his head at the man, then eventually he lowered the weapon as instructed. Jess breathed a sigh of relief as Jase marched off away from the group.

"Where do you think you're going?" Mellor roared, storming after him. "Come back here!"

Jess turned back to the little girl who was now being rushed away by her collar. She clenched her jaw in frustration; she knew that she had to let her go, but that didn't make it any easier. She turned back towards Jase and Mellor who were now practically having a shouting match in the middle of the village. He shouldn't even be here. Even though she knew she shouldn't, she felt angry at Mellor for allowing that little girl to go with that man, probably to receive another beating, and angry at him for allowing Jase out on patrol when he was quite clearly still suffering mentally. They had been here weeks - he should have noticed and called it in. His failure had put them all in danger.

***

As soon as they arrived securely back inside the FOB, Jess marched off towards the medical tent furiously. She had contained her anger at the situation all the way back from the village and now she just needed to get away from them all. Mellor, Jase, and that abhorrent man in the village. She just needed to bury herself in the stock cupboard and take half an hour of quiet. Maybe Jenny would be there to cheer her up. They had become good friends in the past few weeks and it was good to have someone to lean on.

Just as she thought she had got away, Jess heard his voice calling her name. She swore under her breath and then turned around.

"Can I have a word? Mellor asked flatly.

"Can we do it later, Sir, I've got stuff to do."

He raised an eyebrow, and she knew better than to argue with him. Instead, she walked towards him, and then followed him to the command tent. Once inside, he pulled the door flap shut and stood in front of her, his arms folded authoritatively.

"I expect you to follow orders at all times, do you understand me?"

"Yes. But that girl…"

"Is nothing to do with us," he interrupted. "I know it's hard, but we're here to do a job, Medic. If we start getting involved in local matters then we jeopardise the mission and the safety of the platoon. You're here to support us, you do not get involved with the locals unless I tell you to, is that clear?"

She gritted her teeth, then dipped her head

and looked at the floor. "Yes, Sir."

She knew that he was right and it was unfair to resent him for it - it was his job after all, to command them and keep them safe. It just left a bitter taste when she had come out here to help people, and he wasn't allowing her to. He nodded and then raked his hands through his hair wearily, taking a few steps to the left and leaning over the command table.

"That's all."

Jess watched him with concern. "Sir. What about Jase? He's not medically fit to be here-"

"Yeah, I know. I should have called it in, but he assured me he was doing alright. I thought I was doing the right thing, he said he didn't want to go home…"

"He masked it well," Jess replied sadly. "I had started to think he was ok. But after today - there's no way we can allow him to stay here."

"I know that. I'll speak to Swan, he has to go back home and sort his head out."

Jess nodded. "It's for the best, Sir. I love Jase and I care about him, he's a good friend to me. But I can't watch him put himself in danger. He needs help."

He stood up straight, puffing his cheeks out with a long breath. "He's a young soldier and now his career's over before it's even started. All because of what he's seen here. What's this going to do to him? What if he never recovers?"

"We all know the risks when we sign up."

"Do we though? Does an eighteen year old really appreciate what they're committing themselves to when they get on that first aircraft? The things they're going to see? The parts of their own body that they're going to lose?"

Jess shrugged. "I don't know. But he won't be on his own, Sir. He'll get support. There's no reason why he can't get over this if he gets proper support."

He sighed. "Yeah, you're right. Sorry, it's just... it's been one of those days."

"It's been one of those weeks," she smiled weakly, and he smiled back.

They stood in silence for a minute, then he straightened up and cleared his throat.

"Right. I need to go and find Lieutenant Swan."

"You're doing the right thing, Sir," Jess stepped backwards and then opened the door of the tent.

He nodded and watched her hesitate in the doorway. Her fingertips clutched the fabric door and she turned to leave, but then stood there, her gaze returning to him, seemingly unable to leave.

"Was there something else?"

Jess dropped the curtain and took a couple of steps back towards him. She opened her mouth to speak but couldn't find the words.

"It's not often that I find you speechless, Corporal Fern," he joked jovially. Jess suddenly realised that it was the first time she had actually seen that part of his personality shine through since she had returned to the platoon. Jase was right, and she knew that she had to say something. It was her responsibility to keep an eye out for all members of the platoon, not just the privates.

"Are you ok, Sir? Like… really ok?"

"Yes," he glanced at her strangely. "Why do you ask?"

She bit her lip. "I um… I noticed that you haven't been… yourself lately."

He snorted. "In what way? I can assure you, I am definitely myself, thank you very much."

"It's not a weakness to admit you're struggling, you know," she attempted to get through to him, but there was now an atmosphere between them and she could tell that he had closed up. "We all struggle sometimes."

"Thanks for the pep talk," he interjected defensively, straightening up. "But I can assure you, I am perfectly fine. Now, if that's all, I have a lot to do."

Jess pursed her lips. She knew that there was no getting through to him when he was like this. He was stubborn, and he had already made his mind up. But the front he was putting on was not fooling her at all.

"Well I'm always here, if you need to talk. I'll leave you to it."

***

Crouched down in the medical tent, Jess was replenishing the supplies in her bergen when she heard his angry footsteps crunching through the almost frozen sand outside. She knew it was him before she even saw him. She stood up

131

straight and turned to face him just in time.

"How *could* you?!" He roared, squaring up to her, his face just inches from hers. Immediately she knew that this was 100% the right decision. He was barely recognisable.

She raised her hands defensively, shocked at the anger which was radiating from him. "Jase! Calm down."

"Calm down?!" He shouted, still inches from her face. "*Calm down*? Would *you* calm down if it was you who was being marched back home like an invalid?"

"Lower your voice now," Jess ordered firmly, standing her ground.

Jase stood there for a few moments, his chest heaving up and down furiously as his heart pounded in his chest. He had never experienced anger like it. Suddenly something inside him clicked. He realised what he was doing and fell backwards into a chair, his head in his hands, his whole body shaking. "I'm sorry!"

Jess crouched down beside him. "I know. It's ok. I know."

"You couldn't possibly know!" He cried, looking up at her with tears streaming down his face. "You have no idea what's going on in *here!*" He jabbed himself hard in the head.

Jess reached forwards and took his hands in hers. "I do. Because I was there too, remember? I lost them too, Jase. But you have to release some of that anger in there, or it will kill you."

"I wish it would!" He sobbed, his body still shaking. "Every night when I go to bed, I

132

pray it will be me. That I just won't wake up. That I won't have to go through another day like this."

Jess squeezed his hands. It was hard to see him suffering this much. "Why didn't you talk to me? You promised me that you would."

He shook his head angrily and snatched his hands away, wiping his eyes roughly with the backs of his hands. "Because I knew you'd do this. I can't get better at home. All I wanted when I was there was to come back here. I thought coming back here and getting on with things would help, but I just can't do it. Every sound, every smell, every sight that reminds me of that day - and I see them all again. Dead. Right in front of me. And it's my fault, Jess. How can I ever forgive myself? And if I can't function here and I can't function at home, what do I do?"

"You're not well, Jase. You need help. Proper help. And once you get it, it will get easier. I promise."

He scoffed at her. "How can you possibly promise that? You're a medic, you've saved hundreds of lives out here. What have I done? Missed the IED that blew five of our men including my best friend to bits."

Jess watched him dissolve in a fresh bout of tears. She had no idea what to say or what to do to help him. He looked almost beyond help. Instead, she reached forward and held him tightly in her arms until he had no tears left.

"God, I'm sorry," he sniffed weakly when he almost had no energy left. "I don't even know what's happening to me. It's pathetic."

Jess watched him pull out of her grip and look down at the floor, defeated. "It's good to cry, Jase. You need to find some way of releasing that anger... that devastation... or it will consume you. When you get back to the UK you'll see a psych, you must tell them the truth, do you promise me? Tell them everything. The sooner you accept that you need to do that, the sooner you'll recover. You can't keep pretending that everything's ok."

"I don't think I can," he admitted. "I can barely even think about it, let alone talk about it. I'm going mad."

"I know. But it will get easier. Please, if you won't do it for yourself, do it for them. Melon wouldn't want you to be like this. He'd want you to live your life, do all the things he can't. Do you hear me?"

Eventually he nodded. "Yeah."

"Good." She held him close to her again. This time he allowed his body to relax, and he felt as though a huge weight had been lifted off his soldiers. "And you're not going mad, Jase," she rubbed his back gently and held him tight. "It's called PTSD, and it's more common than you think. But there is a way out. Everything's going to be alright."

Chapter Ten

Jess stepped out of the makeshift shower tent, slinging her towel over her shoulder whilst clipping her helmet back on. Luck had turned in their favour, and finally the shower had been fixed earlier that morning. It felt good to be properly clean for the first time in weeks. The weather was milder, too; the sun was out and the warmth on her skin helped her to feel a bit more positive. There was a hint of spring in the air.

She glanced over towards the entrance gates, where an armoured vehicle had arrived laden with supplies. That was another thing to be happy about. A successful delivery of supplies meant that they were good for another couple of weeks, and although it was only standard ration food, Jess was relieved that they wouldn't have to further ration what they had on base.

Turning back in the direction of the tent, she caught sight of a lone soldier approaching the vehicle. She stopped for a few seconds, watching him get closer. It was Jase. He reached the vehicle and leant up to grab on the handle on the back and then looked over in her direction. Jess nodded with a small reassuring smile. He nodded back, his face emotionless, and then jumped up into the back of the vehicle and out of sight.

Jess sighed and began to walk back to the tent. It was bittersweet watching him go. She knew that it was for the best - for him and for the rest of the platoon - but it was always sad to lose a member of the team, especially one who she had served with previously. More than anything she hoped that he would take up the support available to him when he was in the UK. Too often she heard of former soldiers slipping through the support net, leaving the army and not seeking help for PTSD. Jase was clearly struggling and she shivered, contemplating what might happen to him if he didn't seek that support. She made a mental note to check in on him when she could, once comms were back up again. At the moment they had lost their comms link, which was intermittent at the best of times. Now they had no reliable way of contacting the outside world.

She got back to the tent and hung her towel up, then pulled her helmet off and lay back on her cot, allowing her muscles to relax. Today it was her turn for downtime; Jenny was covering the medical centre, not that there should be much action because Lieutenant Swan had decided there would be no patrols that day, to save all available resources for the resupply convoy if necessary. It had come with its very own medic; provided that they didn't receive a mayday call when it was on its way back and still fairly close to the FOB, they shouldn't need to have any involvement.

Jess reached over to the bag she kept by her bed and pulled out her music player and headphones. She put them in her ears and pressed play, then pulled the brown envelope she always kept in her locker out. She turned it upside down and three sheets of thin card fell out onto her stomach. She turned them over and stared at the photographs, skimming the faces of her parents and little brother with her thumb as if they would feel it. She missed them a lot today. She missed them every day, but it was the days when she had time to stop and think that it really hit her.

"I miss you, Dad," she whispered.

She tucked the photographs under her pillow and closed her eyes, allowing her mind to wander off to distant memories as she listened to the music which brought them all back to her.

***

Colour Sergeant Mellor wandered across to the scoff tent, his stomach rumbling. Despite the lack of action it had been a long day of planning, and he had been in the command tent for most of it discussing tactics for upcoming patrols with Lieutenant Swan and the Afghan soldiers. Over the next few days they wanted to press forward towards new villages that they hadn't already visited, building relations with the locals and trying to flush out insurgents who they suspected were using abandoned compounds as IED factories.

He was about to head over and collect his dinnertime rations when his eyes fell on the table which housed most of 1 Section. Everyone was present except for two people - Jase and Jess.

"Alright, guys?"

They all sat up straight as they saw him approaching, "Sir."

"At ease. Where's the medic?"

"I don't know, Sir," Harris replied. "Haven't seen her in hours."

"Hmm. I'll see if I can catch her in the medical tent."

Mellor left, turning right in the direction of the medical tent. Once there he carried out a quick sweep - it didn't take long as it really was just a tent, with a divider in the middle of it - and there was no sign of her. He furrowed his brow while crunching through the sand towards the accommodation tents. There were only so many places she could be on a small base, but it was unusual for her not to sit and have dinner (if you could call it that) with the others.

He lifted the curtain and poked his head around it. "Corporal Fern?"

He could see her still and silent, lying on her cot with her back to him. Her brown hair, which she normally wore tied up, was loose and spread out across her pillow. Walking through the doorway and in her direction, he let the curtain fall back in its place behind him. Once he was a couple of metres away he realised that she was asleep, her chest rising and falling steadily. He noticed a small piece of card sticking out from under her pillow and he reached forwards and pulled it out gently. It was a photograph of two adults - presumably her parents as Jess was a definite mix of both of them - standing in an embrace. Her mother wore a wedding dress and her father was in full military dress. Mellor's chest felt tight at the realisation that she was missing her family. That was an almost alien concept to him; he never missed his parents, not at all. In fact, for him, one of the major bonuses of going on tour was to get away from them and have an excuse not to stay in touch.

Suddenly, she stirred and he tucked the photograph back under her pillow quickly, this time fully underneath so that it wouldn't fall out again. Then he walked to the end of the cot, clearing his throat to wake her up.

"Corporal Fern?"

Her eyes shot open and once she got eyes on him, she sat up quickly, pulling her headphones out of her ears. "What's up? Has something happened?"

"No. It's time to eat."

She frowned, lifting her arm to look at the watch that she wore on her wrist. "Sorry, Sir. I didn't intend to sleep this long."

"It's no problem. I did tell you to get some rest."

Her cheeks flushed a mortified shade of scarlet. "Not that much rest though! I'll be over in five."

He nodded and turned to leave, but upon reaching the doorway he stood still for a moment, almost unable to move. It was like his shoes were stuck in quicksand and the more he tried to muster the energy to break through it and leave, the harder it pulled him back. Brushing her hair back up in a ponytail, Jess watched him silently from across the room. There it was again, that tension between them. Since coming back she had reassured herself that there was nothing between

139

them, that their kiss at the train station was just a product of their grief and an outpouring of all the emotion from that day - combined with a truckload of alcohol. But they were here now, sober; and just like the day they had been reunited at the hospital, she felt herself wondering whether there was something more to it than that. And the thought of that scared her, because the consequences of that could be huge.

She straightened the sheet on her cot and looked up at him again. He had turned now and he was watching, his eyes fixed on her piercingly. She felt like she couldn't breathe for a moment and she swallowed hard, her heart pumping harder in her chest.

"Are you alright, Sir?"

He nodded, not taking his eyes off her. Against her better judgment she took a few steps towards him, taking a deep breath and trying to act completely normally. She was being stupid, reading into things too much. He had pretty much said that there was nothing between them. She had to stop this. And yet...

He nodded. She was within touching distance. "Yeah. Are you?"

She bit her lip. "Yeah. Just missing home. Worrying about Jase."

"He'll be fine," he reached over and placed his hand on her upper arm reassuringly. "It's absolutely the right thing for him to go back."

"Yeah. Yeah, you're right."

He nodded and took his hand back, turning

to leave. Before he had the chance, Jess suddenly lost control of her mind and she grabbed him by the elbow.

"Sir, wait."

He turned to face her again and looked down at her hand, an expression on his face that she couldn't read. "What is it?"

She shook her head and removed her hand, her cheeks flushing again. "Nothing. Sorry, it's nothing."

"You can tell me," he encouraged softly. "Whatever it is, you can tell me. You *should* tell me."

"No, it's fine. Honestly. It's nothing."

"Clearly it is something."

He was so close now that she could feel his breath on her face. Jess wished that he was easier to read. One minute she looked into his eyes and she was sure that he felt the same. And then the next he was just her superior again and she felt like she was being stupid. It was beginning to drive her mad. Her heart was still pumping madly in her chest, and there must have been a shot of adrenaline coursing through her veins because before she could stop it, she had opened her mouth and the words had come out and she couldn't take them back.

"Why did you really ask me to come here, Rix?" She whispered hopefully.

He looked thoughtful for a few seconds, furrowing his brow. "You know why. Because I needed a medic. Someone I and the rest of the platoon could trust. And I knew you'd be a good

141

match for those requirements."

She stared at him for a few seconds, willing him to just tell her the truth. Finally, when he said nothing else she nodded and took a step back. "Ok."

"Why did you ask that?"

Jess took a deep breath and let it out shakily. She wished that she could take it back now, clearly he didn't feel the same and it was all in her head.

"I dunno. Sorry, my head's all over the place today. I'm just tired. I'll be back on it tomorrow, I promise."

He didn't move. His eyes were still locked on hers and suddenly, she felt overwhelmed by the urge to get closer to him. Desperate to suppress it, she lowered her eyes to the floor and then cleared her throat.

"Shall we go then?" She asked brightly, making a move to leave, but he was still blocking her way. She looked up at him again, and this time his eyes had softened and there it was again - that *look* he gave her - like she was the most amazing thing he had ever seen.

"Jess… you know what the regulations state."

"Of course," she answered casually, as if she didn't know what he meant.

"And if I wanted to… act on my feelings… you know I couldn't?"

Her heart was pounding even harder in her chest now - she was right - he *did* feel the same. For some reason she suddenly felt nauseous and flustered, and she nodded and replied quickly, her voice a little quicker and squeakier than she had meant it to be.

"I know."

He nodded and cleared his throat as if he was trying to clear all thoughts and emotions from his mind. "Right. I'm needed in the command room. You go and get something to eat and get some more rest. We're heading out tomorrow at 0500 hours and I need you at the top of your game."

"Of course," she breathed and he nodded, slipping out of the tent, leaving her alone.

Jess stood in silence for a few moments and then shook her head, taking a deep breath. Get a grip, she thought. She caught sight of herself in a mirror which sat next to one of the other cots. She barely recognised herself anymore.

***

The next day went from bad to worse. The FOB suffered an attack overnight and, although they didn't suffer any casualties, it meant that a significant portion of the platoon were up for most of the night and then went straight out at 0500 hours on patrol. It wasn't unusual for them to be up for such a time without any significant rest, and at least they had spent some time at the base the previous day resting. However, as they lined up at the front gate ready to leave in full combat gear, Jess felt as though she hadn't slept for days.

She straightened the helmet on her head

and took a deep breath of the early morning air, trying to clear her head. Usually at the beginning of a patrol she was full of adrenaline, ready to go; this morning she felt as though she could happily have got on a plane back to England without a second thought. It was as though she had mentally checked out of the army last night when lying in her cot, before the shots started.

Ever since he had left the tent, she had barely stopped thinking about him. As an experienced army medic, she was used to compartmentalising, closing off parts of her mind that might compromise a mission until she was in a safe place and ready to open the door again. But something had changed in her since the last time she went home - she found Rix on her mind more and more, and the more she tried to compartmentalise her feelings for him the more they seemed to consume her. He was right in front of her now, trying not to look at her because he felt the same and he was responsible for all of their lives on this patrol. They both knew that they were in dangerous territory - if anyone found out, they would never be able to serve together again and if they allowed anything to happen between them whilst on tour, it could even be the end of their careers with the army. The consequences were massive. Mellor in particular felt conflicted as although he knew that he ought to inform Lieutenant Swan of his feelings, he knew that would mean that Jess would be transferred. Strangely, the thought of her being away from him seemed even worse than the thought of him being discharged. He just couldn't contemplate it at the moment.

The doors of the vehicle opened and they began to climb in. When it was her turn, Jess reached up and swung herself up inside the vehicle, sitting on one of the benches with her bergen between her legs. She straightened her helmet on her head, mentally preparing herself for the conflict they may well face today. There was only one road out of the base and it was quite possible that insurgents would have left IEDs for them, or staged an ambush. They would have to take the journey slowly and they had further to travel than usual. The Afghan army wanted to push towards further villages and today was the first day.

"Ready?" Jenny's voice roused Jess from her thoughts.

Jess nodded, fastening her grip on her bergen. "Mmm. You?"

Now sat opposite, Jenny grinned. "Bring it on."

Last to board was Mellor, and he sat a few spaces along from where they were sitting, on Jenny's side. Jess glanced at him but was very careful not to make eye contact. She needed no distractions. The potential for injuries today was massive and like he had said, she had to be at the top of her game. She would have to deal with her feelings for him when she got back to the UK at the end of her tour, but for now she had a job to do. Mentally, she ran through the kit she had packed in her bergen, and what she would do if there was an ambush, shots fired or an IED blast. She was the lead medic on this patrol and she would not get it wrong. If Corporal Little was watching, she'd do him proud. She was responsible for 1 and 2 Sections as well as leading the trio of Afghan medics who were riding behind them in the second vehicle.

The vehicle's engine roared up, and before long they were immersed in the eerie darkness of the Afghan desert. Jess felt the rumble of the engine in her chest as the vehicle continued its slow journey down the dirt track, spitting up a small sand cloud in its wake. For the second time, Mellor ran through the plan of action. They were simply supporting the Afghan Army, flushing out insurgents in a new village. They were to reassure the locals but keep their eyes and ears out for any signs of insurgent activity while the Afghans took the lead. It was much the same as any other patrol that they had been on recently, except this time it was a completely new village and they weren't entirely sure what to expect. As such, both 1 and 2 Sections were joining together on the patrol, with Mellor in command and Sergeant Kelly of 2 Section as second in command. Lieutenant Swan would remain at the base with 3 Section and the rest of the Afghan soldiers who shared it, in case of an ambush.

The vehicle continued to rumble along the dirt track. It seemed as though they were travelling hundreds of miles but in fact it was nowhere near that far; they could only crawl along as anything suspicious had to be checked out and cleared by the two Vallon men in the front of the vehicles. They stopped at three vulnerable points where the track became narrow and turned, but thankfully no IEDs were detected and they passed through without any issues. By the time the sky turned a lighter shade of blue and the villages they passed began to wake up, they were approaching the village that they were aiming for. Preparing to disembark, Jess kept a tight hold on her weapon.

The vehicle came to a standstill and they jumped down from the vehicle, their hands on their weapons just in case. The village was quiet and had an eerie feel. Many of the compounds appeared to have been abandoned, presumably because the villagers had fled during nearby conflict. This particular village had been under Taliban control just nine months ago, but ISAF had managed to regain control of it and some of the villagers were now beginning to move back in. It was very important that they managed to get the remaining villagers on side, and prevent the insurgents from re-infiltrating.

As Mellor commanded small groups of the soldiers in different directions, Jess looked around her at the squalid conditions the villagers faced. It was clear that anyone living here was very poor, and they had probably had no choice but to return. The chatter of small children turned her head and she noticed a small group watching them from next to a derelict compound. She smiled and waved, and they giggled and waved back. Mellor turned and watched the exchange.

"Right, Peters, Rayan, Harris, you three

patrol this central area and reassure the locals. Medic, you stay with them. Anything suspicious or any useful intel, you call it in immediately."

"Sir," they responded in unison and he nodded, then marched off towards the Afghan commander, who was already talking to a couple of locals fifty metres away.

One of the children approached Jess and tried to reach up for the pen which was shining on the lapel of her uniform.

"You like pens?" She asked with a smile, and the child nodded although she wasn't sure that he understood. After unclipping the pen, she reached down and placed it in his palm. "There you go."

His face lit up with joy and he squealed, waving the pen at the other children who instantly ran over and jumped up at Jess.

She grinned. "Whoa, whoa! Ok! I only have one more spare."

She unclipped her other spare pen from her uniform and then Private Peters was at her side, his hand in his pocket, pulling out a handful of boiled sweets which he had brought especially, all the way from the UK.

"You're a right softie!" Jess grinned, watching him hand them out to the children, whose hands were waving in the air with excitement.

"Everyone likes sweets," he smiled. "Sweets can win wars."

Jess laughed. She soaked in the excitement of the children and tried to block all negative thoughts to the back of her mind. Now they were here, the village didn't seem too bad - no worse than any of the others they had visited. She kept one hand on her weapon but gripped it less tightly; hopefully she wouldn't need to use it. The sweets ran out and Peters tipped the bag upside down.

"All gone. Sorry!"

The children all groaned, but they still had smiles on their faces. One of them stepped forward and tapped Peters on the hip. He looked down.

"Thank you," the child said slowly.

He grinned and ruffled his hair. "No problem, little man."

Jess smiled again and then looked up. It was at that exact moment that something in the distance caught her eye - something glinting in the early morning sun some distance away, but it was coming towards them down the dirt track which led to the village. Focussing on it, she narrowed her eyes. Suddenly she recognised the put-put-put of distant gunfire. Each shot was louder than the last. He wasn't quite in range yet, but Jess and Peters realised that they were quite vulnerable. The rest of the section, with the exception of Rayan and Harris were quite some distance away.

"Contact!" Peters yelled and the soldiers began to hit the ground around Jess.

She looked from the approaching moped to the children who were beginning to scream and run around her like headless chickens. About ten metres from where she was standing, one of the

149

children had dropped to the ground and was screaming in fright, caught in the kill zone all alone. Jess knew that she should take cover herself, but she couldn't just lie there and watch him die.

As soon as Mellor heard Peters shout, he turned to where Jess and the others were positioned. Time seemed to stop. Jess leapt up and sprinted towards a lone child who lay on the floor between the rest of the soldiers and the shooter. The child was about thirty metres away from the nearest compound, in open ground.

"Get down, Medic!" He bellowed into his radio. "Harris, on me!"

He raised his weapon and sprinted towards them. The bullets were getting closer now, deflecting off the sand just metres away from her. She continued to run towards the child as Peters took a shot at the insurgent on the moped. All she could think about was getting to the petrified little boy and hauling him to safety.

She was within touching distance of the child when she fell. The shots were raining down around her from multiple directions. Suddenly the driver fell from his moped, neutralised by a bullet fired by Harris.

"Medic!" Mellor bellowed, so loudly that he felt as though his lungs were about to drop out. She hit the ground in a cloud of dust.

The shots were still raining around her and he held his weapon up, ready to strike the second insurgent as soon as they came within range. All he could think about was getting to her, he was beside himself with worry at what he might find. The other children had scrambled up and scurried away screaming hysterically, but she was still and silent on the floor, the child she had been trying to save concealed from view by her body.

"No," he hissed under his breath.

She was perfectly still and silent. More bullets rained down in their direction and he felt something impact with his thigh, but mid-adrenaline rush, he felt nothing. He got to her and crouched down on the floor, just as the second shooter turned the corner. Mellor raised his weapon and shot him in the head at almost point blank range.

The shots stopped. The streets were now deserted except for the soldiers and he could hear his heart beat smashing away in his head.

"Jess," he croaked.

Lifting her hair off her face gently, he could hardly breathe. Suddenly, he was relieved to see that her eyes were open and she was alive. The little boy cowered underneath her silently, his tiny body shaking with fear.

"The other children," she muttered, a little dazed.

By now, Harris had caught up, and he grabbed the child and sprinted him to safety towards the nearest compound.

"They're fine. No casualties. They're fine, Jess. What were you thinking?"

"I'm alright," she pushed herself off the floor, fighting for breath, her chest heaving. She straightened her helmet and his eyes fell on the circular imprint which had hit her perfectly square, right between her eyes. Just a couple of inches down and she would be lying dead in his arms.

Coming down from the adrenaline rush, Mellor's breathing was shaky. "Luck was on your side today."

"Yeah," she agreed, still a little breathless herself.

"You weren't hit anywhere else, were you?" His eyes skimmed over her, full of concern.

At the same time, both their eyes lowered and fell on the puddle of fresh blood which sat between them on the floor. Jess's heart began to pound in her chest and her stomach turned upside down.

"Jess," he cautioned nervously, his eyes skimming over every inch of her. "Where's that coming from?"

She quickly leant forward to clamp her hand over his leg. "It's not mine."

He looked down and saw that she was right.

Chapter Eleven

The taxi pulled up slowly outside the house of Jase's parents and he stared at it vacantly, not making any move to exit.

"Is this the place?" The driver prompted him and Jase turned his head, still staring blankly. The driver flicked the interior light on and peered at him suspiciously. "Are you alright, mate?"

The light startled Jase and his eyes widened as they came in to focus. "Yeah. Sorry."

He pulled a bunch of twenty pound notes out of his wallet and without even looking at them, thrust them at the taxi driver.

"Hey," the taxi driver called after him. "It was only thirty quid!"

But Jase wasn't listening. He carried on up the path. He barely heard the driver thank him before he quickly drove off.

He saw his mum's face appear in the front window, her eyes wide with surprise. She had no idea that he was due to come home. He had considered calling them when he was sat at the airport in Cyprus, waiting to board the aircraft back to the UK. But he couldn't find the right words. How could he tell them that he had been sent back because he was losing his mind? He had decided to call them when he got back to base in the UK. But when he got there, he still couldn't find the words. He had convinced himself that maybe he could stay on base and persuade the psych he was ok, then he could get back out to

Afghan for the rest of the tour. The thought of being stuck in the UK alone with his thoughts, while the rest of his section were out there together, petrified him. He would prove them wrong - Colour Sergeant Mellor and Corporal Fern - and he would get himself back out there. He would show them.

But it hadn't worked. The psych had been concerned enough to put him on sick leave and a programme of CBT. There wasn't even the option to stay on base - they had decided, without even seeking his opinion, that sending him back home would be the best thing for him. To Jase, it seemed like 100% the worst thing for him right now. Coming back and seeing the house again for the first time since he had left to go on tour instantly brought back memories. The desperation he felt when he was last here, how the thought of getting back out there had comforted him, the night terrors he had experienced when he saw his best friend's lifeless face over and over again. Reaching the front door, he considered bolting. Maybe it would be the best way, he didn't feel like he should be here at all. But before he made a decision the door flung open, and his mum threw her arms around him, tears running down her face.

He stood limp and emotionless in her arms as she held him close and sobbed against his chest. He felt nothing. He didn't feel happy to see her, but he didn't feel unhappy. He felt completely detached.

"Jason! Why didn't you tell me you were coming back on leave?!"

He felt a lump form in his throat and he opened his mouth to talk, but no words came out. How could he possibly explain that he wasn't just back on leave - that he was possibly back permanently?

"What a surprise!" She momentarily released him and stood back to look at him. "Oh, I've missed you more than you'll ever know. Come in, come in. I'll make you some lunch, you must be hungry?"

"Thanks," he managed, following her in.

"You go and sit down," she held her arms out for his bergen. He ignored her and set the bergen down. It probably weighed as much as she did.

Jase sat down in the living room on the edge of the sofa. He had grown up in this house and sat on this old sofa thousands of times, yet he felt unnatural and awkward sitting on it now. It didn't feel like his home. He felt like he was a stranger visiting someone's house. He wondered if this was how it felt for the officers who had to go and visit the relatives of the soldiers who were killed in battle. If this is how they had felt when they had to go to Melon's parents' house and tell them that he was dead.

Elena set a tray of tea and biscuits down on the coffee table. "Here you are."

When Jase looked at the tray, he had a sudden urge to smash it into a million pieces. He couldn't explain why; just that simple notion of a cup of tea and biscuits was enough to fill him with rage.

"Actually, I'm not hungry. I'm filthy, I'm going to take a shower."

He got up and marched out of the room and up the stairs before Elena even had a moment to say anything. She opened her mouth to speak but then closed it, her eyes falling on the full tray on the coffee table. Something didn't feel right. It was like he was there, but he wasn't - if it wasn't for the warm cushion where he had just been sat and his boots and bergen slung in the hallway, she might have thought that she was going mad.

She padded back towards the kitchen in her slippers and sat at the dining room table, listening to the quiet hiss of hot water running through the pipes. She picked her mobile up from the table and hesitated, then dialled her husband's number. She held the phone tighter in her hand, pressing it against her cheek until he answered.

"Hi, love. You'll never guess what's happened. Jason has come home!"

She was about to explain that something didn't seem right, but the excitement in George's voice got to her and she just couldn't. She couldn't spoil that excitement. Instead, she reminded herself that her son had probably had a long, tiring journey home, and had suffered difficult conditions while he was in Afghanistan. He was probably exhausted and keen to get a shower and get some sleep. She was sure that he would seem more positive tomorrow.

***

Jess pressed a dressing hard against Mellor's leg, which was now oozing thick red blood. He was going into shock; his whole body was shaking and she could see his teeth visibly chattering.

"Keep pressure on it," she commanded as Harris placed his hand over the dressing, allowing her to pull a tourniquet out of the bag. "And I need a med-evac organised now. He's Cat-A."

As she pulled the tourniquet on, he groaned, and she placed a hand on his undamaged leg supportively.

"It's alright. You're doing really well. Just keep breathing."

His chest heaved up and down as though he had just run a marathon, and he gritted his teeth hard, fighting past the pain. She could see the young private was starting to panic as blood began to seep through the dressings - silently she passed him another one and he quickly unwrapped it before clamping it down onto the wounds. There were multiple entry and exit wounds and she suspected that at least one had gone straight through his femoral artery.

Jess tried her best to look completely calm. She prepared the syringe and then administered the analgesia. "I'm going to give you a shot of this, you'll feel much better in a minute."

She heard Sergeant Kelly relaying the nine liner over his radio, and she concentrated on taking Mellor's observations in an attempt to keep her mind on the job only. On the outside she was calm and controlled, providing the best medical care she could. Inside she was absolutely terrified. Mellor was ghostly white and sweating profusely, and the huge puddle of blood around them on the floor was an indicator that he needed to get to Camp Bastion urgently. He had already lost a huge amount of blood and she had only limited supplies. If he didn't get on the chinook quickly, she could lose him.

"We're too vulnerable here," Kelly announced, returning from making the radio call. "We need to move to a nearby checkpoint for the extraction. They'll bring in an apache for air support."

Jess glanced down at his leg. "I don't think we should move him until the med-evac arrives. It's too risky. We need to get them to winch him up from here."

"But if we stay here, we're sitting ducks," Kelly muttered quietly, but Mellor still heard.

"Just leave me. Get yourselves to safety. Fern needs checking over."

"Don't be ridiculous," Jess snapped at him.

Kelly turned back to her. "We have to do what's best for the whole platoon, Medic. We need to get back on the vehicle and move. That's an order."

She contemplated what he had said for a moment, then nodded. "Yes, Sir."

The driver began to reverse the vehicles towards them and the other soldiers prepared to move, all the time holding defensive positions in case more insurgents arrived. Whilst Kelly responded to the command room over his radio and Jenny finished checking over the children who had almost been caught in the cross fire, Jess and Mellor had a moment alone. He reached over and grabbed Jess's hand in his, squeezing it hard.

"This is bad," he grimaced. "I know it's bad. I'm sorry, Jess. I really am."

She squeezed his hand back. "Don't be daft, what have you got to be sorry for? You're going to be fine, ok? I'll get you on that MERT if it's the last thing I do."

"Don't say that," his whole face contorted, his chest heaving up and down in agony.

"Shh. Just relax," she reached down to wipe a stray tear from the corner of his left eye, which had managed to squeeze its way out. "The anaesthetic will work in a moment."

"I'm sorry, Jess," he repeated. "I'm sorry, I should have told you sooner how I felt. Now I might not get the chance."

"You can tell me when we get back," she insisted firmly. "Now stop this. I need you to be strong, ok? For all of us."

The vehicles came to a standstill and the rear doors opened, allowing the other soldiers to jump on. Jess heard footsteps behind her and turned to see Jenny jogging towards them.

"They're all fine, Jess. A couple of scrapes but nothing that requires any more treatment."

"Great," Jess nodded with relief. "Alright Sir, I'm going to take this side of you and help you up inside the vehicle. Jenny, take the other side."

"Ok," Jenny immediately wrapped an arm around him.

He cried out in pain.

"Lean on me," Jess ordered. "Put your weight on me. We've got you."

He was heavy, but they used all their might to carry him to the rear of the vehicle where Rayan and Peters were waiting to lift him in.

There were just a couple of soldiers left to board, and on Kelly's command they jogged over. Together with Jenny, they jumped inside the vehicle and Jess swung her bergen into the back, then jumped up behind it. In that split second something caught her eye. A figure appeared in the doorway of a nearby compound, dressed all in black - she could see nothing of him but the whites of his eyes. The driver started the engine of the vehicle ready to move, but at that moment she saw the figure raise an arm and throw something towards the convoy.

In what felt like slow motion, it flew through the air like it was a cricket ball and she was the wicket. It was a perfect shot. Jess watched, her eyes wide, as it got closer and closer. Seconds before it landed she heard Kelly's frantic shout to shut the doors and move the vehicle, but it was too late. It landed with a clatter right by her feet. She stared at it for a millisecond, her body still with shock. She knew she had to give it her best shot - it was their only chance.

With her pulse pounding in her head, she heard Mellor frantically shouting her name.

Before she had time to think about what she was doing, she bent down and grabbed the grenade, using all her strength to hurl it back at the insurgent. Just in time, the vehicle jolted forwards and she watched the grenade fly through the air back towards the compound. Just two seconds after it left her hand it exploded, throwing her back inside the vehicle with tremendous force.

For a few seconds everything looked black and then white spots danced in front of her. She could feel something warm on her face and could hear the buzz of voices around her, but the ringing in her ears was deafening and she couldn't make out who it was or what they were saying. She choked up what felt like a mouthful of sand and tried to sit up.

"Jess, stay still for me."

Jess managed to make out one of the voices - it was Jenny. She blinked hard, and eventually the white spots started to subside and she could see again. Her vision was still blurry, but she could make out the roof of the vehicle and half a dozen worried faces around her.

"Sir," she croaked, still trying to sit up.

"Is she alright?" She heard Mellor's voice now and she tried to turn her head to look at him, but she couldn't see that far.

"She's alright," Jenny reassured him. "She's talking. She'll be fine, Sir."

"Is he alright?" Jess's head throbbed from its impact with the floor. She became agitated at the ringing in her ears and tried to lift her arms to rub them, but she lacked coordination. Lifting her arm to her face, she caught sight of blood running down her arm, from her elbow to her wrist.

Jenny nodded and she reached over to hold Jess's arm. "He's fine, he's stable. Leave him to me and stay still. You've got some shrapnel injuries and I need to try to stem the bleeding from that one, it looks quite deep."

"Medics make the worst patients," Jess muttered with a grin.

"I'm glad you haven't lost your sense of humour, Corporal Fern," Kelly breathed, visibly relieved.

Whilst one of the soldiers updated the nine liner, the vehicle bounced over a particularly large pot hole. Jess heard Mellor groan as his leg moved.

"Leave me," Jess pleaded with Jenny. "Please, sort him out. I'll live."

Jenny ignored her, removing Jess's helmet and inspecting her head, then she finished cleaning the wound on her arm and wrapped a bandage around it. Once she had replaced Jess's helmet, she turned her attention back to Mellor. Jess could see him properly now and he looked bad, really bad. He was pale and clammy and his uniform was soaked with blood. His trousers had been cut away leaving his leg exposed but it was impossible to see a single patch of skin due to all the blood.

"How far to the checkpoint, driver?" Jess forced herself back into medic mode, her mind clearing. She was ok - she *had* to be ok. He needed her.

"Three kilometres," the driver shouted back. She nodded, but she wasn't reassured yet. He needed to be on that MERT now.

The roar of the Apache helicopter overhead reassured them as they continued along the track. They were a medic and a commander down now, and just wanted to get their casualties extracted so that they could get back to base without any further incidents. As Jenny checked over a couple of other soldiers who had been thrown about by the force of the grenade, Jess managed to push herself up and lean against the side of the vehicle, her eyes firmly on Mellor. He looked up and for a second his eyes met hers - more than anything she wanted to tell him how she felt, before it was too late.

He groaned, tipping his head back with the exertion of breathing. "Medic."

Jess managed to get up and shift over to where he was sitting, resting a hand on his forearm reassuringly. "Hang in there."

She wanted to hold him more than anything, but she knew that she had to be careful with the entire section watching on. She couldn't cross that line. Not today. Not with everyone watching.

"You're going to be alright, Sir."

"I don't think I am," he panted through the pain, his head tipped forward. "I'm trying but... I can't."

"Yes, you can," she took his hand and squeezed it hard. "You can and you will. If I can survive a grenade, you can survive a comfortable trip in the back of this to the check point."

He forced a smile, but his head soon fell back again, his chest heaving with the effort of breathing. Jess felt panic rise within her. She could feel his pulse was weakening in his wrist and she was worried. Really worried.

"Wheels down in two minutes."

"Perfect timing. Here we are," Jess reassured him.

To everyone's relief, the vehicle made it to the checkpoint and they were met by a group of soldiers who had a stretcher ready. Jess had no choice but to sit and watch as Mellor was strapped to it and prepared for the lift.

Jenny pulled another stretcher onto the vehicle. "You too, Jess."

"No, there's no need."

"I think we've had quite enough heroics from you today, don't you?" Jenny asked with one eyebrow raised, and Jess gave up quickly.

They didn't have time to argue, she could hear the chinook approaching and they had to be ready. It would be vulnerable when landing and she knew the pilot would want to be on the ground for as little time as possible - preferably much less than a minute. And at least if she went with him, she could make sure that he was ok.

The chinook landed, throwing up a huge dust cloud. The soldiers hastily carried the stretchers to the door, which was open before the chinook even touched down. The ear splitting hum of the rotary blades took over Jess's mind and she closed her eyes, trying her best to relax.

Her head was still throbbing and she could feel the blood oozing through the dressing on her arm. She was in worse shape than she had realised.

Within a minute the chinook lifted off the ground again, and she stared up at the grey patterned roof whilst the cabin filled with dust and then promptly cleared again. She heard the buzz of the medics working around her and it felt strange to be the one on the stretcher for a change. The atmosphere was tense and the sound of the wind rushing through the gun ports and the rotary blades was almost deafening. She couldn't hear Mellor anymore and she couldn't see him either. Sick of the sight of the drip bags hanging from the bars on the ceiling, she closed her eyes again. She thought about how close she had been to losing him, and felt a tear escape from the corner of her eye. How close she still was to losing him. And he had only been shot because he was trying to protect her.

Chapter Twelve

Jess stood in the corner of the operating theatre and watched the surgeon's desperate attempts to revive him. He was losing so much blood that it had saturated the sheets and was dripping down from the edge of the trolley onto the floor. She looked down and saw that the surgeon's white shoes were covered in it. She was fixed to the spot, her heart thumping in her chest; she felt as though she might be sick. She could see him slipping away and as the monitor began to flash and bleep, they desperately tried to resuscitate him.

She watched helplessly as one of the surgeons stood above him and compressed his chest as another squeezed the ventilation bag which dominated his face. His skin was deathly white as though every millilitre of blood had been sucked out of it. The lips she had once kissed were now blue, cold and lifeless. As they gave up on him, she tried to scream his name but no sound came out. It was like she was stuck in a nightmare and couldn't get out. She could barely breathe. She was suffocating in sheets of grief and she thrashed around, trying to fight her way out.

Suddenly, she heard his voice calling her name and she fought harder. It couldn't be - he wasn't dead - he was here, calling her name. She thrashed harder and harder until she felt his hands firmly on her arms. He was here! He was trying to release her! She kicked harder and harder and then she heard the voice again. She managed to break free and she shot upright screaming...

"Jess!"

Her chest was heaving. She gasped for breath and she felt hands on hers as she started to focus. It wasn't him. She panicked, realising that he wasn't here after all and she looked around, her eyes wild as if she was still on the front line and the grenade was coming back at her, all over again.

"You're safe. It's alright. Deep breaths, you're ok."

She listened to the voice and took a deep, slow breath in and then exhaled. Her breathing became more regular and the room came into sharper focus; she realised that she wasn't in the operating theatre at all - she was on a ward at the Camp Bastion Field Hospital. Exhausted, she let her head drop back against the pillow behind her and stared straight up at the ceiling as it all came flooding back to her. The sound of the monitors bleeping frantically as he was wheeled out of the chinook and straight inside the ambulance waiting at the bottom of the ramp. How lonely she felt when she was brought up to the ward without him. The frustration she felt when it seemed as though he had been in theatre for hours, and nobody could give her any news. Her eyelids felt impossibly heavy and she closed her eyes again, her head becoming fuzzy as she was placed under sedation.

Some time later, she heard the steady thump of boots approaching in the corridor outside. It reminded her of him, and she opened her eyes, turning her head towards the door. She knew that it wasn't going to be him but she couldn't stop her heart from wishing that it was. More than anything she wished that she could just wake up from this nightmare and change things, right from the beginning. She should have just told him how she felt the day after the repatriation ceremony in Wootton Bassett, then they probably wouldn't even be here now.

"Corporal Fern," Lieutenant Swan appeared in the doorway.

She smiled weakly. "Hi, Sir."

"How are you feeling?" Hovering in the doorway, he held his cap gingerly in his hands.

"I've been better," she winced, adjusting her arm on the bed in an attempt to sit up.

"Here - allow me."

He walked over and helped her to sit up, then took a seat on the chair next to the bed. "I hear you were quite the hero."

"Any one of us would have done the same, Sir."

"And I have no doubt that you're right. But it doesn't negate the fact that you were very brave, Corporal Fern."

Jess smiled weakly. Her smile quickly faded when she felt that familiar knot of dread in her stomach. It appeared out of nowhere every time she thought about Mellor. "Is there any news?"

"He's still in surgery."

Jess's heart sank. The wait was agonising.

"I hear that it's not looking good for his leg, I'm afraid. They've patched it up for now but they'll have their work cut out back in Birmingham."

Jess looked down at the sheets on the bed sadly. He was going to be devastated if he lost his leg. Maybe if she hadn't been injured then she would have been able to do more to save it?

"He will be very proud of the way you acted, as am I," Swan reassured her, as if reading her mind. "If it wasn't for your actions then I'd be looking at the bodies of eight of my soldiers right now. Brigadier Tompkins and I are of no doubt whatsoever that the fact the MERT was not spooning troops into body bags was down to you."

Jess swallowed the lump that was forming in her throat and she tried and failed to fight back tears which were threatening to fall.

"Sorry, Sir," she mumbled, rubbing at her eyes furiously with the side of her hand.

"Don't be. I think you can be forgiven for showing a bit of emotion, today of all days. I'll probably shed a tear myself a little later."

It seemed strange coming from him and suddenly she felt almost like laughing. She felt like she was on some sort of emotional rollercoaster, one minute relieved and happy to be alive, and the next back in that devastating hole again.

"Brigadier Tompkins will be visiting you later. I know he wants to thank you personally for your actions."

Jess nodded. She wondered what the Brigadier would think if he knew the real reason that Mellor had been injured. Because of her. She was no hero at all, and they had nothing to thank her for. She had ignored his orders, allowed her judgment to be clouded by emotion, and he had been forced to save her.

Swan rose from the chair slowly. "Well, I'll leave you to rest. Take care of yourself and we'll catch up tomorrow."

"Sir," she nodded weakly, watching him leave. She leant back against the pillow with a sigh. There was only one thing she wanted, more than anything else in the world right now, and she knew she couldn't have it. In fact, she might never see him again.

***

Jess watched as Hayley, one of the Nurses she had worked with when she had been based in the field hospital, walked past the ward and then did a double take, stepping through the door.

"Jess?!" She asked incredulously, her eyes narrow as if she wasn't sure and she was still trying to work it out. "What are you doing here?"

"I got caught by a grenade. Long story."

"Oh my God!" Hayley's eyes skimmed over the dressings which covered the lacerations on Jess's face. "How are you still alive?"

"Lucky, I guess."

Hayley sat down on the side of the bed and took Jess's hand in hers. They had become quite close when they worked together, and it was hard seeing her friend look lost and in pain.

"Are you alright? Really alright, I mean? Not just surviving?"

Jess said nothing, but she felt her eyes fill with tears. She felt her bottom lip wobble and she shrugged, blinking the tears away.

"Didn't think so. Come on. Open up."

Through watery eyes, Jess managed a weak smile, recalling all the moments they had spent together in the medics quarters, dunking a garibaldi biscuit in a cup of tea during a break whilst deep in conversation. She missed that. She felt safe with Hayley and she opened her mouth ready to speak, but then she quickly closed it again. Hayley was still in the army and she wasn't sure what she would say if she knew about her feelings for Mellor.

"I'm just worried about the soldier I was brought in with. Colour Sergeant Mellor."

Hayley looked vague but then she frowned. "Oh yeah - I know. Cat-A. Multiple gunshot wounds to the leg?"

Jess gulped back the lump in her throat. "That's the one. Nobody seems to know anything. When I was caught in the blast from the grenade, I was in the middle of treating him. Now I feel guilty because I didn't do a good enough job."

Hayley rolled her eyes. "Well, that's ridiculous! Why do you always do this? Criticise yourself? You're your own worst enemy, do you know that?"

Jess shrugged, but she knew that it was

true. If it was the other way around, she would be the first one telling Hayley that she wasn't to blame.

"I'll see what I can find out. On one condition."

Jess looked up hopefully. "What?"

"Stop blaming yourself for things that are out of your control. Some soldiers live, some soldiers die. We do our best to put them back together but we can't save them all."

"Ok," Jess nodded, although the thought of him dying was too much for her to bear.

***

"Two minutes, ok?" Hayley muttered, pushing Jess along the corridor in a wheelchair.

"Yeah. Thanks for this, Hayley. I owe you one."

"You owe me more than one!" Hayley said as they approached the doorway to intensive care. "Now if anyone finds you here leave me out of it, ok?"

"Of course."

Hayley pushed open the door and then wheeled Jess inside. She couldn't even see his face - all she could see was a figure mostly covered by a white sheet, his face covered with various tubes and his body crossed with wires. Hayley pushed the wheelchair over to the bed and then stood next to Jess for a few seconds.

"Are you sure you want to do this?" Hayley asked.

Jess took a deep breath. "Certain. I'll be fine from here, thanks."

"I can stay if you want?"

"No, no. It's fine. I'm sure you've got loads to get on with."

Hayley shifted on her feet awkwardly, then sighed. "Yeah. Alright then, I'll come back in a few minutes, ok?"

Jess heard the click of the door closing behind Hayley, and then she pushed the wheels of the wheelchair around to move it closer to the bed. It was awkward because her arm hurt and she was still weak from being sedated, but she was determined. She glanced back over at the window - nobody was around. Then, being careful to avoid the drip and the pulse monitor which was attached to one of his fingers, she carefully reached over and took his hand in hers.

She ran her thumb gently along the side of his hand. "Hi. It's just me."

The steady bleep of the machine and the rise and fall of the ventilator matched the steady thump of her heart. She glanced down at the sheet which covered his limbs, and squeezed her eyes shut as tears began to spill. "I'm sorry. God, I wish I'd just been honest with you from the start. Then we wouldn't even be here now."

His chest continued to rise and fall slowly in time with the ventilator. He was perfectly still, and she had no idea if he could even hear her. Probably not, with his current level of sedation.

"I hear you're going home tonight. The lengths some people will go to get a bit of extra leave, hey?"

Realising that this would probably be the very last time he ever set foot in Afghanistan, or any other war zone for that matter, Jess felt a lump erupt in her throat. One split second, one decision and potentially his career in the army was being snatched away from him.

"I wish I could come with you," she whispered, raising his hand gently to her lips and kissing it gently. "More than anything. I promise that the minute I'm back in the UK I'll be knocking on your door. You better have some decent coffee ready."

She heard footsteps coming down the hallway and she quickly kissed his hand again, then placed it back on the bed gently. At the click of the door opening again, she looked around to see Hayley standing in the doorway.

"Are you ready?"

Jess nodded. "Yeah. Thanks."

She glanced over her shoulder at him again just as Hayley wheeled her out of the room. It was agonising having to let him go back on his own, and she knew that it would probably be several weeks until she saw him again - she still had weeks left of this tour. Her own injuries were superficial, and it was very unlikely that she would be able to persuade anyone to give her some leave. It would be reckless to do that anyway - they were already short on base, especially now that they were another soldier down.

"What's the deal with him?" Hayley

probed curiously, pushing the wheelchair quickly down the corridor towards the ward. "You seem... really upset. I know it's upsetting to see one of your team hurt, but... it feels like more than that?"

Jess paused for a moment. She knew that she had to choose her words carefully. She felt a little sick as she realised that Hayley had noticed that something wasn't quite right.

"You remember I said that last time I was here, it was just me, my boss and a couple of privates left out of our whole section?"

Hayley nodded as they reached the ward and she put the brake on the wheelchair, then helped Jess back into bed. "Yeah?"

"He's the boss," Jess explained sadly.

"Oh!" Hayley's eyes widened. "Sorry... I didn't make the connection."

"That's ok. It's just extra hard... you know... he was the last one left from our section. One of the privates has left for special forces and the other has been sent back to the UK because he's medically unfit."

"He'll be ok," Hayley reassured her. "He'll be back in Birmingham tomorrow, they really are the best."

"Yeah. I know. It's just hard... I feel like I've failed to keep my section safe, you know?"

Hayley rolled her eyes again. "Oh, don't start this again! Injuries happen, this is a war zone. You can't blame yourself."

"I do though. It was my fault he was shot. He told me to get down but I carried on running."

Hayley frowned, placing her hands on her hips firmly. "And if you hadn't? What about the little boy you saved? Yes, I know all about that - everyone's talking about it."

Jess blushed. She didn't want to make this all about her when he was lying in there, fighting for his life. "I just did what any decent soldier would have done," she mumbled.

"Exactly. So you weren't to blame, were you? The child survived, you survived, he'll survive too. It will be ok."

***

Jess lay in bed propped up on her pillows, staring at the shadows on the ceiling. She was exhausted but every time she closed her eyes, all she could see was the insurgent's evil eyes staring at her through the slit in his clothing, the look of panic she saw in Mellor's eyes when he realised he might not make it, and the pounding of the medics on his chest when he almost gave up on life during the short chinook journey to Camp Bastion. Just thinking about that took her breath away, and instead she tried to force her mind on to other things.

She closed her eyes again and focused on a memory of her dad. It was one of her most vivid childhood memories - she could still smell the scent of freshly cut grass and hear the sweet sound of birds singing outside whenever she thought about it.

As the front door opened, she almost burst

through it with excitement. She ran down the garden path towards him. He crouched down at the side of the road in his fatigues, his arms stretched wide ready to receive her. Throwing herself at him, she squealed with delight. Then he stood up, hoisting her high up in the air and spinning her around like an aeroplane, then pulled her back into his arms and gave her a hug so tight she could hardly breathe.

"That's to make up for all the hugs I've missed," he held her tightly and she breathed in his scent deeply, savouring that smell which she associated with the love and safety of her dad. At that moment it was like they had never been apart.

She laughed with delight as he carried her back up the garden path towards her mum, who was standing in the front doorway with tears of happiness and relief running down her face. He set Jess down on the path momentarily and wrapped his arms around his wife, kissing her hard on the lips, one hand resting on the growing bump of their second child who was nestled between them both.

"Ewww!" Jess squealed, and they both laughed. Then they broke their embrace and went inside for dinner.

Jess's mind wandered back to Mellor again, and what he had said about his parents. Would they be there for him when he got back? She pictured him alone in a hospital bed in Selly Oak, coming to terms with his horrific injuries and the end of his career as a soldier, completely on his own because his parents were too useless to care.

She couldn't bear to sit and think any longer, and she swung her legs round and sat on the edge of the bed, stretching her calf muscles. Her whole body ached and every time she sat up her head started banging again, but she just needed something to take her mind off this before she made a decision she might regret. She put her feet down on the floor and inched herself off the bed, waiting for her legs to give way - but thankfully they didn't. Holding onto the end of the bed for support, she began to walk over to the window which offered a fairly good view of the airfield. She wondered if he was out there now, being wheeled onto a C-17 bound for the UK.

Slowly, she lowered herself onto the windowsill and sat silently, staring out into the darkness, the moon lighting up parts of the base hauntingly. She leant her forehead against the glass and watched the glowing lights of the air strip in the distance. They twinkled like stars against the darkness of the rest of the base.

"I wish you were here, Dad," she whispered. "I don't know what to do."

She thought about the colleagues she had lost over the past year, how quickly their lives were wiped out, how life just seemed to carry on once they were gone. She thought about Jase and for the first time since he had gone, she felt glad. If he hadn't have gone home when he did, perhaps it would be him that was being loaded onto the C-17, but not on a trolley. In a box.

Chapter Thirteen

George bolted upright in bed, confused and disorientated. His wife was sat next to him, white as a sheet, gripping onto his arm in terror.

"What was that?!"

"I don't know, love," George pushed the duvet back and leapt out of bed, picking up a heavy book from his bedside table.

"Be careful," Elena hissed as he made it to the doorway and crept out on to the landing.

All the lights were off upstairs and there was just the faint glow of the downstairs hallway light. Elena decided that she couldn't let her husband face whatever it was alone. Hesitantly, she followed him out of the bedroom and along the hallway.

They crept down the stairs. Everything was still and silent except for a strange crackling sound coming from the living room - it sounded like a cross between water dripping and something creaking. They had almost reached the bottom of the stairs when George trod on the creaky step at the bottom and then he charged through the living room door, holding the book high above his head ready to face an intruder.

Elena's eyes fell on the bay window and she gasped, a hand clamped firmly to her mouth. Although the window was still in one piece, the glass had been shattered in a perfect bullseye and it was still crackling as tiny fault lines continued to spread across its entirety. On the floor at the bottom of the window was the coffee table, which had lost one of its legs on impact. George looked from the coffee table to his son who was sitting on the sofa in front of the television, a vacant expression on his face.

"What on earth is going on here, son?!"

Jase didn't look up. His eyes were fixed on the television and his hands were stuck to the games console controller. George took a few steps towards his son and stared at the screen. Jase was playing a graphic war game; the character on screen was lying on the floor in a pool of blood, presumably having been shot by the enemy. George could see the reflection of the screen glowing in his son's eyes. He almost looked like he had been hypnotised. Elena stood next to him, her hand still clamped over her mouth, her body shaking with shock.

The sound of footsteps on the stairs cut the feeling of intensity in the room for a moment as Katie and Louise, their daughters, were woken by the noise. George looked at Elena and she immediately left the room to send them back up to bed.

"Come on, back up to bed you two. There's nothing to see down here. Just an accident," George heard his wife say as she climbed back up the stairs with them.

George paced across the room and closed the living room door with a quiet click. Then he looked back at his son who still had his eyes fixed on the screen and the controller sat in his hands as though it was stuck like glue. Suddenly he realised that he'd had enough of this. All of it. Two months his son had been back, and at first he had made allowances but he just seemed to be getting worse.

"I said, what has gone on here, son?! George raised his voice again. Jase didn't move or even acknowledge him, and he felt his blood boil. "Look at me when I talk to you!" He strode forward and snatched the controller from his hands.

Jase looked at him then. He turned his head and stared at George, his eyes full of anger and contempt. George barely recognised him.

"*Talk* to me, son!" He shouted.

Jase stared at him blankly, and then went back to staring at the screen. George moved in front of it, leaving him no choice but to look at him.

"It's 3am," George tried very hard to keep his voice level so as not to frighten the girls. "What are you doing down here, playing that, at 3am? No wonder you can't be arsed to get up until God knows what time of the day."

"I can't sleep," Jase replied quietly, his voice flat and emotionless.

"Well you won't sleep, will you, if you stay in bed until one in the afternoon!"

George was shaking with frustration. He was absolutely seething. However, he took a deep breath and forced himself to calm down. "What happened to the window?"

Jase looked over at the window as if it was the first time he had seen it. Examining the broken glass and the broken table lying underneath, he frowned. But he said nothing.

"Now you listen to me," George placed his hands firmly on his son's shoulders. "This has got to stop, you hear me? You need to see someone. What you're doing... how you're *behaving*... it just isn't normal."

Jase blinked at him, lost for words. He couldn't possibly articulate how he was feeling. He knew that it wasn't normal - he knew that it wasn't right. But it felt like he was in a huge black hole, and no matter how hard he tried to climb out he would just slip right back down again, even deeper than before. Gaming was the only escape he had, the only way he could feel even remotely in touch with the army life he missed.

George rubbed his brow exasperatedly. "I don't understand. If you would just *talk* to us about what happened, maybe we would understand."

"What's the point?" Jase muttered. "Talking won't change what happened."

"But if we understood, maybe we could help you. We love you, son. We always will, no matter what."

Jase's eyes slipped back on the screen again, at the dead soldier lying in a pool of blood on the floor. How he wished that he could be that soldier, put out of his misery. He fantasised about being that soldier almost constantly. One of his favourite ways to occupy his mind when he needed to, was to day dream about all the ways he could die.

"I just couldn't sleep," he stood abruptly and pushed past his dad to get out of the room.

"Don't walk away from me, son," George protested. "We haven't finished!"

"Yeah, we have," Jase opened the living room door and sloped up the stairs to his room.

George stood in silence in the living room for a moment, examining the photographs on the wall - his son in his school uniform on his first day of primary school, another photo of him on his last day at secondary school, and finally, one of him proudly wearing his army uniform on the day of his passing out. It had been his son's lifelong ambition to be a soldier. That was what he didn't understand. Two months ago Jase had returned from Afghanistan unexpectedly, apparently on leave, but he had never gone back. Countless times they had tried to ask him what was going on, when he was going back, but he had never explained it. To start with they had thought nothing of his unusual behaviour - going to bed in the early hours of the morning and waking around lunchtime, not really leaving the house - they had simply put it down to jet lag, and him making the most of his downtime before he returned back to the front line. However, as time went on it had become clear that he was not going to be returning any time soon, and things had got even worse.

He was distant and angry all the time and he didn't seem to want to do anything besides play computer games and sit on the sofa all day, eating whatever he could find in the cupboards. It was like he had reverted to being a teenager again, and it was quite apparent that he hadn't done a jot of exercise since the moment he had stepped off the plane - he had lost his muscle definition and his t-shirts were stretched over a small pot belly which had sprung up in place of his six-pack. Worst of all, it felt like he wasn't really there. It was as though he had put up a screen and wouldn't allow anyone in, not even his parents.

Initially they had hoped that the situation might resolve itself in time, and he would start to get back to normal. But he was just getting worse and worse. Now they had a broken window and a coffee table to sort out - and who knew what or whom the next casualty would be.

George knew that he had to do something about it. But he just didn't know what. How could he fix the problem if he didn't even know what it was? He pressed his fingers to his temples frustratedly, his eyes still on the shattered window that he would now have to find the money to replace.

**

One month later.

Jess stepped out of the taxi and looked nervously up at the block of flats that greeted her. She had waited for this moment for what felt like forever, ever since Rix had been repatriated without her. Her heart had ached for him every day since he had left. They had been able to briefly keep in touch a couple of times, but the lack of communications at the base had made proper communication almost impossible. In any event, they were still both serving soldiers pending the outcome of his medical board meeting. Jess could not do anything to jeopardise that. He was in for a long road, and the last thing he needed was for it to be complicated if their feelings for each other came to light. Not to mention the fact that if anyone in the company got wind of the fact that their relationship whilst on tour was not strictly professional, she could lose her job too.

Taking a deep breath, she pressed the door buzzer. Butterflies of anticipation danced in her stomach. Suddenly she realised that she didn't know what she was going to say. She hadn't seen him since she sat by his bedside at Camp Bastion whilst he lay there unconscious. What if he wasn't the same person anymore?

"Hi," his voice came over the intercom and she smiled with relief. He sounded just the same.

"Hi."

The door buzzed, and Jess pushed it open then pressed the button for the lift. Twelfth floor. She wondered how he was getting on here on his own - all that way up, unsteady on his feet. The lift climbed quickly and before she knew it there was a ping as the doors opened, and she was there. She could see his door right in front of her. Flat 124. She stepped out of the lift and stopped a few paces behind the door, taking a deep breath in an attempt to steady her nerves. Suddenly the door opened, and there he was, right in front of her.

"Hi," she repeated, smiling nervously.

She could tell that he was nervous too. It almost felt ridiculous - they had spent months together on tour, and now they felt awkward around one another?

He stepped backwards awkwardly with his crutches. "Come in."

Jess followed him inside and closed the door behind her. Her eyes fell on the loose leg of his shorts which hung below the bottom of his stump. She swallowed hard. She wasn't sure why the sight of it affected her this much - she already knew that he had lost his leg. For some reason it was just a shock to see it in the flesh.

"How was your journey?" He hobbled down the hallway with her closely behind.

"Oh, it was fine thanks."

When they got to the living room she saw the view that the flat enjoyed over the parkland and river beyond and she smiled, taking a few steps over towards the patio doors.

"You have an amazing view."

"Yeah, I like it. Much better than the view of my mum's sour face, anyway."

Jess grinned. It was good to hear him sounding more like his normal self. The small talk was uncharacteristic of him and it was making her nervous. "Things aren't going great with them then, huh?"

He shrugged. "Are they ever?"

Their eyes locked together again, and this

time, for the first time, Jess let herself be drawn into him. They were safe here, locked away in his flat on the twelfth floor, with nobody to catch them. She took a few steps towards him and brushed her thumbs along his fingers which were clutching the handles of his crutches. He slipped one hand out and reached up to brush his thumb across the faint scar on her cheek. His touch was electric and she savoured the sensation of energy building between them.

He leant forwards, knocking one crutch to one side, and his lips brushed against hers. Jess closed her eyes and reached up, cupping the edge of his face with her hand gently. It felt like a current of electricity ran through their bodies as their tongues made contact and their kiss deepened.

"I missed you," he breathed, his lips just millimetres from hers.

"I missed you too," she replied, making the move this time as their lips collided again.

As things got a bit more heated she stepped back, worried that she might make him unsteady.

"It's ok. I won't break."

She cupped both hands around his face this time, kissing him again, and tiptoed back towards the sofa. When they got to the sofa she ran her hands down his forearms and he slipped his arm out of the handle of his remaining crutch, lowering himself down onto the sofa next to her.

"Sorry. It's not exactly the sexiest way of moving about."

"Don't be silly."

His hands were free to hold her this time and they kissed again, this time their bodies started to entwine and Jess leant back against the cushions of the sofa, his body pressing against hers. She had only been in his flat a few minutes and yet it felt entirely natural, as though she had been there for days.

"I've waited for this for a long time," he whispered against her lips, running his hands up inside her top and across her ribs, underneath the underwire of her bra.

Lifting her arms so he could remove her top, Jess felt her pulse quicken and something stir inside her. The sight of her long hair cascading down her bare chest brought out something animalistic in him. He practically ripped his own shirt off, placing his hands on her waist and trailing kisses from her jaw down to her cleavage.

She groaned, pulling him closer to her and then leant back further against the sofa, enjoying the sensation of his weight pressing down on her. Kissing each other deeply, their tongues danced together, exploring each other for the first time. Then suddenly, just as quickly as it had started, she felt his whole body tense up and he groaned, pulling away from her.

"What's wrong?" She asked as he writhed in pain next to her, pressing a hand hard to his stump.

"I can't explain it," he choked, holding his breath and throwing his head back, his back arched. She could see that he was in agony.

"Breathe through it," Jess took control, holding his hand in hers and squeezing it supportively. "Just breathe through it, it will pass."

He lifted his head and looked into her eyes and took a deep breath then let it out slowly, again and again. Slowly, his muscles started to relax. He leant back against the sofa with a sigh.

"Are you alright? Do you need me to call someone, or…"

He shook his head. "No, I'm fine. God, I'm sorry."

"Why would you be sorry?" She frowned.

"Talk about kill the moment," he shook his head with frustration.

"It's fine. Honestly, it's fine. Don't worry about it. I didn't come here with the intention of sleeping with you anyway, I just wanted to see you. I just… couldn't keep my hands off you."

Rix smiled at her but when she looked closely, she could see sadness in his eyes. She leant forwards and kissed him gently on the lips, then curled up under his arm, her head on his shoulder. She heard his heart still racing in his chest and she covered it with her hand protectively.

"I get these… pains," he admitted eventually, once he felt able to open up. "I can't describe them… it's like I can feel the pain in my leg all over again, but it isn't there. I feel like I'm going crazy. How can I feel pain in something that isn't even there?"

Jess frowned and tilted her head to look up

189

at him. "You're not going crazy. They're phantom pains."

"They're what?" He frowned as though she was talking in a different language.

"Phantom pains. It's a thing, I promise you. You're not going mad. Lots of amputees get them."

He shuddered at her choice of label. He hated that word. *Amputees.* It made him feel like he was being put in a box that he never wanted to be in.

"Have you spoken to your doctor about it?"

He shook his head.

"You need to," she replied, gently running her thumb in circles on his chest. "They'll be able to help you. You can take medication to help. Why didn't you mention it sooner?"

"I don't know. I just… thought it was in my mind, you know. I just need to get over it. I can't go on like this, I just feel stuck… stuck in this flat, on my own… I can't even go anywhere because the pain is awful some days. I don't want to get stuck somewhere and then it starts and I can't get back. At least here I can deal with it on my own."

"But you shouldn't be on your own," Jess whispered, a lump forming in her throat at the vulnerable tone of his voice. "People want to help you. I want to help you."

"You are," he replied, lacing his fingers with hers. "Just by being here."

She smiled and tilted her head up to kiss

him again, snuggling up close to his chest, breathing in his scent. It was her new favourite place, right beside him. Now that she was here and they could do whatever they wanted, she wasn't sure if she would ever want to leave.

Chapter Fourteen

Jess woke up to find a chink of light streaming through the gap in the curtains, straight onto the pillow between them. She turned her head and watched the steady rise and fall of Rix's chest whilst he slept, his head lolled to one side. She studied every inch of his face. He looked completely different when he was sleeping; his usual stern, war hero appearance was replaced by a more vulnerable look. She wished that she could see inside his head. He had been upset last night, confused and embarrassed that he hadn't been able to perform. Of course it hadn't bothered her at all and she had meant what she said - coming here to sleep with him hadn't been her intention. She had just been desperate to see him after all that time apart.

He stirred in his sleep and rolled over; slowly and carefully, she moved across the bed to spoon him from behind. The contours of their bodies seemed to fit together as though they were made for each other and she lay her arm over his chest protectively, her face buried in his neck. It surprised her how quickly she felt comfortable with him. This was the first night that they had shared a bed and they hadn't even had sex, yet sleeping and waking up together seemed like the most natural thing in the world.

She felt him fidget and then he turned again, this time to face her. She watched as his eyes snapped open and once he registered where he was he smiled, stretching his arms and wrapping them around her.

"Morning," he mumbled huskily, tucking his hands up the back of her t-shirt to rest on her bare back. His touch gave her goosebumps and she smiled as his lips met hers for a lazy kiss.

"Morning," she replied, her face close enough to his on the pillow that their noses were almost touching.

"Did you sleep well?"

"Mmm. Very. You?"

"Better than normal. *Much* better than normal. You should stay more often."

His lips brushed hers again and she pushed her body closer to his with a smile. It wasn't a lie - he had slept much better than normal, although to be fair 'normal' wasn't much to compete with. A typical night involved a few hours of broken sleep and then sitting on the edge of the bed, rubbing his sore stump after being woken by the pain. He had woken up in pain a couple of times in the night but having her there was comforting, and he had managed to sleep for at least five hours. That to him was a very good night's sleep, and he felt quite refreshed.

Jess's thigh brushed against the end of his stump and he winced, causing her to jump backwards quickly.

"Sorry! Sorry, I didn't mean to hurt you."

"It's ok," he grimaced. "It's not your fault. Come here."

She was hesitant then though - too scared of hurting him again to come too close. "Does it

193

hurt a lot?"

"Yeah."

"When's your next appointment?"

"Friday," he answered abruptly, not offering any more information than she asked.

Rix didn't like to think about his appointments. Thinking about them reminded him of his time at Headley Court, and how strange he had felt there. The medical treatment he had received whilst at the facility had been fantastic, he couldn't deny that. It was just that being there had made him feel out of sorts, he couldn't really explain it. He had spent three weeks on the ward there undergoing intensive physiotherapy. It was there, while lying in his bed one night after a gruelling day of exercise, that he had realised his head wasn't in the army anymore. He had mentally checked out. He listened to a few of the guys there, some of whom had far worse injuries than his - double or even triple amputations - talking about how much they missed it, and how much they wanted to go back. And he realised that he no longer felt the same. For the first time in his life he didn't crave the structure and the excitement that the army brought him - he dreaded it. All he wanted to do was go home and lock himself away in his flat, waiting for Jess to return. He knew that things would be better when she was back. He just had to keep going until that time.

Jess reached under the duvet for his hand and took it in hers, lying back against the pillow again. He could still see the faint marks left by the shrapnel injuries on her face. The wounds were healed now but the scars seemed just like the wounds Afghanistan had left inside him - you could barely see them, unless you really looked. But they would always be there.

"They're fitting me with a socket," he confided eventually. "I don't really know how that's going to work when it feels like a bolt of lightning goes through my body every time it touches something."

Jess frowned. "Every time?"

"Yeah."

"Have you told them?"

"Yes and no. They know I'm still in pain. They probably don't know the full extent. If they did, I'd be asked to stay there again for a bit and I don't want that."

"But you need to do what it takes to get better. To get strong again."

Rix clenched his jaw. He knew she was right but there was something in his mind, like an invisible barrier, stopping him from accepting it. It was like he couldn't allow himself to look to the future, all he could think about was now - and the most important thing to him now was distancing himself from what had got him here in the first place.

"Once you've got the socket fitted you can start working with the prosthetics, it won't be long before you can come back to the regiment," she suggested.

Rix was silent and she blinked at him. Eventually he looked down at the floor. "I won't be coming back, Jess."

"Why?"

"We can't serve together now, and it's best for everyone if I just call it a day."

"Best for who?" She frowned. "Not best for you. You can't just give up. We can serve in different companies, we'll find a way."

He shook his head and turned onto his back, staring up at the ceiling. He ran a hand through his hair in frustration. She wasn't listening, she wasn't hearing him.

"My medical board hearing is next week. I'll get a medical discharge, I'll get my compensation, I can start again."

"Doing what? If that's what you want then fine, but… you need a plan, Rix. You can't just lock yourself away here for the rest of your life."

"What do you *think* I'm trying to do?" He snapped, raising his voice slightly in frustration. She instantly looked disappointed and he shook his head. "I'm sorry. I didn't mean to…"

He sat up then and leant over the edge of the bed, his head in his hands. Jess watched him for a few seconds unsure as to what she should do, but then she got out of bed and walked across the room, kneeling down between his legs on the floor.

"Hey," she took his hands in hers as tears began to spill from his eyes. "It's ok. I'm sorry."

She leaned up and took him in her arms and before she knew it, he was holding on to her with all his strength, squeezing her tight and letting out a series of strangled sobs. Her heart

196

broke at hearing him in such excruciating pain and she held him for as long as it took, until she felt his grip loosen and his sobs grew weaker.

"I'm sorry," he sniffed eventually. "I don't want you to see me like this. I don't know what's happening to me."

"You've just lost your leg, Rix. You almost died. Everything you thought you knew has turned on its head. It's quite normal to feel confused, angry... upset... honestly."

He reached down and cupped her jaw with the palm of his hand. Jess couldn't help but nuzzle against it, enjoying the warmth of his skin on hers. Every hour she spent with him she felt herself getting pulled in closer and closer. He was like a forbidden quicksand she just couldn't escape from, and nor did she want to.

"I just don't know how to stop feeling like this. I thought coming home would... fix me, you know. I'd start to feel like myself again. But I don't even recognise myself anymore. I feel like I'm going mad."

"You're not going mad," she stroked his cheek with her thumb softly. "But it will take time. And you might never be that person you were, again. You need to concentrate on feeling better, taking little steps. And in time you'll feel better, I promise you."

"You sound like the psych," he smiled weakly as she climbed onto the bed next to him.

Jess put her arm around his shoulders and held him for a few minutes, neither them saying anything.

"I'm going to see Jase later," she said eventually, breaking the silence. "Why don't you come with me?"

"I don't think that's a good idea. We can't let anyone know about us, not yet."

"He wouldn't know. Why would he?"

He shrugged. "I don't know. I'm not sure I can keep my feelings for you hidden."

"Well, we both managed fine in Afghanistan. Nobody had a clue."

"Yeah but... things are different now. I can't lie to myself anymore, Jess. I don't want to. I've spent the best part of a year hiding my feelings, I just can't do it anymore. The safest way is to keep my distance. At least for a few months, until it isn't blatantly obvious that this all started when we were on tour."

He felt her gaze on him as she realised what he had just said, and he felt his pulse quicken and his cheeks flush slightly. Pulling his hands away from hers, he cleared his throat and reached for his crutches.

"I'm going to take a shower."

"Rix..." she called after him. He turned away and left the room without looking back. It was the first time he had admitted how long he had felt this way, even to himself.

***

The high street was busy and they sat in silence at the table. Jase watched as person after person walked past the window in the afternoon sun. He had never really paid much attention to other people before returning from Afghanistan, but now it seemed to have become a bit of a fixation. It always went the same way. Firstly, he would focus his attention on strangers going about their daily business, either to distract his mind from things he didn't want to think about, or to break himself out of an awkward social situation. Then he would become fixated and over invested, silently analysing each person and wondering what they might be doing or where they might be going at that moment in time. Finally, he would become angry. Angry that the person was going about their life without a care in the world about the soldiers who were dying all around the world. Angry that his friends would never be able to walk down the high street like that again. And angry just for the sake of being angry - because it had become a default emotion for him these days, and it was hard to find something that didn't trigger it off.

Jess watched him. He gripped his fork hard in his left hand, scrunching the napkin that was folded next to his plate with his right. He barely even noticed her watching him, he was too busy watching the people passing the restaurant window. They had been sat at the table for almost half an hour now, and yet they still hadn't really talked about anything.

Jess turned her fork in the middle of her plate of spaghetti. "I heard that Raj is doing well with selection. Have you spoken to him lately?"

Jase barely took his eyes off the window.

"No, I haven't. I haven't really heard from anyone at all."

"No? What about your sessions with the psychiatrist? How have they been going?"

Jase snorted. "Yeah, great. Just what I need. I can feel the anger and grief pouring out of me with every session I go to."

Chewing a mouthful of spaghetti, Jess raised an eyebrow then glanced down at his barely touched plate of food. She had almost finished hers, yet she had only seen him eat one or two bites since it had arrived. Suddenly, he seemed to snap out of his day dream and he looked back down at his plate, pushing his food around with the fork and then setting it down on the edge of the plate with a clatter.

"How are things going for you, *Corporal* Fern? No doubt you'll be making Sergeant next year, now it's just you left. Maybe you'll even get Mellor's job."

"Aren't you hungry?" Jess asked, not rising to his scathing tone.

He shook his head and looked down into his lap.

Suddenly she didn't feel hungry either, and she set her own fork down on her plate, then screwed up her napkin and dropped it on top. Jase looked up again.

"How is Mellor, anyway?" He asked, his voice a little less barbed.

Jess opened her mouth to answer honestly, but quickly closed it. She had to think very carefully before she told him anything. She could tell he was angry, and if she even gave him the

200

slightest hint that something might be going on between her and Rix, he might become fixated on it. That could have disastrous consequences for all three of them.

"Last I heard he was going for a medical discharge. I think he's back with his family. I'm not really sure. They didn't really keep us updated after he left."

"Yeah, well. At least he knows how it feels to get sent home, now."

In silence, Jess watched the corners of Jase's lips turn into a very brief smile. It was gone again so quickly that she wasn't certain that she had even seen it. But she couldn't ignore it.

"He had no choice, Jase," she argued. "You know that. You weren't well, you needed support. Support we couldn't give you in Afghanistan."

"At least when I was there I had a purpose. It was my home. The platoon were my family. I've lost everything, because of him and Swan."

"His hands were tied," Jess retorted. "You know he was just following protocol? If he had let you stay and something had happened, it would have been down to him? Your mental wellbeing was his responsibility."

"Yeah, well. He cocked everything up. I'm not who I used to be."

Jess sighed. "I understand that you're angry. But it isn't his fault, Jase. He just did what he thought was right."

"I didn't know you were his biggest fan," Jase replied cuttingly. "You know your next promotion won't be his decision now he's had his leg cut off, right?"

Shaking her head, Jess stared at him, stunned. He seemed incredibly callous and closed. She had been expecting him to be different today, but never in a million years had she expected him to be this hostile. Clearly he wasn't coping well with being back at home.

She reached down and picked up her bag from the floor. "I think it's time I left. I don't think me being here is helping you very much. I'm sorry, I shouldn't have come."

"Yeah, maybe you shouldn't," he mumbled, even though he felt a little guilty.

Jess pulled some money out of her purse and set it down on the table. She knew that he wasn't well, but that didn't mean that his words stung any less. She had too much going on in her head already, she didn't need to be made to feel guilty for making what had certainly been the right decision.

"If you ever want to talk properly, I'm always here. But I'll give you some space. I'm sorry you feel how you do, I really am. But in time you'll see that it was the right decision."

Jase turned his head and looked back out of the window as she picked up her bag off the floor and stood up. "Bye, Jase."

And then she turned and left, without him saying another word. Jase sat at the table and watched her leave the restaurant and walk past the window, blending in with the other passersby just getting on with their own business without a care in the world.

Chapter Fifteen

Jess watched the countryside fly past the window as the train rushed along the tracks. She savoured the greens and golds of the fields and crops which whizzed past, blowing gently in the wind. She had missed the colours of the British summer last year when she was out in Afghanistan. Apart from the reds and greens of the poppy fields, Helmand Province was overwhelmingly beige for the summer months. And the heat was unbearably hot. The last two weeks had been hot by British standards, but by Jess's standards it felt cool and refreshing.

She'd had a busy two weeks. Normally she spent her leave pottering around in the garden with her mum, spending time with Liam and catching up with friends from home. This time she had done that as usual, but with the added commitment of spending time with Rix. She hadn't minded at all, of course; it had been hard saying goodbye to him that morning. His lips lingered for a little too long when he kissed her goodbye, and he held her gaze longingly when she left. She didn't think it had truly hit her yet, that once she was back on base she would be without him, and she would have a new boss - and quite soon, Colour Sergeant Mellor's way of doing things would be a distant memory. Two weeks were never enough and she found herself day dreaming about the time they had spent together.

Her mind wandered back to earlier that morning, when they had lay under the duvet in his bedroom, the cool morning breeze blowing through the open window, the curtains floating lazily through the air like ghosts. She had traced every inch of his body with her fingertips, faltering over the indent in his upper thigh, where one of the bullets had entered his body. She remembered the look of utter terror in his eyes at the realisation that he might bleed to death, and suddenly she felt as though she was back there, reliving it all over again.

"Did you think I was going to die?" He asked softly as if he could read her mind.

Jess pressed her lips together and then blinked at him. "No."

"I did."

She didn't know what to say. The thought had crossed her mind, when she was pushing dressings to his leg and the blood was seeping out faster than she could get pressure on it. Even once the tourniquet was on, he was still bleeding out. She was lying in a way, at more than one point she had thought that she was going to lose him. In fact, when she lay in the MERT staring up at the ceiling whilst the medics worked around her, she had been almost certain that he was slipping away right next to her.

"I was close, in the MERT," he admitted. "I felt like I was going down. My whole body was tired and heavy... it was like it was willing me to let go. But I couldn't. I knew I had to fight."

"And fight you did," she smiled weakly,

taking her hand away from his leg and settling it on his chest right next to his heart.

She felt the steady thump of his heart under her hand and she skimmed her thumb over his chest gently. The thought of losing him was almost too much to bear.

"I thought I'd lost you," he confessed. "Twice, in fact."

"Twice?"

"When I saw you on the ground with those kids... I thought you'd been shot. I saw it hit you and you fell, I honestly thought that was it. And then when you were thrown back by that grenade..."

His voice trailed off and she could feel his heart thumping harder in his chest. She knew that he struggled to think back to that time too. It was still very raw for both of them. Jess said nothing and instead held him close to her, her cheek resting on his chest. She closed her eyes and breathed in his scent, savouring everything about him for the last time before she went back to base.

Rix ran his fingers through her hair gently. "All I wanted when I woke up was to know that you were alright. I couldn't remember much about the journey back - the MERT... the last thing I could remember was the blast. I was convinced you were dead."

Jess turned her head to make eye contact with him. "I'm sorry I wasn't there. I wanted to be."

"I know. It almost killed me lying in that bed in Birmingham for two weeks, not knowing where you were or if you were ok. I was convinced something was going to happen to you and you'd be the next face I saw on the news."

Jess reached down and placed her hand on his reassuringly. "I wanted to call. But the signal was awful, and I didn't even know where you were, really. It was such a relief when you got in touch and I knew you were doing ok."

Rix linked his fingers with hers and then turned his face to kiss her. He tilted her chin up gently with his hand and pressed his lips to hers as her body tightened to his. He felt his desire for her growing and the pressure from his lips intensified as she felt it too. Placing a hand either side of her jaw, Rix rolled onto his back, expertly pulling Jess with him. She landed on top of him and continued to kiss him as he brought his hands down and squeezed her tightly. He wanted her so much it hurt. He tried to relax and push any thoughts which weren't related to what was happening now to the back of his mind, desperate that he would finally be able to give himself to her. He had been trying for two weeks and the frustration he felt every time he was unable to was getting unbearable.

Momentarily she broke away from his kiss and sat up, pulling her t-shirt over her head, dropping it off the edge of the bed and leaning back over him, her breasts contacting with his bare chest as his mouth kissed hers hungrily. The feeling of her bare skin against his drove him wild, and he felt a groan rise up from his stomach at the sensation of her fingers edging their way down to his shorts. Her hand slipped inside and at that exact moment, the pain appeared out of nowhere again, travelling up what was left of his thigh and then shooting through his groin area. She felt him tense up immediately and broke the kiss, withdrawing from him, her eyes full of concern.

"It's ok," he grimaced. "Don't stop."

But she could tell that he was in agony again and she couldn't ignore it. Instead she placed her hands just above his stump and massaged the muscles hard. He cried out in pain and arched his back, but gradually she felt his muscles relax and he sighed frustratedly, draping his arm over his face to cover his eyes.

She placed a hand on his belly and rested it there, not sure what to say. Every time they had tried to have sex this had happened. It was frustrating for her, she couldn't imagine how frustrating it must have been for him, not even being able to control his own body.

"For God's sake," Rix muttered. "Why does this *keep* happening?"

"I don't know."

"As if it's not bad enough that I'm missing most of my leg, I can't even get that to work either. Brilliant. I haven't got much going for me really, have I? Maybe they should have aimed for my chest, done the job properly."

"Don't say that," Jess frowned, mildly irritated. She hated it when he was morbid. The five platoon members they had lost on their last tour of Afghanistan would surely give anything to be here now, missing leg or not. She knew that she shouldn't think like that, because she had no idea what was going on inside his head right now, but she couldn't help it.

When he didn't answer, Jess leant down and picked up her t-shirt from the floor. Once she was dressed, she sat on the edge of the bed hesitantly for a minute or two and then stood up.

"I'm going to take a shower."

"Ok," he answered, his voice completely emotionless.

She picked up her overnight bag and carried it with her to the bathroom, closing the door behind her and sitting on the lid of the toilet, her head in her hands. She hated having to leave him like this but she had no choice. She had to go back to the garrison today. This day was going to come eventually but she had put it out of her mind for the last two weeks, concentrating on getting by on a day to day basis, every time she was back at home counting down the time until she would see him again. She felt completely infatuated, like a love-struck teenager, and that scared her. She didn't think that she had ever felt so deeply about anyone. Sometimes she thought he felt the same but then sometimes he became distant and detached. Why did things have to be this complicated?

A clatter and then a bang outside startled her and she stood up, opened the bathroom door and peered around the corner. There was nobody there but she could hear a noise coming from the bedroom. It was quiet at first and she took a few steps down the hallway. As it became louder, she realised what it was. He was crying.

Her stomach turned and she rushed back through the bedroom door, where Rix was curled up in a ball on the floor, one crutch a couple of metres away from the bed where it had fallen. He was sobbing with frustration, his arms firmly clamped around his remaining knee. She immediately jumped forward and moved the crutch out of the way, then leant down to help him.

"Come on," she soothed, taking his hands in hers and lifting him up onto the bed. She dried his tears with her thumbs and then put her arm around his shoulders, pulling him tightly against her as his frustration and devastation poured out of him like the floodgates had well and truly been opened.

"It's ok," she whispered softly. "Things will get better, I promise."

***

"Corporal Fern," Brigadier Tompkins remarked. She stood to attention in front of him, her eyes fixed firmly ahead. "Stand at ease."

She dropped her gaze and widened her step, placing her hands behind her back. "Sir."

"Take a seat," he instructed, and she complied.

"So," he mused, flicking through the paperwork on his desk and then focusing his attention on her. "I hear you were quite the hero in

210

Afghanistan."

She shifted in her seat awkwardly. "Well... I did my best Sir. We all did. In extremely difficult circumstances."

"Quite. Well Corporal Fern, firstly I'd just like to thank you personally for your actions. There's no doubt in my mind that 1 and 2 Sections would have suffered many fatalities if it wasn't for your quick action in removing the grenade."

"Any of us would have done the same, Sir. It just happened to land at my feet, that's all."

He raised an eyebrow and then nodded, flicking through the paperwork again. "And Lieutenant Swan informs me that you also saved the life of a civilian child, despite the threat to your own life."

"Yes, Sir. But again, any of us would have done the same."

"Give yourself credit where credit is due, Corporal. I certainly am."

"Sir," she nodded gratefully.

"It's not the first time that I have heard good things about you in recent months."

"Sir?"

"Lance Corporal Fern is an outstanding Combat Medical Technician and displayed exemplary gallantry during active operations in Afghanistan in June 2009," he read from the sheet of paper in front of him. "On a routine patrol out of the FOB we were caught in a daisy-chain explosion from multiple IEDs which resulted in multiple Cat-A casualties and KIAs. Despite the threat to her own life and the loss of her leading CMT, Lance Corporal Fern maintained a professional and cool composure and provided the highest standard of medical care to the wounded, saving the life of Corporal Jones. This was not the first occasion during the tour upon which Lance Corporal Fern had put herself in the line of fire in order to treat her colleagues, and no doubt it will not be the last."

Jess sat silently, taking in what he had just read. She felt a small blush rise up from her neck and through to her cheeks, and she pressed her lips together nervously.

"Is that about the size of it, Corporal Fern?"

She nodded. "Yes, Sir. But I was just doing my job. Just like everyone else in the platoon that day."

He smiled and placed the paper down on the desk, clasping his hands together. "I think, Corporal Fern, that if I asked Colour Sergeant Mellor about your actions on your most recent tour of Afghanistan then he would say exactly the same thing as Sergeant Kelly has. And for that reason it gives me great delight to be able to inform you that you have been put forward to receive a Military Cross. The announcement will be published in the London Gazette tomorrow."

Jess was speechless - she opened her mouth to talk but no words would come out. Instead she shook her head, struggling to make sense of what he had just said.

"I… don't understand," she managed

finally.

"You have been awarded the Military Cross, Corporal Fern," he beamed, an unusual sight. "I received this recommendation from Lieutenant Swan back in September last year, and it gives me great pleasure to be able to inform you of it now. I hope it goes some way to confirming to you just how highly regarded you are by the whole company."

"Thank you, Sir," she managed, still almost speechless.

She knew what he was saying but she didn't understand why. There were dozens of brave soldiers in the platoon, many of whom she thought deserved an award much more than she did. She felt completely overwhelmed.

"I'm sure the new recruits you will be training in the coming weeks will find your story truly inspirational. Once again, well done Corporal Fern. Very well deserved."

***

Jess fidgeted with impatience until she heard Rix pick up the phone. "Did you know?"

"Know what?"

"You *know* what," she hissed with excitement.

She was standing outside in the gardens, enjoying some fresh air after a busy day of introductions with a new set of privates, fresh out of their initial training. It was her job to get them ready for life as medics on the front line.

Tomorrow the work would really begin.

"Did you know that Swan had put me forward?" She asked impatiently when he didn't respond.

"Yes," he replied, and she could tell that he was smiling. The thought of his smile made her miss him all over again.

"How could you keep it from me all this time?! Major Tompkins said that Swan put the recommendation to him in September?!"

"He did. But you know I couldn't tell you. That's the rules. If I told you I'd have had to kill you."

"Shut up!" She laughed. It was good to hear him joking around. She had been really worried about him when she left, he had seemed incredibly vulnerable. "How are you doing?"

"I'm alright. Missing you."

"Me too," she breathed. "Have you packed your things?"

"Yeah, all packed."

Rix was going back to Headley Court tomorrow for a short stay while he got used to his new prosthetic leg which was being fitted. He hoped that things would become a lot easier once he had two legs again. He knew that it would never be as easy as life had been before, but he was fed up of moping around on crutches.

Jess quickly glanced around to check that she was still alone. "Don't forget to mention the pains you've been having. They'll be able to give you something to help."

"I won't forget. You wait, I'll be a

214

changed man next time you see me."

"I'm not sure I want you to change," she smiled. "I like you just the way you are."

He went silent on the end of the phone and she watched as a little bird flew from a nearby tree across the evening sky.

"I'd better go. Let me know how tomorrow goes, yeah?"

"I will," he promised. "Bye."

"Bye," she echoed, and with a click on the other end of the phone he was gone.

Jess held the phone in the palm of her hand and stared at the screen for a few seconds, then she locked it and slid it back inside her pocket. She had been dreading this, leaving him and coming back to the base without him. But now she was here and she was doing it, things didn't seem as bad. Especially now that she was going to get a Military Cross, she couldn't wait to see her mum's face. Suddenly it struck her that she hadn't even called her mum yet - the first person she had wanted to speak to after receiving the news was Rix. Walking back towards the building she mulled that thought over in her mind, wondering what it meant.

Chapter Sixteen

Jase fell against the bar as the lights flashed around the club, and the music thumped in the background. He was having a good time now. It had taken a while. When he first arrived he had almost left; the heavy base of the music and crowds of people had made him anxious and his mind had been screaming at him to leave. But he had come with a group of old friends and they had persuaded him to stay, providing a constant supply of beers and shots to encourage him to loosen up and have a good time.

He ordered another round of drinks and then glanced back at the booth where his friends were chatting up a couple of girls. One of them smiled at him suggestively and he grinned back, admiring the bare skin of her legs under the table. Once the barman had made the drinks, Jase picked them up and edged across the room to the booth, clumsily spilling one of the pints over the sleeve of his shirt. Not that he noticed.

"Here you are!" He announced jovially, handing the drinks out.

The girl's hand brushed against his and she took one of the shots from him, then downed it. "Thanks."

"You don't waste much time!" He grinned.

"No. I don't. Now drink up, let's dance."

He downed his pint and then followed her onto the dance floor. The music was booming, and he could feel the bass coursing through his body. The vibration in the pit of his stomach set off something in his mind and suddenly he was back there again, the vibration of the IED blast rumbling through him, knocking him backwards. His head was spinning and he could hardly breathe. He stumbled through the crowds of people packed tightly onto the dance floor, ignoring the protests of those he shoved out of the way in his desperation to escape. Finally, he got to the door of the club and he stumbled down the steps, flying round the street corner and down an alleyway where it was still and quiet, and he felt safe.

He leant his back against the wall and tilted his head to the sky, gulping in air. The air had been unbearably thick in the club just like it had been in Afghanistan and he felt like he had been starved of oxygen. Eventually his breathing levelled and he focused on where he was right now, trying to force all thoughts of Afghanistan out of his mind.

The clip clop of heels approaching the alleyway broke him from his thoughts and he looked up to see her walking around the corner. "There you are. Are you alright?"

Jase stood up straight and moved away from the wall. "Yeah, sorry. Just needed some air."

"Are you coming back in?"

He shrugged. "I don't know."

"Was it something I said?" She frowned.

"No. It wasn't you. Look, I'm sorry. I'm

not in the best place right now, I just got back from Afghanistan… I lost some friends there. My head's all over the place."

The distant glow from a street light at the end of the alleyway lit up her eyes, which widened with surprise. "You're a soldier?"

"Yeah."

He felt the heat from her body and she leant up to kiss him. He kissed her back, his head still spinning from the excess alcohol he had consumed.

"You need to relax. I know just what you need."

"Do you?" He asked. "Because I haven't got a clue."

She smiled, and then plunged one hand down her cleavage, pulling out a small plastic bag full of half a dozen coloured pills from her bra. She opened the bag and held one pill in her palm.

"Here. Take it."

Jase looked down at the pill in her hand. "What is it?"

"Just take it," she urged. "*Trust* me. If you want to relax and have a good time, just take it."

She placed a pill in his hand. He hesitated. Part of him was telling him not to, and part of him wanted to at least give it a go. Surely anything was better than how he felt now? "I'm not sure."

"Look, just give it a try, yeah? If you don't like it you don't have to do it again. But just take it and come back inside. I promise you'll have a good time."

Jase hesitated for the last time, then tipped

his head back and swallowed it. It was just one - he didn't really have anything to lose.

"There," she grinned. "Give it half an hour and you'll be like a new person. Now come inside."

***

It wasn't long before Jase started to relax. It felt like an overwhelming wave of happiness gradually took over him, pushing out every inch of anxiety from his body. It felt amazing to be free of it, he let himself be consumed by the music and he danced crazily on the dance floor as she laughed next to him.

"What's your name?" He yelled over the music.

"Shelly," she grinned, shrieking with excitement as he spun her around on the dance floor.

It felt as though they were the only ones there, spinning around and having the time of their lives. But in reality they were beginning to irritate other people who were being barged around by their flamboyant dancing. Within a couple of minutes, one of the bouncers came over and shouted in Jase's ear. "Come on, mate. It's time to go!"

"What?!" Jase cried.

"Come on."

He felt himself being rough handled off the dance floor and he began to flail about, trying to resist. He started to feel confused and his heart was now pounding in his chest. Where were they taking him?

"Get off me!" He shouted.

Shelly followed him towards the doors. "Jase, it's ok. Just leave it. Let's go."

"Where are you taking us?!" He yelled, still flailing in the bouncer's grip.

Just as he was really starting to panic, they reached the door of the club and the bouncer pushed him out onto the street. "Time to go home."

"What?!" Jase protested incredulously. "But it's not closing time yet!"

"You've had enough. Go home, mate."

Shelly took his arm and guided him away from the club. "Jase, it's fine, come on. We'll go somewhere else."

They walked for minute or two before they got to the alleyway and came to a stop. Jase could feel his heart pounding in his chest and he felt as though he had run a marathon - he could feel beads of sweat forming on his forehead.

"It's boiling," he complained, tugging at his shirt and unbuttoning the top few buttons.

Shelly smiled at him and then leant forward, unbuttoning the next few buttons suggestively. Jase's eyes connected with hers and at that moment, he felt as though she was the most beautiful woman he had ever seen. It felt unreal that he could feel so strongly for someone he had met just hours ago. Gently he lifted his hand and skimmed his thumb along her jaw. "Um…"

Suddenly he couldn't resist the urge

anymore. He pressed his lips to hers and kissed her furiously, they staggered back until her back was resting on the wall of the nearest building and he ground his body against hers as their lips crushed together. He felt a furious desire rising up within him and he slipped his hands under her dress. He was about to lift and carry her down the alleyway when he heard the sound of laughter behind them. "Look at that tart!"

Turning around to see who it was, Jase broke their kiss. Then he glanced back at Shelly who was pulling her dress down quickly, her face turning a mortified shade of scarlet, and he felt an overwhelming urge to protect her. As the group of men walked past he narrowed his eyes and marched up behind them, his fists clenched by his sides.

"*What* did you say?!" He spat, grabbing the man by his shoulder firmly.

"Alright, mate. Calm down."

"Who do you think you are, talking to a lady like that?"

"*Lady*?!" The man raised an eyebrow and looked around the rest of the group. They all laughed. Jase felt even more furious then, and he glared at the man, his fists clenched.

"You need to learn some manners," he growled.

Jase was shaking with rage and the man could see it. He looked around the group again and then shook his head, turned and walked away. Jase stood rooted to the spot. He felt torn yet again - part of him wanted to chase after the man and teach him a lesson, but part of him knew that he should just let it go. There were about eight of them and one of him. His chances probably weren't great.

He turned back to where Shelly had been standing and saw that she was gone. He swore and rammed his fist against the wall furiously. They had been having a good time, why did something always have to come along and spoil it? He pushed his bleeding hand in his pocket and walked down the street, looking for something else to smash up.

***

As Rix approached the grand red brick building on his crutches, he felt a trickle of sweat run down his back, following the curve of his spine. It had been several weeks since he had left Headley Court, yet being here again just made it feel like he had never left. Suddenly he realised that he hadn't really made much progress since leaving. When he had stayed here he'd had a fixed routine, just like in the army. They were up early, doing set exercises throughout the day. When he was here the idea of leaving and going home and waiting for Jess to return from tour had given him the motivation to work hard so he could get home. When he had got home, he had allowed things to get on top of him.

But today was the day that he would have his new prosthetic leg fitted, and he was trying to be optimistic about that. He couldn't deny that he was nervous. He knew that it was going to be hard work getting used to using it, but he hoped it would be the first day of the rest of his life.

"Hi," he cleared his throat, approaching the reception desk. "Colour Sergeant Mellor."

"Ok, Sir. Welcome back," the receptionist smiled, tapping on the keyboard of her computer. "Do you want to go through and someone will be with you in a minute."

"Thanks."

He travelled down the hallway on his crutches, his rucksack a dead weight on his back. Then he sat in the waiting area with his rucksack down by his side, and he wondered what Jess was doing right now. Was she thinking of him? Did she think about him as much as he thought about her? Suddenly he heard the sound of footsteps approaching and he turned around, expecting to see the prosthetist. Instead he did a double take as someone familiar entered the room and then broke out in a grin.

"Mellor," he said brightly. "How are you, mate?"

Rix stood up on one crutch and reached forwards to shake his left hand. "Gav. I wasn't expecting to see you here."

They sat down side by side in the waiting room and Gav's eyes fell on Rix's crutches and his stump, which was visible at the bottom of his shorts. "Sorry, mate. I heard what happened."

"Thanks. Bit of a nightmare. But I survived, that's the main thing. What have you been doing with yourself, anyway? It's been ages."

"Yeah, I've been busy. I'll be back on base soon, I've just been signed off here. I'm good to go." Gav raised his prosthetic arm. "These things are amazing."

"You're staying in?" Rix asked.

"Yeah. I can't wait to get back with the guys. Aren't you?"

Rix looked down at the space below his stump and shook his head. Seeing Gav so determined and desperate to get back to the platoon only emphasised to Rix how much things had changed in his own mind. Once upon a time he would have felt the same, desperate to get his strength back and get back to what he loved. But now he wasn't even sure how he felt about the army anymore, whether it was love or hate. One thing was for certain, he didn't want to go back.

"I'm ready for something new," he muttered, eventually.

Gav smiled genuinely. "Good for you. What's your plan? What's next for you?"

Rix didn't know how to answer. He opened his mouth, cobbling together something non-committal, but thankfully before he had to answer, the door opened and he heard his name being called.

"We should catch up properly some time," Gav suggested as Rix stood up next to him. "Go for a pint or something. Maybe get some of the others together, it would be good to see the medic and Jase too? I haven't spoken to them for ages. And Raj, if he's not out on some covert mission by then, I heard he's doing great at selection."

"Yeah," Rix nodded, although that was the last thing he and Jess needed. "Well, it was great to see you. I'll give you a call."

They shook hands again and then he slung his bag over his shoulder and pushed his hands back through the handles of his crutches. Reaching the doorway, he breathed a sigh of relief. He had escaped just in time.

***

Rix sat on the bed as the prosthetist examined the newly fitted socket. He glanced over at his new leg which was leaning up against the wall a couple of metres away. It was strange to think that it was going to become a regular part of him very shortly.

"Great," the prosthetist smiled. "That looks like it fits perfectly. How does it feel for you?"

Rix ignored the dull ache in his stump. "Fine."

"Excellent. Well, we've obviously gone through the technical side of how the leg works, and how to care for it and yourself when you're using it. We have an hour or so left, I would propose that we do a short stint of exercises with the parallel bars to allow you to get used to walking on it. Over the next two weeks you will work with the physio team to build that up, then you should be able to use the leg successfully when you go home."

Rix glanced at the parallel bars which cluttered up the corner of the room. "Great."

He sat and watched as the prosthetist showed him how to fit the leg and then set up the bars within a reasonable distance, allowing him to stand up and support himself, not yet bearing any weight on the leg. It didn't feel very comfortable and it felt almost alien, like he couldn't trust it. However, it wasn't anywhere near as painful as he had expected. The pain was manageable, if it meant that he could start getting back to normal.

"Ok. To start with, I want you to just walk to the other end of the bars, holding on with both with your hands, and put very minimal weight on the leg. Just to get used to how it feels."

Rix nodded and held on tight to the bars, skimming his hands along it slowly. He moved the prosthetic leg forward. It felt odd and heavy, like he had no control over it. His arms trembled with exertion, taking almost all of his weight whilst he walked his remaining leg forward.

"Good. Now another step."

He tried again, this time trying to put more pressure on the leg. The knee joint buckled and his hip gave way; he managed to grab hold of the bars and keep himself upright, but he had lost his confidence and he stood still for a few seconds, trying to psyche himself up for the next step.

"That's ok. The knee joint will take a lot of getting used to."

Rix looked up at the prosthetist with his smug, immaculately shaved face and took an instant disliking to him. That's easy for you to say, he thought, you have both legs. Remembering the coping tactics he had learnt in the army he gritted his teeth and channeled his frustration into getting the job done. He took another step forward, this time he was a lot steadier and although he wasn't putting much weight on the knee joint, it was a start. He got to the end of the bars and quietly smiled to himself, feeling his first triumphant moment of the day. Maybe this wouldn't be as hard as he had anticipated after all.

***

After an exhausting day, Rix was glad to be in his bed. He had spent a couple of hours practicing on the prosthetic leg, and he felt as though he had made a lot of progress. Whilst he was still relying on both bars for support, he felt himself almost looking forward to tomorrow - he set himself a personal challenge that he would walk with the support of just one bar, instead of two. There was no point in hanging around. He wanted his life to get back to normal, and he knew that this was what he had to do.

He scrolled through the news on his phone for a few minutes, then found himself scrolling through his contact list. Jess was right at the top. How he wished he could hear her voice again - he almost ached for her. The lights were out on the rest of the ward and it was too late to call her, so he sent her a text instead.

Hows the training going?

He pressed send and then lay in the dark, his phone lying next to him on the bed. Within a minute the screen lit up and he lifted it up.

Fine thanks. Sorry didn't text earlier been crazy busy. How's the bionic leg?

He grinned, typing his response back.

Better than my real one. I'll be back next weekend I'll show you then.

He set the phone down again and wondered what she was doing right now. Was she lying in bed like he was, thinking about him? He couldn't wait to spend the night with her again. The soft glow of his phone shone off the ceiling again and he picked it up.

Sounds good. Hopefully I can get away from here. Look forward to seeing you again x

Chapter Seventeen

Unlocking the front door of his flat, Rix sighed with relief. The door got stuck on a pile of post and he awkwardly managed to squeeze through the gap, pushing the pile of post out of the way with one of his crutches. He closed the door behind him and tried to bend down, leaning some of his weight on one crutch. He couldn't quite get low enough and he gave up, deciding that he would retrieve the post once he had removed his prosthetic leg.

He walked through to the living room and set his crutches down, lowering himself down on the sofa. It was good to be home. For almost two weeks he had worked hard getting used to his new leg. He disconnected the leg from the socket and then removed the socket, rolling the liner off to expose the bare skin of his stump. It was red and tired from the busy day and the journey home and he massaged it gently, enjoying the sensation of fresh air on his skin.

He lay back against the sofa and closed his eyes, allowing his mind to wander. Jess was already on her way and he couldn't wait to see her. Then he remembered the post and he picked up the crutches then hobbled back down the hallway. It felt like a step backwards removing the leg and relying on the crutches, but he knew it was going to take a long time to get used to the leg, and sometimes he just needed to use the crutches for speed. He had become used to them over the last couple of months and at the moment they were the easiest option.

Without the leg he was able to bend down with ease and pick the post up, leaning on one crutch for support. He flicked through the post - most of it was bills and junk mail - and set it down on the sideboard. There was just one official looking envelope which was of interest and he stared at it for a few seconds, wondering whether it was what he thought it might be.

Rix ran his thumb through the top of the envelope to open it, and pulled the paper out. Recognising the letterhead, his pulse quickened slightly. He was right. He skimmed through the letter and then set it on the side next to the other post. He had expected to feel relieved at having a date, but it just filled him with dread. In four months' time he would be discharged from the army, the only adult life he had ever known. And he had absolutely no idea what he was going to do.

***

The doorbell rang and Jess got up to answer it. She took the pizza boxes from the delivery driver and paid him, then carried them over to the coffee table and grabbed two plates from the kitchen cupboard.

"Thanks," Rix muttered, taking one of the plates from her.

She watched him open one of the boxes and put a few slices of pizza on his plate. There was something on his mind, something bothering him; he had barely spoken since she had arrived. She knew that he would be tired after returning from Headley Court, but it was definitely more than that.

They ate in silence. He only ate two slices before he set the plate down on the table and leant back against the sofa with a sigh.

"Aren't you hungry?" Jess asked, half way through her fourth slice of pizza.
He shrugged. "Not really."

While she ate, Jess watched him out of the corner of her eye. He looked quite unhappy. Once she had finished she put his plate on top of hers on the coffee table, and then leant back on the sofa, placing her head on his shoulder. "Is everything ok?"

"Yeah. Brilliant," he retorted.

Jess frowned slightly but said nothing. Instead she placed her hand on top of his and entwined their fingers, squeezing his hand slightly.

"I got my written notice today," he volunteered eventually. "Sixteen weeks, and that's it. I'm out."

She squeezed his hand again. "Isn't that what you wanted? Some certainty? So you can move on?"

He shrugged. "I don't know what I want at the moment, Jess."

"What do you mean?"

"One minute I'm glad that I'm leaving… but then I realised today that I have absolutely no

231

idea what I'm going to do when I'm out. In sixteen weeks my life turns upside down again and I have no plan whatsoever."

"You still have plenty of time. And you'll have your compensation package to keep you going until you get things sorted."

He put his arm around her and held her tightly to him, burying his face in her hair on the top of her head. The smell of her calmed him slightly and he didn't ever want to let her go.

"I'll go mad sitting in this flat," he said quietly. "On my own."

"You don't need to sit in here on your own. You'll go through resettlement, they'll help you decide your next steps. You don't have to decide now. At the moment all you need to think about is getting strong and getting your head straight. The rest will fall into place."

He didn't feel like it would, not at all. Since his conversation with Gav two weeks ago, he had become increasingly anxious about the fact that he didn't seem to have a plan. He had always had a plan, ever since he was old enough to want to leave his parents. For the first time in his life, he had absolutely no idea what he was going to be doing in six months' time.

"The army's all I've ever known," he confided. "What if I can't cope without it? I keep thinking… only another few weeks and I'll be out of hospital, only another few weeks and I'll be up and about on my prosthetic leg… and things can go back to normal. But each time one of those things happens I still feel the same. Like nothing's changed and I'm still stuck in the same position, with no idea of what I'm going to do if I don't have the army."

Jess looked up at him and leant her chin on his shoulder. "I know it feels like everything's really uncertain at the moment, but that's natural. I know I'd feel the same if I was leaving. But you need to try to focus on the positives. Yes, it's scary leaving all you've ever known but you're going to have a big lump sum behind you - you can do whatever you want. Retrain in anything you want. And you'll be brilliant."

He held her tightly and mulled over what she had said. It all sounded incredibly easy, and every day he promised himself that the next would be the first day of his new life. But then every day he woke up scared and uncertain, constantly thinking about the what ifs every time he thought about a new avenue he could go down.

"What would you have done if you didn't join the army?" She asked. "What did you want to do when you were a kid?"

"I don't know. I don't really remember. All I can remember is wanting to get away from home as quickly as possible. The army made that happen."

"And you achieved what you wanted. You have this place, you're independent from your parents, you're a brilliant soldier."

"Was a brilliant soldier," he muttered, then shook his head. "I just… I wish I had a choice, you know. But I don't really, I have to leave. Even leaving the flat at the moment is such an effort, I can't imagine being in a position that I can just do all the things I used to do without even thinking about it."

"You will get there," Jess insisted. "There are triple amputees who go on to compete in the Paralympics. Don't you think they felt just like you do one day?"

He hadn't really thought about that and he nodded slowly. She was right, of course she was right. He had to stop this self-pity - he had never been one to wallow in misfortune, he had always done what was necessary in order to achieve what he wanted. He never let things get in his way. He supposed that was why he felt this low at the moment, because he felt out of control - he felt physically weak like he had done as a child, and that scared him.

Jess pulled away from him and sat up straight, looking him right in the eye. "What did you used to do before you joined the army? Like, as a hobby?"

Rix snorted. "You really don't want to know."

"Yes I do," she argued.

"Well... let's just say I wasn't quite the upstanding citizen I am now. I used to get in trouble. Dad tried to get me interested in various hobbies... shooting, golf, cricket... but I wasn't interested. All I wanted to do was hang around with my friends and make trouble."

Jess bit her lip. It was hard to imagine him being that person now, she had only ever known him as the calm, collected and professional sergeant and then colour sergeant he was now. She knew about his past because he had told her snippets, but she still found it hard to believe sometimes. "What about property? You could invest some of the money you get as compensation, start a property portfolio?"

"I guess. I don't know though. I wasn't always the best with paperwork."

"You could get someone to manage it for you. You buy one, you rent it out, then you can mortgage it and the rent covers it. Then do it again, and again. Before you know it you'll have your own little empire."

"Yeah…" he muttered vaguely.

She took his hand again and threaded her fingers through his. "Like I said, you don't have to decide now. You've got four more months before you even leave, and by that time I'm sure you will feel completely different to how you do now. Something will come up, it always does. Everything happens for a reason."

That he did believe. Sometimes he struggled to understand why he had been dealt this card, why after twelve years of service his army career had to end like this. But then he had met Jess, and lost her, and got her back due to his poor medic's misfortune, and they were able to be together now because he was no longer serving with her. Maybe that was what was meant to be out of all of this - maybe it had been them all along, and as a result of that their paths had to vary slightly. This way she could continue to serve, and he had a chance to do something else and go out on an honourable note, not a dishonourable one like he would have if their relationship had developed during their period of service together. Maybe his whole life up until now had been leading up to this point, when they would be together. He just wished that he felt some sense of direction so that he knew where he was headed next, because at the moment their relationship was new and he felt quite lost. He hadn't even been able to make love to her yet, and he didn't want her to get bored and move on before he had the chance to show her the man he could be.

Chapter Eighteen
Two months later

Elena dropped the washing basket and wrestled with the door of the machine. It was annoyingly stiff these days and it seemed to be irritating her more each day, especially now that Jason was home and she had another adult's washing to do. It felt as though she was forever washing and drying - as soon as she dried one lot of clothes, it was time to wash the next. She felt guilty for being petty about such a menial thing; she had spent months wishing that he would come home to her when he was in Afghanistan, but now he was back and the reality of it had hit her it wasn't quite how she had expected it to be. She hardly even felt like she knew him anymore; if he didn't look exactly the same, she could have sworn that her real son had swapped with another soldier and they had come home in his place.

She crouched on the floor with her knees either side of the basket and pulled the clothes out of it, pushing them through the door of the machine. In the bottom of the basket were two pairs of jeans, and she checked the pockets of the first absent-mindedly, then pushed them into the machine too. There were a couple of coins and a short, stubby pencil. She tutted. George was always leaving things in his pockets, at least she had thought to check today and he wouldn't have to take the machine apart later to clear them when they got stuck. She pulled out the last pair of jeans and checked the pockets quickly. Her fingers brushed something thin and plastic in the back pocket and she pulled it out. It was a small rectangular plastic bag.

At first she assumed it was just rubbish and she threw it down to one side on the floor next to the pencil and coins, but once she had loaded the jeans into the washing machine and shut the door, her eyes fell on it again and she realised that it wasn't just any plastic bag. She picked it up and held it up to the light in between her fingers, she could just make out a white powdery residue inside. Her heart began to pound in her chest as she remembered a documentary she had watched several years ago, when Jason had been at school and she had been worried about the company he had kept. And then he had left school and joined the army, and she couldn't have been prouder - he had come home from basic training a different person, he had gone from a boy to a man, who was able to iron his own clothes, take responsibility and act responsibly. Which is why it came as such a shock to her when she realised what the little bag had contained.

Suddenly she felt an unexpected rage rise from her stomach, and she clenched her hand around it. She strode out of the kitchen, down the hallway and up the stairs. It was almost lunchtime and he was still in bed. Suddenly all the little things that had been irritating her over the past couple of months came to a head and bubbled over. She swung open his bedroom door and ripped the duvet off his sleeping body. He

238

groaned and tried to pull the covers back over himself.

"Get up!" She ordered. Jase opened his eyes and looked at her, they were still bleary from sleep.

She suddenly felt an emotion that she had never felt before when looking at her son - disgust. He looked and smelt like he hadn't showered for weeks, his face was covered with an unkept stubble and his bedroom surfaces were thick with dust.

"I said, *get up*!" She shrieked, and his eyes snapped open again. Rubbing his eyes, he sat up on the edge of the bed.

Elena marched over to the curtains and pulled them open so abruptly that the curtain pole nearly fell off the wall. Jase shielded his eyes from the sun as though it was blinding him.

"Mum, what are you doing?!"

"It should be me asking you that!" She cried.

"Sleeping," he muttered, bemused.

That just served to anger her further, and she thrust the little bag at him. "What is *this?!*"

Jase looked from her furious face, to the little bag in her hand, and back again. "No idea. Where did you find it?"

"In the pocket of your jeans!"

He shrugged. "I don't know how it got there. Must just be rubbish."

"I am not an idiot, Jason! I know exactly what this is. Don't lie to me!"

He said nothing, but she could see it in his

eyes. He was lying. He knew exactly what had been in the bag, she was right. She looked around his room and suddenly it all became blindingly obvious - if she had just taken a good look around his room before now, she would have known. On the bedside table were several dirty tissues, most filled with snot but some covered in little spots of blood. The waste paper bin in the corner of the room was also overflowing with similar tissues, and furiously she tipped it over, rooting through the contents manically as though she was in some sort of trance.

"I knew it!" She screeched when she found a clump of similar bags in the bottom of the bin. "Why would you lie to me?! Why would you do something so stupid?!"

Jase didn't move from the edge of the bed, he just leant his head on one hand and rubbed his eyes wearily with the other. Elena looked at him again, and it suddenly hit her that she couldn't stand him anymore. He was filthy and disgusting as if he had slept rough for the last three weeks. His room was filthier than a teenager's, and he did nothing but game all night, occasionally slope out for a bit and then come home and sleep for most of the day. She was disgusted. They had put up with an immeasurable amount of stress caused by him during the last few weeks and this was the straw that broke the camel's back. They couldn't live like this anymore.

"Explain yourself Jason, please. Because I can't help you if I don't understand."

She sank down on the side of the bed and

he watched her sob, her shoulders heaving up and down. Jase looked up at her, and he realised that he felt nothing. He felt completely empty, hollow… he didn't even know how to react. The level of detachment he felt scared him. He had always been close to his parents. Yet here his mum was, sat on the edge of his bed absolutely distraught because of him, and he felt like he didn't care anymore. At all.

Eventually, he shrugged. "You're right. It's cocaine. What else do you want to know?"

His voice sounded detached and callous, and Elena recoiled from him as though he had hit her. Realising that he didn't even feel sorry for what he had done, her devastation turned to disgust yet again.

"What's *happened* to you?! Talk to me Jason, please. I need to understand. You're killing me."

His eyes widened and then he shook his head, a strange smirk on his face. "I'm killing *you?* Yeah, alright then."

Elena reached forwards and tried to grab his hands, but he pulled them away too quickly. "I love you, you're my son. But I don't understand why you won't talk to me. You're not the same person anymore. I don't even recognise you."

Jase sniffed and wiped his nose with the back of his hand. Elena looked down and noticed that his leg was shaking slightly. He was tapping his foot on the floor over and over again, as if he was a small boy who couldn't sit still. He got up and pulled a pair of jogging bottoms over his boxers. They were stained and they smelt disgusting. "I'm going out."

"Don't you want to take a shower?" Elena exclaimed, horrified that he would even consider going out in such a state. She remembered the first time that he had come home from basic training, immaculate in his uniform - even his beret had been in exactly the right position. He had proudly explained every part of his uniform to them and his sisters, and when he had returned to base a few days later he had spent hours before he left getting his uniform washed and ironed perfectly, ready for his return.

Jase shook his head, pulling on a screwed up t-shirt off the floor and snorting back a throat full of snot. Just the sound of it turned Elena's stomach.

"We need to talk about this," she pleaded. "You don't get to run away from this, Jason. You need help before it's too late."

He laughed then, a laugh she didn't recognise. For a second he sounded almost hysterical. "Too late? It's *already* too late, Mum. Don't you see? It was too late when I set back in this dive of a house. Why do you *think* I'm off my head on coke most of the time?"

Before she knew what she was doing she heard the loud crack of the palm of her hand striking his left cheek, leaving a glowing red mark. They both stood in silence, her struggling with what she had done, and him realising that he had pushed her too far.

"J- Jason…" she stammered, lifting her

hand up towards his cheek again, horrified as it glowed brighter by the second. "I'm sorry…"

In silence, he turned and left the room. Elena stood in horror, the thump of his footsteps down the stairs and the slam of the front door echoing through her body.

She knew that he was right. It was already too late. She had already lost him.

***

Jess arrived home just in time for dinner. She smiled, the comforting smell of barbecue chicken hitting her nostrils, and her stomach growled with hunger. She set her bergen down in the hallway just as she always did and followed the scent of the food through the kitchen to the back garden.

"Jess!" Liam smiled. "You're back!"

She beamed, her eyes on the chicken which was sizzling away on the grill. "I am. That smells delicious."

"My finest barbecue chicken," he joked, although he wasn't wrong about the chicken - it really was good. "Are you hungry?"

Jess nodded. "Starving."

"Good. Because I think I've cooked too much - what do you think? Have I cooked too much? Argh, I'm really nervous!"

Jess put her arms around her little brother and squeezed him tight. "It'll be fine. He's a lucky man, chicken or no chicken."

Liam laughed, pulling out of her grip and

turning back to the chicken with his barbecue tongs. Jess looked around the garden. "Where's Mum?"

"She's gone to get lemonade," Liam rolled his eyes. "I told her, he's fine with cola, but she's stressing about there not being any lemonade."

Jess grinned. She could just imagine Jane now, buzzing around the kitchen, stressing about whether everything was just right. It was only going to be the four of them tonight but she would still want to make the best impression possible. She worried about the smallest things.

"What time is he going to be here?" She asked, slipping the elastic from her hair and allowing it to tumble down her back. It felt good to let it loose after a busy day.

Liam looked at his watch and pulled a nervous face. "In about... half an hour! Oh my God! I'm not sure I'm ready!"

"I'm sure he's more nervous than you. Stop worrying!"

Liam set the tongs down on the tray next to the barbecue with a clatter. "Yeah, yeah. You're right... I just want everything to go well, you know? I really like him! You know when you just like... really, really like someone... and you want everything to be just perfect?"

"Yeah," Jess answered honestly, and suddenly she noticed that Liam had turned to her and was watching curiously. She tried to ignore him, but after a couple of seconds his smile widened and she couldn't ignore him staring at her.

"What?"

Liam raised one eyebrow curiously. "Is there something you need to tell me?"

Jess shook her head and shrugged nonchalantly, pulling her hair back up in a messy bun.

"There is!" Liam cried theatrically, his eyes wide. "It's that sergeant you've been spending time with, isn't it? I *knew* it!"

"Colour sergeant," Jess corrected. "And there's nothing to tell."

Liam poked her playfully. "There *so* is. I *know* you, Jess! And there's something going on, I know it!"

She shook her head, but she couldn't help but smile at the thought of Rix.

"Why didn't you tell me about him before? And why didn't you bring him today?"

Jess stuffed her hands in her pockets and shuffled from one foot to the other, looking down at the floor. "It's... complicated. We're not really together yet... I don't know. It's all a bit confusing really."

"In what way?" He pressed. "You're at his house like *all* the time - what's wrong with him, is he married?!"

"No, no. Nothing like that. He's just... I don't know. It's not that simple. It's a long story."

Liam glanced at his watch. "Well, I'm not in a rush. It'll help me take my mind off my nerves! Come on!"

Jess glanced at the chicken still sizzling on the barbecue and the back to Liam, who was still peering at her expectantly. "I was going to have a shower before Aaron gets here. I don't really want him meeting me in my sweaty old fatigues."

"He won't *care* about your uniform, Jess. He knows what you do for a living. He thinks it's cool, actually. Now, spill."

"Alright," she took a deep breath.

This was the first time that anyone had asked Jess about Rix since they had started seeing each other. She didn't really know why she found it almost impossible to articulate. Perhaps it was the fact that she wasn't sure exactly where they stood - she didn't think of him as her boyfriend, yet it didn't feel official enough for him to be her partner either. All she knew was that every day her feelings for him seemed to strengthen, and she couldn't picture her life without him in it.

"He's not really my boyfriend as such...we've been seeing each other since I got back from Afghan but I don't know... we've known each other for ages. It's just complicated really because we didn't meet how normal couples meet. So, we're not really... I don't know... a proper couple yet?"

Liam cocked his head. "So like friends with benefits?"

"No... no, not like that. We haven't...." her voice trailed off.

Liam's mouth almost dropped open. "Really? But you've been back for like - three months! And you stay at his house all the time! Why haven't you?"

Jess shrugged. It was hard to explain to

someone who had not experienced the realities of war. Rix was working really hard to battle his demons but he still wasn't quite there. There was always something that stopped him - either his phantom pains would start up or something mentally would get in the way, and he panicked. She knew that he wanted to and that it greatly frustrated him when he couldn't give her what he wanted to. She couldn't deny that it frustrated her sometimes too. She fancied him something rotten and they had got close more times than she could count - but then, right at the last minute, he hadn't been able to.

Liam could tell that she was clamming up trying to answer the question, and he quickly changed the subject. "Was he like… your boss? Out in Afghanistan?"

"Yeah, pretty much," she replied, and then laughed as his eyes widened and his mouth dropped open comically as if he was in shock. "But nothing happened until… well, let's just say we were professional when we were out there."

"Yeah, right." Liam playfully nudged her. "Come on. How did it start?"

Jess thought back to the first time she realised that she had feelings for him. She had thought about it so many times and struggled to put her finger on it, but recently she had remembered exactly when it was. It was watching him read the eulogy at the memorial service in Camp Bastion, listening to the words he had painstakingly put together in memory of their fallen soldiers. She had realised then that he had a big heart, and from then on there had always been something there, even though she hadn't realised exactly what it was at the time.

"We went through some difficult times in Afghan. It just brought us together, really. I can't really explain how it started. And then he almost died, and I realised how I really felt about him."

"Wow," Liam exclaimed. "Did you save his life?"

"Well... sort of. But he sort of saved mine too."

Liam grabbed her and shook her theatrically. "Oh my God! It's like something out of a novel or something! Him taking a bullet for you and then you are pumping on his chest and bringing him back to life so he can profess his love to you!"

Jess rolled her eyes sarcastically. "Oh yeah, it was exactly like that! Anyway. I really need to get out of these stinking clothes. Keep it to yourself for now, ok? We can't risk anyone from the army finding out about us, not yet."

He nodded. "I don't even know anyone from the army anyway."

Jess smiled and pecked him quickly on the cheek. "Thank you."

"I'm not done with you yet!" He called after her.

As she got to the door she turned around and stuck her tongue out at him and they both laughed, then she ducked through the doorway and headed through the kitchen towards the stairs.

The barbecue went well. After the initial awkward introductions, Aaron seemed to slip well into their family dynamic and they all had a lovely evening. At ten o'clock, Jane decided to call it a night and went up to bed, leaving Jess, Liam and Aaron sitting around the fire pit at the bottom of the garden in the dark. Jess was sat in a big circular camping chair which could have fitted two of her in it, wrapped in a blanket enjoying the warmth of the fire. Liam and Aaron were sat side by side in a love seat the other side of the fire, a blanket lazily draped across their laps. Liam watched his mum go inside and close the back door behind her, and then he turned to Jess, a mischievous glint in his eyes.

"Where were we earlier. You need to tell me all about this guy." He turned to Aaron. "Jess was telling me earlier about her boyfriend. It's all a big secret."

Aaron nodded and they both looked at her. Suddenly she felt under interrogation. She wrapped the blanket tighter around her and hugged her knees up to her chest.

"I don't know what you want me to tell you. We met on tour, it's early days... we're supporting each other. That's all."

"Yeah, but I need to hear the whole story. About how you saved each other's lives! It all sounds incredibly dramatic!"

Jess rolled her eyes but she couldn't help but smile. She always found it difficult to talk

249

about what happened on tour. She was very aware of the fact that her mum had never liked her being in the army and putting herself in harm's way, after losing her dad. She didn't like to worry her by telling her about all the things she had seen and the near misses she'd had - and there had been many. Instead she tended to play down what happened in combat, because she believed that what Jane didn't know wouldn't hurt her.

"It really isn't as dramatic as you make it sound. I save lives every day out on the battlefield, it's my job. Anyway. We were on a patrol in a village. Out in Afghan it's hard to tell who's on what side. The Taliban don't wear a uniform, you see a guy riding down the street on a bike and it could just be some local going about their everyday business, or it could be someone who's got a weapon stuffed up their trousers ready to blow your brains out."

Aaron and Liam were looking at her wide eyed, desperate for her to go on. She knew that she had them captivated already. She glanced back at the house to make sure that her mum hadn't returned before she went on with the story.

"Everything was going fine, and I was just talking to these local kids... probably only about five or six years old. And then out of nowhere, this guy started shooting at us. We were right in the open and the poor kids didn't have a chance. There was one stuck right in the firing line. I had no choice, I had to go and grab him. And then I was knocked down, he shot at me - luckily it hit my helmet and I wasn't hurt - but I was a bit dazed, the shots can really knock you for six if they hit you just right. Rix ran over and he shot the guy dead. I was fine... but then I realised that he had been shot. And it all blew up from there really."

Liam and Aaron were practically on the edge of their seats. "What happened next?"

"Well, we had to get him back to the main base, Camp Bastion. It's the one you've probably seen on the news."

They both nodded, still captivated. Describing it in detail took her back there again - she could almost smell the arid desert sand and feel the grit in her mouth as the chinook took off and covered them in a plume of dust. She shivered, reliving the petrified look in Rix's eyes when they had been travelling in the vehicle to the extraction point, and he hadn't known whether he was going to make it.

"I stemmed the bleeding and then we got on the vehicle and had to drive to the place where the helicopter would land and pick him up."

"They land helicopters right in the middle of a battlefield?!" Aaron asked.

"Yeah, of course. They have to. If there's a seriously injured soldier they have to get him out, as quickly as possible. It's that or they die."

Jess consciously chose not to mention the grenade - there was no need for them to know at all, and she didn't want to worry Liam unnecessarily - and continued with the next part of the story.

"Then we both got on the chinook and

went back to Camp Bastion. He went for surgery on his leg, then he was brought back to the UK and I didn't see him again until the tour finished."

"Wow," Liam's eyes widened. "How did you get together, though? Did you just like... declare your love for each other when you saw each other again?"

"No. I just went back to his flat and it all went from there really."

Liam frowned. He was putting two and two together and he couldn't make four. He definitely wasn't stupid, he was a very analytical sort of person and Jess knew that he would have pieced it all together in his mind, and it just didn't fit.

"I just don't get it though. How did you know to go back to his flat? How did you know he felt the same?"

Jess shrugged. "Just a feeling, I guess. And we would have met up at some point anyway, when you spend six months eating, sleeping and breathing with the same people you tend to catch up when you're back home."

He eyed her suspiciously again but then Aaron shifted in his seat, lying back against the side of the chair and stretching his legs over Liam's lap. She let out a deep breath she had been holding as Liam got distracted and moved the blanket around, then picked up the beer he had placed on the floor by his chair. "What does he do now? If he's lost his leg?"

Jess hesitated, struggling to put it in to words. "He's... just trying to sort his head out at the moment. He leaves the army in two months, he needs to decide what he wants to do next. And he's obviously building up his strength on his prosthetic leg, he's doing really well at the moment. I'm proud of him."

And proud she was. She felt a little ball of pride swell up inside her at the thought of how far he had come since that first day she saw him after returning from deployment. He was getting about well now, he hardly used his crutches during the day when he was at home. He was even managing to get to his physiotherapy appointments without them.

Liam took a swig of his beer. "When do we get to meet him?"

Jess relaxed slightly at the thought of being with him again. "Hopefully soon. Well, I'll be getting my medal soon and he'll come when I get that so... you'll definitely get to meet him then. At the moment we're just taking things slowly... like I told you earlier, nobody can find out about us. I don't want people putting two and two together and getting five, nothing happened on tour but that doesn't stop people assuming."

"But that might be ages!" Liam protested, turning to Aaron who was looking curiously at him.

"Jess won an award for bravery," he explained, matter of fact. "The Military Cross."

"That's amazing! Well done."

Jess smiled proudly. "Thanks. And it won't be long, because I got the letter today. The ceremony is in November."

"Do you actually get to meet the Queen? Will you have to kneel down in front of her so that she can tap you on the shoulder with a Royal Sword?"

Jess laughed. "No, you muppet. They use the sword when you get a knighthood! But yeah, I might get to meet the Queen. Or maybe Prince Charles or maybe someone else, I don't know yet."

"That's amazing!" Aaron said. "I'd love to meet the Queen!"

Jess smiled and watched as her brother stretched his arm around Aaron and gave him a loving squeeze. It warmed her inside to see him this happy. She could just tell by looking at them that they were a good match - good for each other. It felt like she and Rix had never ending hurdles to overcome before they would be able to act like a proper couple, proud to show off their feelings for each other when they went out. Keeping their feelings for each other a secret was quite wearing sometimes.

Jess yawned and stretched, knocking the blanket off her lap. "Well. I'm heading on up. I'll see you in the morning. Good to meet you, Aaron."

"Yeah, you too," he smiled as she got up out of the chair and tossed the blanket over the back of it.

As Jess walked through the kitchen doorway and closed it gently behind her, she stood in the kitchen for a few seconds, staring at her phone. She scrolled through her most recent photos - she had taken some last time she stayed at Rix's flat of the two of them, lying in bed looking quite content in each other's company. She smiled, tracing her thumb over his face absent-mindedly. She really missed him. She really seemed to have fallen for him.

Chapter Nineteen

It was Saturday evening, and George and Elena were watching the television together with Katie and Louise when they heard the doorbell. They exchanged a hopeful look. Elena jumped out of the chair and raced to the front door, wondering whether it would be Jason. He had been gone for ten days now and she was getting frantic. They had tried all of his old friends and everyone that they knew may still be in touch with him, but there was no sign of him at all.

Elena swung open the front door to find two police officers standing on the doorstep. Leaning against the doorframe for support, her hand shot to her mouth and her eyes filled with tears.

"Oh, no," she gasped, choking back tears. "Please, God, no."

"Mrs Coulson?" One of the officers asked, his hands clasped together in front of him.

"Yes," she managed, feeling George brush up behind her. She leant against him for support, her legs shaking.

"We're here to see Jason Coulson," the officer replied, and she let out a huge sigh of relief at the realisation that they had not come to tell her that he was dead.

"He… he's not here. We haven't seen him for ten days now."

The other officer stepped forwards. "Can we come in?" Her voice was softer and she seemed a lot friendlier. Elena looked up at George and he nodded, standing aside to allow them entry.

"Come through," he mumbled gravely, walking towards the kitchen.

Elena watched the officers through the door and then closed the front door behind them with a gentle click. Passing the living room, she glanced at their daughters who were no longer engrossed in the television and were instead sitting in nervous silence, their eyes fixed on the doorway.

Elena forced herself to sound a lot brighter than she felt. "Don't worry, nothing to worry about. They'll have just come to see if they can help us track him down. We'll be back in a moment."

"Mum," Katie interjected, climbing out of the chair and meeting her in the doorway. "What's going on?"

Elena glanced back to Louise who was watching them, her young features etched with worry. It was like looking in the mirror.

"Why don't you open the chocolate?" Elena suggested optimistically. "You can share it. We'll talk later, yeah?"

Then she gave them both a big reassuring smile and went through to the kitchen, closing the door behind her. George was sat down at the dining table with the officers, the kettle was already boiling.

"Take a seat," George instructed, his voice flat. Elena sat. She kept her eyes on the officers, one of whom seemed to be analysing every inch of their home and the other who still had a fake smile stuck on her face. Clearly it was going to be a good cop, bad cop set up.

The male officer returned his eyes to the table. "We need to find your son, Mrs Coulson. Do you have any idea where he could be?"

"No," she almost whispered, her voice shaking. "We had an argument, and he left. I haven't seen him since. We've tried everyone we know, but… nobody knows where he is."

"Your son is facing serious charges. We have been asked to track him down by some of his officers who are very concerned that he has gone AWOL. He is in breach of his duty to the Crown, Mrs Coulson, he could go to prison, do you understand?"

Elena nodded and felt fresh tears forming in her eyes. She clasped her hands together on the table so tightly that she could feel her nails digging into the palms of her hands.

"Mrs Coulson," the second officer continued. "I understand that you're worried about Jason, and you have tried to track him down. But is there anything you can think of that you might have forgotten? If Jason returns voluntarily, any sentence is likely to be a lot less severe."

George's face contorted in a frown and he trembled, trying his best not to shout. "She *said*, she doesn't know. If we knew where he was, my wife wouldn't be crying herself to sleep every night, would she?"

"I understand," the second officer sympathised.

Elena looked up at her. She didn't look much older than Jason. Elena was sure that she didn't even have toddlers, let alone her own grown up children to worry about. How could she possibly understand?

"We want to help you find Jason. Please help us to help you."

Elena looked at George, who still looked furious. She slowly nodded. "I just want him home. Whatever it takes."

"And we will do our best to get him back for you," the officer pulled out her notepad. "Now, if we start with a list of everywhere Jason goes, everyone he knows... and everyone you have already tried to contact. We can fill in the gaps. Then we will go through a timeline, and you can tell us everything we need to know about your son. What he likes, what his hobbies are... what he doesn't like. That will help us to build up a profile of him, and that will help us to locate him."

Elena nodded. "Ok. Just tell me where you want to start."

***

Pressing himself to the wall, Jase's chest heaved with exertion. He had only seconds until he needed to move again. He made the most of it, keeping his eyes on the corner of the wall just in case he was being followed. Once his breathing had levelled slightly he crept back towards it, keeping his body flat against the brick work. When he got to the end of the wall he peered around and then took off, running through the crowds of people as fast as he possibly could.

The noise was unbearable, it felt excruciating. He kept his eyes fixed ahead and sprinted through the crowds, keeping his arms out in front of him to brace himself against anyone he collided with. At the sight of him running, wild-eyed, straight towards them, the crowd began to clear - he ignored the protests of several members of the public who had to almost jump out of the way to avoid him. He could barely hear them, and to be honest he didn't care. He just had to get to safety. He was on his own, greatly outnumbered and he just had to stay under cover until they managed to locate him.

He broke free from the crowd on the high street and ran down a narrow alleyway, avoiding various bins which were scattered throughout. He glanced over his shoulder every couple of seconds, ensuring that he wasn't being watched. When he was sure that he wasn't being followed he found a large wheelie bin and checked behind him again, then opened the lid. Perfect. It was only half full and there was plenty of room inside. He hoisted himself up and jumped inside, pulling the lid back down on top of him. Once he was still, in the dark, he felt safe. He curled up in a ball and wrapped his arms around his body, closing his eyes. He had lost count of how many nights he had been awake. That was when they liked to strike, at night. He had to be on high alert at all times, in case of an attack - then he could catch up on an hour or two of sleep in the day until he had to get on the move again. They could be tracking him - what if they were using infrared, what if they had drones? He couldn't be discovered now, he was ridiculously close. They would be coming soon. They would extract him, and he would be safe.

***

Rix sat opposite his parents at the cramped dining table. He watched Lynne prod around in her takeaway curry carton with a fork, as if she was highly suspicious of the contents. She forced a smile. "Well, this looks… lovely."

Her obvious discomfort over something so normal almost made him laugh, but he was careful to hide his amusement and sarcasm in his voice. "Glad you like it."

It wasn't lovely at all. He hadn't even wanted them to come, they had sort of invited themselves. She had asked him about four times now to come and visit them, and each time he had come up with an excuse. Being the dutiful parent that she liked to make out she was, she had turned up on his doorstep, his dad in tow. Clearly, Gerald didn't have any complaints about the takeaway curry because he was already shovelling it in, like he hadn't eaten for weeks.

Lynne stabbed a piece of chicken and nibbled off a piece very carefully, as if it might be poisonous. "So. What have you been doing with yourself?"

Rix shrugged, finishing the mouthful he was chewing. "Not much really. Same as always. Gym. Catching up with stuff."

"Like what?"

"Paperwork," he replied vaguely.

"And have you decided what you're going to *do?*" Lynne emphasised the last word as if it was of great importance. At the moment, getting out of bed in the morning and finding the energy to get up and go to the gym took all of Rix's determination.

"Not yet," he answered coolly, scooping up another mouthful of curry on his fork.

They all sat silently around the table. Rix could tell that his dad was trying very hard to keep his eyes on his dinner and not say anything that might inflame things. As always, the atmosphere between his wife and son was tense to say the least.

"Why don't you come and stay with us for a bit?" She asked, and for a fleeting moment it seemed as though she actually cared. "Being here on your own must be... hard."

"I'm not on my own. I have friends, colleagues."

"Not for much longer," she muttered, and Rix put down his fork on the plate with a clatter.

Gerald looked up from his plate and sighed. "What your mum's trying to say...Is that we're here for you, son. Whatever you need."

"Whatever I need," Rix repeated. "That's

funny. Because you weren't interested when I was flown back to the UK with half my leg missing, were you?"

"We visited!" Lynne protested, her brow furrowed.

"Once. I was in hospital for weeks. And the whole time you were there, all you did was tell me how this was bound to happen at some point, and it's a blessing in disguise because now I'll have some money behind me, and Dad needs help with the family business anyway."

"Well he does," she replied curtly. "And it is. If you push hard, you'll get hundreds of thousands of pounds, Richard. You can do anything you want to."

Rix snapped. "Well, money doesn't buy happiness, does it? You can't fix everything with money. Just like you can't force me to find a wife who meets your strict requirements."

Lynne put down her fork too and sighed theatrically, her eyes rolling at him just like they had when he was a little boy and had done something wrong. "Richard, I thought we were over this. If you don't want to see Charlotte again, then fine. She's a nice girl, that's all. Plenty of ambition. You didn't have to be rude, did you?"

"Rude? What did you expect? I came to see you and you pretty much ambushed me with someone I'm not remotely interested in. It was humiliating! We have absolutely nothing in common."

"Fine," Lynne raised her hands in the air as if in surrender. "Fine. I won't interfere with your love life again. But you do need to sort your life out, Richard. You're out of the army in a couple of months, and you keep saying that you don't want to join the family business, but what are you going to do instead?"

Getting on a plane and disappearing, never to have to see her again seemed like a good option at that moment. But he bit his tongue, instead choosing to shrug and mutter that he wasn't sure yet.

"Your father and I were talking. He'd like to wind things down now that he's getting older, he wants more time to pursue his hobbies. It makes *sense*, Richard. You'd be set for life!"

Rix shook his head. "No."

She recoiled as if she had hit him, and he watched her sit taller in her chair as she took a deep breath and her body bristled. "Why not? Why won't you even consider it?"

"Because I don't *want* to," he insisted, exasperated. "I've got plans, I'll find my own way."

"But don't you think that's going to be a little harder now? I don't understand why you are opposing this. You're being given an opportunity, Richard. An opportunity to *make something* of yourself. Let's face it, it's not like you're going to be inundated with offers…"

He saw her eyes fall on his prosthetic leg, and at that moment he realised that he couldn't possibly like her any less. He would have been quite happy if she fell off the face of the earth and he never saw her again.

"I think you should go," he spat, completely astounded that even she could be so callous.

She sat at the table, not making any move to leave. Her presence at the table irritated him further and he slammed a fist down on the table, making everyone jump. "Now!"

"Richard... please," she stuttered. "Let's talk about this calmly. You're not thinking straight..."

"Now!" He shouted.

Gerald put his fork down and scrambled out of the chair. Momentarily, Rix felt a bit sorry for him, but then again, he had chosen not to stand up to his wife for all these years, which meant that he was complicit. Reluctantly, Lynne picked her handbag up from beside her chair and clasped it to her chest, while rising from the chair slowly.

Rix walked over to the doorway and stood there, waiting for them to walk past. Eventually they did, and he followed them down the hallway and opened the front door.

"Bye, son," Gerald sighed reluctantly, his face troubled.

"Bye."

As she walked past him Lynne paused, looking up at her son with a look of confusion and upset in her eyes. He honestly didn't care. She had done so much to put him down, and this was the last straw. Her eyes were glassy with tears. "I didn't mean..."

"Yeah, you did," he cut her off dismissively. "But do you know what, I'll prove you wrong. Because I have someone who believes in me, no matter what. Losing a leg won't define me. And the fact that you think it will say more about you than it does about me. I don't need your help. And I don't need you to give me a job. I'll get one myself."

She opened her mouth to protest but he closed the door before she got a chance to speak. Then he leant against it, his pulse racing in his chest. It felt good to shut her out. He should have done it a long time ago.

He walked down the hallway, feeling as though he was stronger on his leg than he ever had been. He had joined the army as a young man, desperate for a way to escape from his parents because he didn't have the strength to just leave. But here he was, having almost lost everything, but he had done it all by himself. Even without the army. Every day he was growing stronger and stronger, sometimes when he was busy with something he almost forgot for a few seconds that the leg was not his own. Sure, at the end of the day his stump was tired and his muscles ached, but he was able to walk almost normally now - if he wore long trousers and a proper shoe, to the average passerby he didn't even look as though he only had one leg.

After picking up the other plates from the table and scraping them into the bin, Rix threw them at the sink triumphantly. That was it, they were gone. He had been putting off seeing them for weeks. And now, if he had his own way, he wouldn't have to see them again. Still, there was a niggle at the back of his mind, a niggle of self-doubt. Although he was getting physically stronger, he couldn't say the same for his mental state. Despite the temporary sense of euphoria he felt for finally standing up to Lynne, it was still there - the nagging self-doubt, the black cloud of lowness that always seemed to be hanging over him. He had good days and he had bad days. On the good days something would happen to give him a boost and he could almost forget it was there - but on the bad days it seemed to dominate whatever he did, robbing him of his motivation and persuading him that whatever he had achieved wasn't quite good enough.

Rix turned away from the worktop and caught sight of himself in the mirror, his prosthetic leg visible under his shorts. He felt it seeping back in - covering the good thoughts up like thick black ink, immersing him in hopelessness. He clenched his jaw, fighting back the tears which were prickling in his eyes. Maybe she was right. How could he expect anyone to believe in him, when he couldn't even believe in himself?

***

"Morning," Jess said brightly.

Leaning on the balcony, Rix clasped the phone to his ear and savoured the positive tone of her voice. A cool early morning breeze ruffled through his hair and he took a deep breath, enjoying the fresh autumn air.

"How was last night? You never called."

"Oh…" he hesitated. "Yeah, sorry. I must have fallen asleep."

He didn't like lying to her. But sometimes trying to explain how he really felt was just too difficult, and it was easier to simplify things. He knew that he should open up; she would listen, better than anyone else he knew. But for some reason he couldn't explain, he just couldn't.

He could hear background noise, the noise of the occasional car whooshing past and the sound of footsteps. "What happened, then?"

"Where are you?" He asked.

"Oh, I'm just meeting some old friends for breakfast."

"Sorry, I didn't realise. Don't let me keep you."

"No, you're not," she encouraged. "I haven't got to be there for twenty minutes. I just thought it would be nice to walk. Anyway. Tell me about last night."

He tapped the palm of his hand on the railings of the balcony whilst biting his bottom lip. Where would he begin? Tongue tied, he eventually let out the breath he had been holding and managed to find the words to describe the unexpected evening in with his parents. Once he was done, he heard Jess puff out her cheeks and whistle just like she always did when she was surprised about something. "Your mum really is something else. Don't take any notice, ok? I'm sure she doesn't mean it."

Rix tightened his hand around the balcony

railings. "Oh, she does. She definitely does mean it. That's all she thinks of me, the soldier who got blown up. Well now she can say, *I told you Richard,* because this is exactly what she said would happen when I joined up. I'm sure she's loving it."

"I'm sorry. I thought maybe things would turn around with her... you know. Maybe you could patch things up."

He sighed. "Yeah, well. It doesn't look like it. And to be honest, I'm glad. If I never saw her again, I wouldn't care."

Jess pressed her lips together, feeling torn. It was hard to hear him say that. On one hand his parents sounded absolutely awful - especially his mum. But she would give anything just to have one last day with her dad, and hearing someone else with that opportunity say that they would gladly throw it all away was hard. They were still his parents after all.

"Are you still there?"

"Yeah," she muttered. "Yeah, sorry. I just got a bit distracted."

He got the sense that he'd annoyed her, and he tried his best to sound more positive. "How are things back at home?"

Jess's mood lifted at the change of subject. "Yeah, good. I met Liam's boyfriend yesterday. He's really sweet. I think he's good for him. They're good for each other, actually."

"That's good."

"Liam asked when he's going to meet you?" Jess asked.

Rix ran his hand along the railings and turned to rest the bottom of his back against them, facing the patio doors which led to his living room. He didn't really know what to say. He had mixed feelings. He was glad that she was thinking about him seriously enough to want him to meet her family, yet he was nervous too. What if they didn't like him, what if they didn't think he was good enough for her? What if his leg locked and he got caught in an embarrassing situation?

Jess could sense his apprehension. "Do you want to meet them?"

"Of course."

"Good," she replied. "Because I got my invitation through yesterday, for the investiture ceremony. It's in November. The 26th. And I want you to be there, Rix."

He clenched his jaw and felt his pulse quicken at the thought of having to go to London, in amongst all those people. He had just about got used to travelling on the train to his appointments, but this was whole different ball game. And not only that, but in the same week that his time in the army would come to a definite end. It seemed almost ironic that whilst his career was about to implode, Jess was climbing higher and higher.

"Ok," he said.

She paused and he knew his reaction wasn't what she had been hoping. "Ok?"

He opened the patio door and slipped inside to the familiarity of his apartment. "Yeah, I'll be there."

"You could sound excited about it."

She sounded mildly annoyed. He clenched his jaw, closing the door behind him. "I am excited. I'm just... I'm just tired, that's all."

"But you went to bed early?" She accused.

He didn't really know what to say. He hadn't gone to bed early because he knew that even if he tried to sleep, he wouldn't. It was depressing lying in his bed on his own, staring up at the dim reflection from the lights outside the window on his ceiling, occupied by his own thoughts. Most of the time he tried to keep his mind busy until he was physically exhausted, because he knew that then he would be able to fall asleep more quickly. Lying alone with his own thoughts was dangerous. Then again, even sleeping was dangerous. It only took a second for him to slip back there; some nights he woke up in the middle of the night, his heart pounding in his chest as if he was sprinting towards her again, waiting for her to be shot down in front of him.

Sometimes his mind wandered back even further and he was right at the beginning, watching most of his section being blown to bits right in front of him. Sometimes it only lasted a matter of seconds and sometimes for longer. Sometimes all he could see was their faces, or what was left of them, lifeless on the floor in front of him.

"I've got to go," she said eventually.

She sounded disappointed and he knew that he had let her down. Sometimes he didn't know why he bothered, as all he ever seemed to do was let people down these days.

"I'm sorry. I am pleased for you, you know. And really proud of you."

She paused and he could hear her breath at the other end of the phone. "I'm proud of you too."

"Talk later?" He asked, hopefully. Hearing her voice was one of the only things he had to look forward to right now.

"Yeah. Talk later."

And then she was gone. Rix held the phone to his ear for a few more seconds, longing to hear her voice for a bit longer. Eventually he placed the phone on the coffee table and sat back down on the sofa, pulling his laptop off the cushion and onto his lap. He opened it and began to scroll through the pages he had started reading yesterday, the research he had been advised to do by the resettlement advisor he had seen earlier in the week. He was growing conscious that time was ticking and he needed to come up with a plan. Once he was discharged, he knew that his appointments would dwindle considerably because he would be transferred to NHS care, and he would no longer have resettlement meetings. He would be on his own, expected to function in a world which was alien to him. It would be his first taste of adult civilian life, and if he was completely honest it scared him.

With every day that passed he became increasingly anxious about that date in November that was etched in his mind, his last serving day. Financially he would be fine - he was expecting a considerable lump sum payout and would also receive monthly payments which would more or less cover his rent and bills. He would survive. But he wanted more than that - he didn't just want to survive. He felt the weight of all the soldiers he had lost bearing down on his shoulders, expecting him to make the most of his life because they hadn't been able to. And he felt totally overwhelmed because now, with a little more than eight weeks to go, he was still scrolling through webpages, reading up about hypothetical careers, none of which seemed to quite fit his idea of what he wanted for the rest of his life. And he was running out of time.

Chapter Twenty

The air was thick with sand and explosives. Jase choked as it saturated his lungs, rendering him unable to breathe for a few moments. It began to clear and his heart almost stopped. Their stricken bodies were spread out in front of him, arms and legs missing, even part of a head missing. He looked down at his uniform and saw that it was splattered with blood and human tissue. At first he thought he was the only person still alive but then he saw Jess scramble through the dust to get to the first of the bodies, and he heard Sergeant Mellor's voice as he tried to gain control of the situation.

Jase stood rooted to the spot, unable to move. He gripped the Vallon hard as if it was the only thing holding him upright. This was on him. How had he possibly missed a device this big? He watched as Jess fruitlessly tried to save them, and he would have given anything to swap places. Some soldier he was.

He watched as Jess got up off the floor and came at him, screaming words he couldn't understand. He stepped back but she cornered him, shouting in his face, screaming that it was his fault. He tried to push her away but she was too strong, she had all her weight on his face now and he could hardly breathe. He thrashed around trying to escape but he couldn't - her eyes were wild and she looked ready to finish him off. He screamed in desperation and before he knew it his eyes had snapped open and he realised he wasn't in Afghanistan at all, he was back in the UK and someone was on top of him, their hand firmly pressed to his mouth.

He tried to struggle but he had very little energy; it had been weeks since he had eaten properly and his muscle was wasting away. His filthy clothes now fell off his skinny frame, and when he wasn't off his face on drugs, he was almost permanently either intoxicated or hung over.

"Please!" He begged, trying to wriggle out of their grasp. "Please, don't."

He watched as a second person rifled through his jacket pocket and pulled out the last bag of cocaine he had kept for later, for when he was desperate. Then they released him and quickly ran, leaving him crumpled on the cold alleyway floor in his soiled clothes.

Eventually, when Jase was sure that they were gone he got up, his body shaking. He gazed down at his sweat and urine stained clothes and wondered how he had got himself in such a mess. He had only intended to leave home for a short while to sort his head out, but days had blurred into each other and he had ended up in a drug and alcohol induced coma for so long he couldn't even remember what day of the week it was, or where he had been for the past few weeks.

He thought about Melon and what he would say if he could see him now. He would be disgusted - they all would. Their lives had been torn from them, they hadn't had a choice; and here Jase was, destroying his own life one step at a time. In the last few months he had lost not only himself, but his family, his home and his self-respect. Thinking about Jess and Mellor, he scratched at his patchy beard. He was certain that they wouldn't be kicking around in a dark alleyway, stoned and drunk, trying to blot out that disastrous day. Sometimes he wished that he hadn't burnt his bridges with Jess. He had been angry, bitterly angry. But she was probably just about the only person that would understand, if he told her the truth.

Jase was tired and he needed to find somewhere safe to sleep for the night. Now this place had been compromised, he couldn't stay. He crawled out of the alleyway and pulled his hood up, making his way out towards the busy high street. It was packed with people making their way home, going about their daily lives. One of the things he had struggled with the most since coming back to the UK was seeing civilians just walking around, completely oblivious to what was going on out in Afghanistan. The day of the repatriation, the whole of Wootton Bassett high street had come to a standstill while the procession ran through it. And yet, within minutes of it finishing, it was like it had never happened; there were people walking down the street again, seemingly oblivious to the massive loss of life.

Jase walked down the high street deep in thought as crowds of people parted around him. He barely noticed the scowls on their faces as they deliberately avoided him; he was filthy and the stench rising from him was pungent. Suddenly he heard a loud bang behind him and he froze, his heart suddenly racing in his chest. He darted past a group of civilians and pressed himself to the nearest wall, turning to look. His eyes frantically darted around the crowd of people who were still ambling along as if the noise was all in his head. He heard it again, this time it was even louder and he felt the rumble in his stomach. He looked frantically around him. Why were they all ignoring it? He wanted to scream at them all to run but every time he caught someone's eye and they looked up at him, all he could see in their face was disgust. He shrank down in a nearby doorway and sank to his knees, his eyes tightly shut and his curled up fists pressed to his temples, wishing that it would just stop.

He wasn't sure how long he had been there when he heard footsteps approaching. His heart leapt again - this was it, he was sure of it. He kept his eyes closed for a moment, trying to get his head straight so that he could decide what to do. He began to bash his fists hard against his head, trying to wake himself up from this nightmare. He heard a voice this time but the echo of nearby traffic and pedestrians was ear splitting, and the voice sounded distorted as though he was underwater. He made a split decision and reacted, suddenly leaping from the floor and throwing his arms out in front of him to knock the person out of the way.

There was only a split second between him opening his eyes and throwing the person off their feet for him to realise how wrong his judgment had been. He saw her eyes open wide with fear as he approached her and pushed her straight backwards; she landed on the hard concrete path with an awful crack and he stood there for a couple of seconds, unsure as to what he should do.

"I'm… I'm sorry…" he stammered, but every part of his body was telling him to run.

People began to stop and rush over to help her and all he could do was stand there in absolute horror at what he had done. And then he heard the noise again and he had no choice - this time his body chose to escape and he sprinted away.

He ran and ran, until he had escaped the crowds of people and the path became emptier. His lungs felt fit to explode and he could feel his pulse thumping in his head, but he kept going. He knew that he wasn't safe and all he could do was keep running and running. Eventually he had left the town behind completely and he was running along a cycle path next to a main road. A large lorry whizzed past kicking up a plume of dust, and he froze. He was back there again; the dust infiltrated his lungs and he choked, leaning up against a lamp post. Gripping onto it for dear life, his fingertips went white with pressure. As the dust cleared he could see their faces again, but this time they were on the other side of the road.

They were trying to say something to him, he could see them shouting. He shouted back, the dust clearing as cars continued to whizz past. He didn't know how he was going to get to them but he knew he had to; he could help them this time, he could do the right thing, make up for all the things he hadn't done in Afghanistan.

"I don't know how!" He looked up and shouted, his body shaking with adrenaline. He had to be quick. As the air cleared further they seemed to be getting further and further away. Melon was shouting something he couldn't quite hear.

Jase's chest still heaving up and down with exertion. "I can't hear you! I can't... hear you!"

He let go of the lamppost and took a few steps towards the kerb. He could see them better now - the air was a little clearer and apart from the occasional car whizzing past, he had a clear line of sight over to the bushes where they were waiting for him. Suddenly he realised what they were saying. They wanted him to come.

"Roger that!"

Before he even knew what he was doing, he had left the kerb and was striding across the carriageway, all his attention focused on them. They were just a few metres away now - he could see their faces. It was definitely them. He could hear them better now too, they were all screaming at him to come, unanimous.

Then he felt a rush of air, the deafening roar of a horn ringing in his ears and a bright light shining in his eyes. In a split second he turned, shielding his eyes but the light was blinding. He staggered backwards and for the first time in weeks he could see clearly. But it was too late.

***

The boiling kettle bubbled away in the background, but Jess barely noticed. She sat at the dining table, her phone in her hand, staring into space. She didn't even look up when her mum entered the kitchen, took the kettle off the hob and stood in front of her, her hands on her hips.

"Jess? What are you doing?"

Jess looked up, her eyes startled as if she her mind was still elsewhere. "What?"

"The kettle," Jane scowled, mildly irritated. "I'm surprised it hasn't boiled dry. It's like a sauna in here."

She swung open the back door and let some of the steam out. As a wave of fresh air hit her, Jess looked around her and realised that Jane was right. The kettle had clearly been boiling for quite some time. She blushed slightly. "Sorry. I was miles away."

Jane softened slightly. "I can see that. Are you ok?"

Standing up, Jess pushed her chair backwards with a loud scrape. "Yeah." She crossed the kitchen to the empty mug which she had placed on the side in readiness. "Do you want one?"

"Please," Jane replied and sat down at the table.

Jess took another mug off the mug tree, picked up the tea bag canister and opened it, placing a bag in each mug. Jane watched her fill each mug with water and stir it. Something wasn't right with her daughter. She had known it since the minute she had come back to the UK. She was always a bit closed when she came back from a tour, it took her a couple of days to settle back in. But this time was different. She felt like she barely saw her these days, and when she did spend time with her it was like she wasn't there. Her mind was clearly on something, or someone, else.

Jess placed one mug in front of her and sat opposite, cradling her own mug between her hands. They both sipped their tea in silence. Then Jane watched as Jess's gaze wandered to the window.

"Jessie," she said softly, placing her hand on top of her daughter's. Jess looked back at her, the deer in the headlights look back again.

"Mmm?"

"Is everything… alright?"

"Yeah. Why'd you ask?"

"You just seem a bit… preoccupied lately. Distracted. You can talk to me, you know. About anything?"

Jess smiled weakly. "Yeah, I know. I'm fine, Mum. Don't worry."

Jane nodded and took her hand back, lifting the mug to take another sip of her tea. She knew her daughter, and she knew when she wasn't telling the truth.

"You would tell me wouldn't you, if there was something bothering you?" She probed gently.

Jess raised her eyes off her mug again and their eyes met for a few seconds. Those eyes.

281

Whenever Jane looked into them deeply like that, it was like they were the eyes of her husband. They were stunningly similar, sometimes it took her breath away just how similar.

"Did something happen? When you were deployed? You can talk to me, you know. I used to listen to your dad's war stories."

She watched Jess's eyes soften momentarily at the mention of her dad. Jane had retold many of the stories to her when she was a child, and Jess had loved to hear all about them. All the countries he had visited, all the good things he had done to make lives better.

"How did you know? That Dad was the one for you?"

Jane smiled, her gaze wandering momentarily as she became lost in memories. She could see him clear as day, right in front of her, in his camouflage uniform with his beret balanced on his head. "I just did. Not at first. It took a while."

"How long?" Jess asked.

Jane ran her thumb up and down the handle of the mug thoughtfully. "I thought he was an idiot at first. He used to drink at the pub I worked at, when he came back from tour. He always used to try to chat me up, but then, he used to try it on with lots of girls. He was popular."

Jess smiled at the thought of her dad trying to smooth talk her mum. She knew that they had met at the pub but she had never really been told the whole story.

"One evening he said he was going to be

deployed the next day. Suddenly I realised I didn't want him to go. I didn't love him then - not really... I hardly knew him. But we talked all night and when I finished work he was waiting outside for me. He walked me home. When we got to my front gate he kissed me, and he asked if I would meet him at the airport when he came back. It was just a short tour then, only four months, but it felt like a lifetime."

Jess's smile faded as she remembered how agonising it had been when Rix was brought back to the UK and she couldn't see him until she returned from Afghanistan. It must have been even worse for her mum, being stuck at home.

"He wrote to me. He talked about coming back and making a go of things. I wasn't sure how I felt... but I went to the airport. When he saw me his face lit up. And it was then that I realised I wanted to spend the rest of my life with him."

Jess couldn't help but smile again. "Aww. That's really romantic. I can just imagine you jumping into his arms and him spinning you round in the middle of the airport."

Jane took a sip of her tea. "Yeah well, it wasn't quite like that. I was a bit shy. Things got serious a bit later." She looked over the rim of the mug at Jess, who was still smiling absent-mindedly. "Why do you ask? Have you met someone?"

Jess shifted in her chair awkwardly and then looked down at the table. "I don't know. Maybe."

"Who is he?" Jane asked. "Is he a

soldier?"

"Yeah. Well, for now anyway. Not for much longer."

"He's leaving the army?"

"He's being medically discharged. He was shot when we were out in Afghan. He lost one of his legs."

Jane nodded sadly. She was all too aware of the sacrifices that servicemen and women made when they were deployed. Unfortunately for her, it hadn't just been a leg that her husband had lost.

"That must be hard for him."

Considering just how hard it really had been for Rix, Jess felt a pang in her chest. "Yeah. It is. He's doing really well with his physio... but mentally, I just don't feel like he has fully come to terms with it. I don't really know how to help him."

"Just be there for him," Jane placed her hand on top of her daughter's. "Listen to him. Encourage him. But let him find his own way. That's all you can do."

Jess nodded. "It's hard... not being there to help him. But I'm on base all week and I like to come home too. I always just feel torn, like I'm not 100% anywhere. And I don't really know where we stand, you know... one minute he seems like he loves me, the next he doesn't really seem to care for anything. He's really hard to read."

Jane squeezed her hand reassuringly. "If he's struggling, he probably doesn't know what he feels. But love isn't plain sailing. It's not all flowers and chocolates. Sometimes you love each other, sometimes you hate each other. It's peaks and troughs. But just be there for each other, and be honest. That's all you can do."

Jess nodded and placed her other hand on top of her mum's. Jane squeezed her hand back.

"Thanks Mum. You're right."

"I'm always right," Jane replied, and they both laughed. "Is that where you've been lately?"

"Yeah. He lives in Reading."

Jane nodded. "How did you meet?"

Jess hesitated, then she cringed. "He was in charge of the section. I know that sounds really bad. But it wasn't like that."

Jane raised an eyebrow, and Jess bit her lip. "Nothing at all happened when we were on tour. We lost a few of our soldiers last year when we were out in Afghan. It sort of brought us together."

"Last year?" Jane asked. "But you served again together this year?"

"Yeah."

"Blimey, Jess," Jane's eyes widened in disbelief. "Why would you put yourself in that position? If anyone had found out you could both have been court-martialled!"

"I honestly thought nothing was going to happen between us. I thought it was just the shock of what happened last year, bringing us together. I went back to Camp Bastion and I saw him again there. And he asked me to go back to the FOB with them and I couldn't say no, they'd just lost their medic."

Jane was shocked. She had always had her daughter down as the sensible one - completely dedicated to her career. Definitely not one to risk it all for a man. Liam had always been the more romantic one, always going with his heart instead of his head. But not Jess.

"When we were at the FOB everything was normal. I thought I'd got it wrong... I got stuck into work. Everything was fine until that day when he almost died, it was like it brought it all back to me. How I felt. I just couldn't deny it anymore."

Jane sighed. "I understand. Sometimes it takes something big to make you realise how you really feel."

Jess nodded. "Exactly."

"Does anyone else know?"

Jess shook her head. "No. We've both been really careful not to give anyone a reason to suspect us. But we've done nothing wrong, honestly. Nothing happened at all until we were both back home. Well... except that he kissed me... but... like I said, nothing happened after that, I thought it was just because we were both grieving, you know... We were nothing but professional while we were serving together."

Jane took a deep breath and then, much to Jess's surprise, she smiled. Although she wanted to interfere, she knew that she had to let Jess find her own way. Just as she had. "When do we get to meet him, then?"

Jess smiled nervously. "He's going to come to the ceremony. You'll meet him then."

"I'll look forward to that."

Jess sighed. "I'm sorry, Mum. I should have told you sooner. I didn't deliberately keep it from you."

Jane reached forwards and took Jess's hands in hers. "It's fine. It's your life. You don't have to tell me anything. But just know that you can always talk to me, Jessie. No matter what it is. I'm always there for you, good or bad."

Jess got up and wrapped her arms around her mum, pulling her close. Jane relaxed in her daughter's grip. It didn't seem that long since it was the other way round, Jane putting her arms around her young daughter and holding her tight. Yet now here they were, Jess a grown woman with her own life. It was like she had blinked overnight and she had gone from a little girl to the spitting image of her dad. Jane knew that he would be proud if he could see her now.

***

George sat by his son's bedside, watching the steady rise and fall of his chest on the ventilator. It had been a week since they got the phone call, the one that they had been dreading since he had seemingly disappeared off the face of the earth. At the time they had thought that it was the worst moment of their lives, finding out that their eldest son had been hit by a lorry on a road miles from home, all on his own, and was holding onto life by a thread. Later they realised that they were wrong; it wasn't receiving the phone call that was the worst moment of their lives, it was seeing him in hospital just a couple of hours later, when it had become starkly obvious just how fragile he had become.

At first when they had got to the hospital and seen him for the first time, they had thought the police had got it wrong. It couldn't be their son lying on the bed in front of them. He looked nothing like Jason, he looked like a shadow of a man in the bed underneath the tubes and wires. His face was unrecognisable from the trauma of the accident but he was sporting wild hair and a beard which their son had never had. But on further inspection they had realised that it was in fact him. The elation of knowing that he was alive was quickly replaced by devastation when they were informed just how close he was to death. Given the speed and nature of the impact, it was a miracle that he hadn't been killed instantly. Someone had been watching out for him that day.

George leant forwards and took his son's hand in his. He felt incredibly guilty. This was his son, the same boy he had held in his arms twenty three years earlier and promised that he would always keep him safe. And he had failed. Jase had been failed by his mind, he had been failed by the army, and worst of all he had been failed by his own parents. George wasn't sure that he would ever be able to forgive himself for that.

The door clicked open quietly behind him and George turned, coming face to face with his wife. She looked exhausted, she had deep purple indents beneath her eyes which were bloodshot from crying and lack of sleep.

"I thought you were going to get your head down for a few hours?" George questioned.

"I tried," Elena muttered miserably. "But I just couldn't be away."

She had spent the past week at Jase's bedside for twenty four hours a day, with the exception of two short trips home to take a shower. Today was the first day that she had been persuaded to go home and get some rest. Jase was stable, and there was no real need for her to be there. George had promised to call her if there was any change at all, and Katie and Louise were missing their mum. They were used to having her around and suddenly their lives had been turned upside down, not only by their brother being on life support, but also by the fact that their parents had more or less disappeared.

Elena felt terribly guilty about leaving them, but she also felt responsible for what had happened to her son - and she had promised him that she would never, ever leave him on his own again. Ever since the day he left, she had run their last conversation over and over in her mind, as if it was possible to change what had happened if she went over it enough times. George had been dropping the girls to school in the morning and then either going on to work or coming to the hospital, before going home at dinner time to make them dinner and be there for a couple of hours until they went to bed. They had visited a couple of times in the evening, but should the worst happen Elena didn't want their last memories of their brother to be him as he was now. She was very proud of the way Katie had stepped up in order to look after her little sister; she had been collecting her from school and walking her home every day since the accident happened. If it wasn't for her then Elena wasn't sure what they would have done.

George turned back to his son. "Where are the girls?"

"They stayed at home. They asked to come but... I can't bear them seeing him like this."

George said nothing and continued to watching the rise and fall of his son's chest. In a way he felt like Elena was being selfish, although he would never have said that. He wanted to be with Jase too, yet he was still having to go to work and be there for their daughters. He knew that the girls were finding it hard without their mum, but it was like Elena had become completely blinkered to everything else in her life. She was obsessed with being around Jase.

"Maybe you could go home to them tonight," he suggested. "I'll stay here with Jason."

Elena pulled the other chair closer to Jase's bedside and sat on it. "No need. I've brought some bits, I'm happy to stay."

"But I want to. He's my son too, you know."

Elena's eyes narrowed and she stared at him. She knew he was right but it was hard to hear. She felt like she was doing the right thing by sticking at her son's bedside, making up for all the weeks she could have been there for him, but she wasn't.

"I don't know if I can let him go, George," she faltered, heartbroken.

Chapter Twenty One
One month later

Rix stood in front of the mirror in his suit. Tightening his tie around his neck, his hands trembled. He was clean shaven and he had been to the barbers the previous day, so his hair was neat and tidy for the first time in months. On the outside he looked neat, tidy and well presented. But inside he felt like he was falling apart.

He stood still for a few minutes, staring at his reflection. He was wearing a charcoal suit with a copper coloured tie which brought out the brown of his eyes. He felt like an imposter. It was the first time in his adult life that he had worn a normal suit. For every wedding, funeral or other event in the past twelve years he had worn service dress. The fact that his first formal event in civilian wear coincided with his first week as an actual civilian seemed almost symbolic. He could have been staring at any other person in the mirror; it was as though all the years he had spent fighting for his country amounted to nothing. With shoes on it wasn't even possible to tell that one of his legs was made of metal.

The vibration of his phone on the bedside table startled him and he turned to look at it. He knew that it would be Jess, texting to confirm what time they would be arriving to pick him up. They were going to travel to London on the train together, all four of them. He had not met her family yet and that made him even more nervous;

he wasn't good with families. His own parents had hardly set him up with a good knowledge of family etiquette. He had been putting off meeting them for ages and now he wished that he had just got it over with previously.

He walked across the room and picked up the phone, staring at the screen blankly. It was her. One hour. He sunk down on the edge of the bed and dropped his head into his hands, his heart pounding in his chest. He had never felt this conflicted. On one hand he wanted to be there for Jess and watch the proudest moment of her life so far, but on the other hand the thought of travelling to central London, meeting her family and functioning normally for an entire day seemed insurmountable. He had absolutely no idea how he was going to get through it.

***

"Knock! Knock!" Liam grinned, appearing in the doorway of Jess's bedroom. He caught sight of Jess in her dress uniform. "Wow! How posh do you look?!"

Jess turned from her dressing table and raised an eyebrow. "You don't look too bad yourself. Come in."

She patted the edge of her bed and he crossed the room, then sat gingerly on the edge of it. He watched her apply mascara to her eyelashes and then twist the lid back on, blinking at her reflection in the mirror.

"Are you nervous?"

"Petrified," she admitted, and then she laughed. "God. What if I trip up on my way up? Or do the wrong thing?"

"You'll be fine. Everyone will be in the same boat, remember. Apart from the Queen, obviously."

Jess laughed. "When did you get so wise? I thought I was supposed to be the older one, looking out for you?"

"You do. Every time you go and fight for our country, you do."

Jess picked up her cap from the bedside table and placed it on her head gently. She was really nervous. Every time she thought about the ceremony she felt sick. She tried to remind herself that it was just like being on parade; she was well versed in drill, she could do it almost with her eyes closed. Surely it wouldn't be much different than that?

Liam watched her straighten the cap on her head until it sat perfectly. "I'm proud of you. Dad would be, too. Imagine if he could be here today to see this."

Jess's throat suddenly felt tight and she quickly swallowed, taking a deep breath. "I wish he was. More than anything."

She glanced at the framed photograph she kept next to her bed of her dad in his uniform. She had looked at that photograph every night that she slept in her bed since he had died, kissed it goodnight and talked to him when times were hard.

"He'll be there. Watching it all, from up

there. I'm sure of it."

Jess nodded. She hoped that he was right. Feeling her dad right beside her would be the best gift of all, even better than the Military Cross she was about to receive. How different things could have been if he hadn't have died.

"Right," she cleared her throat to get rid of the lump that had formed unexpectedly. "Are you ready?"

Liam nodded, then stood up and offered her his arm. "Yes. Come on, my lady. This way."

"Lady?!" She snorted. "I told you, it's a Military Cross not a knighthood!"

"So?! If I can't treat my sister like royalty on a day like this, when can I?"

Jess rolled her eyes with a smile, linking her arm with his and stepping away from the dressing table. Just as they left the room, she heard her mobile bleep and she pulled it out of her jacket pocket. She read the message which popped up on the screen and her face immediately fell.

"What's up?"

Jess shook her head. "It's Rix. He's not coming."

"He's not coming? Are you serious? Why?!"

Jess stared at the message on the screen. "He um... he's not feeling up to it."

"Not *feeling* up to it?"

Jess forced a smile. "It's fine, it's fine. He's not well. He'll have to meet you guys another time."

Liam frowned and placed his hand on her forearm gently. "I'm sorry. I know you really wanted him to be here. It sucks that he's let you down."

"It's fine, honestly," Jess brushed him off, but her voice was a little too high pitched and she knew that she didn't sound at all convincing. "I have you and Mum with me. That's all that matters."

At the top of the stairs, Jess pulled her arm away from his and looked back towards her room. "You go ahead. I forgot something. I'll be down in two minutes."

Liam hesitated and then began to descend the stairs. "Ok. If you're sure."

She watched him go and then walked back to her bedroom, closing the door quietly behind her. She took her phone out of her pocket again and stared at it, contemplating whether or not to call him. She couldn't deny that she was absolutely gutted that he wouldn't be there to see her receive the award. Just last night they had discussed how much it meant to her, and he promised he wouldn't miss it for the world. It was supposed to be a fresh start for both of them, her starting the next stage of her career and him marking the start of his life outside of the army. She just didn't understand.

Jess realised that she wouldn't enjoy the day at all if she didn't at least find out what was really keeping him. She dialled his number and then held the phone to her ear, listening to the dial tone while she waited for him to pick up. It rang and rang. Eventually the call went through to voicemail and she stuffed the phone back in her pocket frustratedly. She heard her mum calling her from downstairs and she took a deep breath as she opened the bedroom door again.

"Coming!"

***

Standing on the balcony of his apartment, Rix took a deep breath of winter air. It was a gloomy morning and the sky was grey and full of ominous looking clouds. It was as though the weather was a reflection of what was going on in his mind. He looked out across the misty fields towards the river and loosened his tie. It was suffocating him.

When he had built up the courage to text Jess and tell her that he wouldn't be attending the ceremony, he thought that it would be a great relief. In actual fact it had made him feel infinitely worse. He had let her down now, on the biggest day of her life after she had been there for him ever since they had met in Afghanistan. He hated himself for not being able to support her on the one occasion that she needed him. All he could think about were the numerous occasions his parents had let him down as a child, when he had sat at the front of the school hall as all the parents arrived, watching them walk through the door one by one. Each time, the hall filled with parents and one by one the children waved. And each time, as the queue had become shorter and shorter his hope had dwindled and the result was always the same. He was always part of the small group of children who were left alone, because the people he loved most in the world couldn't be bothered to attend. He couldn't risk that for Jess. It was better that she knew now that he wouldn't be there.

He allowed his muscles to loosen, and he gripped the top of the railings as tears began to stream down his cheeks. He had no other option now. He had come close to this point countless times over the past few weeks, yet Jess had managed to stop him every time, even though she wasn't aware of it. It was almost like she had a sixth sense when it came to how he was feeling. Every time he felt himself getting lower, she seemed to turn up or give him a call and change his mind. This time would be different, he knew that. She had to put herself first today, and he would hate himself even more if anything came between her and that medal. He had come to realise in the last couple of months that he loved her - *really* loved her, and now he knew that it was time to let her go. She would move mountains on her own, but not if he was there tying her down. There was no other option.

After clearing his throat, Rix used his arms to hoist himself up high on the railings. He knew that he wouldn't be able to do it as easily with his prosthetic leg attached and, in any event, it felt strange ending things with that attached to him, since he still didn't consider it to be part of his body. In fact, it felt strange having anything attached to his body that wasn't actually part of him. He had even removed his watch and placed it carefully on his redundant service dress which he had folded carefully on his bed, together with his military issue dog tags and medals. It seemed fitting in some way to leave it all lying out like that, together with a letter addressed to Jess which he had hand written that morning. The military had been his life ever since he was eighteen, and it was the only identity he knew.

His abs trembled slightly with exertion as he lifted his legs over the railings and steadied himself on top of them, his one remaining leg swinging back and forth gently. He felt almost weightless up there, it was a relief. He felt as though he was on the edge of leaving all the angst he had felt while in the apartment behind, ready to start again. He watched the wind blow through the empty branches of nearby trees and felt the fresh air on his face. He made sure that he really looked around him and took in the beauty of the view one last time. Because the trees were bare of leaves, he was able to see further than in summer - all the way to the town centre and beyond, the rolling hills of the countryside. He pictured Jess on the train, flying through those hills on the way to London. The thought of leaving her was almost too much to bear, but he knew that he had to do it for her. If he didn't, he would end up dragging her down with him.

He took a deep breath and contemplated how far he should push himself. Was it better to just drop straight down like a stone, or push himself off like a bird? He didn't want to end up splattered up the ground floor flats or landing on some poor unsuspecting resident putting their washing out on their balcony. He wondered how quickly he would die. He wondered who would find his body and felt momentarily guilty. Mind you, he had given his life to the military for the benefit of every person in this building. They didn't feel guilty about that, why should he?

He loosened his grip on the railings and closed his eyes, ready to let go. He filled his mind with thoughts of Jess, the first time she had stepped off the chinook when arriving at the FOB on their first tour together and he had seen her hair framing her face in the downdraft. The first time he had seen her work her magic on the soldiers with whom they served, and the huge smile on her face when they survived. The devastation when she wasn't able to save them all. The heat that seemed to radiate from her when she was around. The way she had looked at him when he had kissed her for the first time. The pure beauty he enjoyed when he woke first and lay next to her, studying her sleeping features.

As though she could read his mind, he felt his phone buzz in his pocket. He cursed himself for leaving it in there. He had intended to leave it on the bed. He tried to pull it out of his pocket, but his body slipped slightly and his hand automatically gripped back onto the top of the railings as his phone slipped out of his pocket and fell all the way down to the ground below where it smashed on the floor, a scattering of unrecognisable pieces. Yes, it would be quick.

Very quick. He closed his eyes again and took a fresh breath, bracing himself for what was to come.

***

The minute the train approached London Paddington, Jess stood up, desperate to get off. All the way there she had felt the empty space next to her that should have been occupied. The emptiness greatly unsettled her, and she had felt a sense of dread creep over her. At one point it had become so consuming that she had locked herself in the train toilet and tried to call him, but he hadn't taken her call. Now his phone was going straight to voicemail and she didn't like the way she felt at all. She had a terrible feeling that something was going off. She had always followed her gut instinct, it was something that she relied upon in the army for survival; more than once it had saved her skin and multiple other soldiers in her platoon. Ignoring it whilst flying through the countryside on a high speed train in the opposite direction went against every fibre of her being.

Striding down the platform, she could hear Liam and Jane behind, discussing where they would need to go next in order to get to the palace. Right now, that didn't seem to matter at all. She was in her dress uniform, ready to go, yet at that moment nothing seemed to matter to her apart from getting to Rix. With every second that passed she felt more and more uneasy. Something wasn't right.

"Jess!" Liam shouted as she stopped underneath the departures board. "It's this way, I've already checked."

She was rooted to the spot, her eyes frantically scanning the board for the next train back to Reading. There it was. Ten minutes and she could go back. She could be at his flat within the next hour. She held her mobile to her ear again and tried to call him, but it went straight to voicemail.

She felt Jane's presence behind her. "Jess? Come on, it's this way. Liam's checked."

Jess turned to face them and shook her head. "I can't," she declared breathlessly.

Jane's brow furrowed in a concerned frown. "What do you mean?"

"I um... I can't. I need to go back."

"What for?" Jane asked, slightly exasperated. "We need to be at the palace in less than two hours. If you've forgotten something don't worry about it, I'm sure we can find a replacement somewhere on the way."

Some things aren't replaceable, thought Jess. She looked down at her uniform and shook her head. None of this really mattered at all. She should have known something was wrong when he had texted this morning, she should have gone straight there.

Jane placed her hands on both of Jess's shoulders. "Jess, talk to me. What's wrong?"

"It's Rix. Something's wrong. Really wrong."

"What do you mean?"

Jess hesitated. "He isn't taking my calls, now his phone's going straight to voicemail. This isn't like him. I'm really worried about him."

"He's probably fallen asleep!" Liam chimed in. "You said he wasn't well, he's probably gone back to bed."

Jess shook her head. "I've just got this feeling... I can't explain it. I'm sorry. I have to go."

Jane gently shook her shoulders. "You're not going anywhere. You deserve this award. And he wouldn't want you to miss it, would he? Not if he loves you. You won't get this chance again, Jess. You'll regret it for the rest of your life if you pass up this chance."

Jess looked around her, spotting the Reading-bound train which was pulling up at the platform. Every fibre of her body was screaming at her to get on the train and go back to him, but she couldn't deny that her mum was right. She wouldn't get this chance again. And if they were right, and he was in bed sleeping off whatever was wrong with him, she would probably regret missing the chance to receive this medal for the rest of her life.

"Put yourself first for a change," Jane reached up and straightened the cap on her head. "Please."

Chapter Twenty Two

The wind whistled through the trees vigorously. He opened his eyes and could see the branches waving above him ominously. Even just the effort of opening his eyes was too much and he closed them again, allowing his body to relax and his mind to wander. This time he was back right at the start, lying in a muddy field with a rifle he had barely known how to hold just six weeks ago. Yet here he was firing at targets on a training exercise. The brutal winter wind swept across the hills and he fastened his grip on his weapon, narrowing his eyes. It felt as though his whole life had been building up to this moment; he truly felt as though he had made it. Lying in a field with a real weapon, training for the job he had always wanted to do filled him with a warmth he could barely even explain, he couldn't even feel the frost below him on the ground.

His mind wandered again and this time he was jumping off the chinook at Camp Bastion, ready for his first tour of Afghanistan. He was in the zone and ready to go. He hoisted his bergen high on his back and followed the others away from the chinook and towards the tents where they would be sleeping until they were transferred to the FOB. He felt as if he was home. Watching the other soldiers on the base going about their business, adrenaline coursed through his veins. He couldn't wait to get stuck in.

Then he was in the sleeping tent at the

FOB, laughing and joking with Melon and Cal, exchanging stories about what they had done whilst on leave. He felt as though he had known them his whole life, not just the relatively short years during which they had served together. He thought of them as brothers - he would die for either one of them, and he knew they would do the same for him.

He could hear them now, calling him, and he used all the energy he had to try to sit up, but it felt as though his body was paralysed. Every inch of his body felt heavy as though he was being pressed to the floor by a tonne of lead. He opened his eyes again and now the trees were gone, all he could see was a bright light above him and he winced, trying to lift his arm to cover his eyes but he just didn't have the strength. The only thing he could make out was a strange pattern through the light above him, and he could hear the distant sound of voices as though he was under water. He thought it was Melon at first but then he realised it was a female voice and he squinted, trying his best to focus on the coloured shadows dancing around him.

"Jason?"

Finally, he managed to open his eyes wide enough to focus on the person standing over him and he realised that he didn't recognise them at all.

"He's back," he heard another voice from across his bed and turned his head to look. He heard the sound of hysterical tears from a distant corner of the room and he narrowed his eyes, trying to squint in that direction but they were too far away - he couldn't see.

"It's ok, Jason. Just relax. Can you squeeze my hand if you can hear me?"
He realised that someone was holding one of his hands and he squeezed it.

"Excellent, well done. Just relax, no need to do or say anything else right now."

He opened his mouth and tried to talk but no words would come out. Instead, he felt a trickle of dribble run out of the corner of his mouth and down his chin, before the woman who he now recognised to be a nurse wiped it away gently with a cloth. The two voices were talking in some sort of technical language he barely understood, and he relaxed, realising where he was. Suddenly, another face appeared in his view and he knew who it was straight away.

"Jason!"

It was his mum. Her eyes were filled with tears and she took his hand in hers, holding it to her cheek, nuzzling against it as if she was savouring the feel of his skin on hers.

"Thank God!"

He blinked her into focus. He barely recognised her. She looked as though she had aged about ten years. Her usual positive and friendly expression was replaced by one wrought with worry. He reached up with his free hand and haphazardly wiped the tears from her eyes. "Mum…"

The sound of his voice only served to make her cry even more and she reached over to him, running her hand through his hair just like she had when he was a little boy.

"I've been worried about you," she whispered, her eyes still leaking as her expression turned to a wrought smile. "I'm so sorry, Jason. We let you down. All of us."

He tried to shake his head but barely had the strength. Instead, he felt a single tear escape from the corner of his eye. "Help me, Mum," he begged.

***

Rix tried to let go, but he couldn't do it. Every time he closed his eyes, all he could see was Jess. He could almost feel the softness of her hair on his fingertips, taste the sweetness of her lips on his and smell the reassuring scent of her body in his nostrils. Eventually he swung his legs around off the railings and sunk to his knees on the balcony, bashing his head against the cold metal, sobbing out a torrent of grief.

Where could he go from here? For the past few months, his focus had been on his last day of service. Now that had passed he felt empty. It seemed as though there was nothing to pass time anymore, just the next time Jess would visit him. He hated being reliant on someone that much. He felt as though he was a cancer to her, leeching on to her existence and zapping all her energy. Every day she came to see him, he worried that it might be the last - that she might tell him she'd had enough and she wasn't coming back to him. She was going from strength to strength, she still had her career. On the other hand he was stuck in his flat, all alone during the week, with nothing but his exercise routine to give him any purpose.

He felt much better once he had sobbed out the tension that had been building within him for the last few months. Knowing that he couldn't actually sink much lower than this was strangely comforting. He no longer felt fragile, he no longer felt scared. He was at rock bottom, yet he still couldn't end it. Surely that had to mean something?

Wiping his eyes on the back of his hand, he reached up and grabbed onto the railings, steadying himself and reaching for the crutches he had left in the corner of the balcony. Slowly he made his way back inside and his eyes fell on the medals lined up on top of his uniform. He picked them up and ran his thumb along the smooth metal rim of each medal, then placed them back on the bed with a sigh. It hurt him that he would never acquire another one, but at that moment he realised that he had to be thankful for those he already had. Many soldiers never got the chance to be presented with more than one, and some didn't even return from their first tour. He thought about the young soldiers he lost and sank down on the edge of the bed, in a bout of fresh tears.

***

Jane waved, then headed inside the ballroom with Liam. Together with the other honours recipients, Jess stood in the lobby, still slightly shaky with nerves. It felt totally surreal to be there at last; she had waited for this day for months, ever since she had learnt about her recommendation back in June. And now here she was, in the lobby of Buckingham Palace, surrounded by beautiful paintings, ornate decor and one of the most beautifully decorated Christmas trees she had ever seen.

Once all the guests had been shown to the ballroom and the large wooden doors were closed firmly behind them, the recipients were shown to a nearby room which was equally as ornate. Jess gazed around at the historic decor and the magnificent paintings which adorned them, before the introductions began. It struck her that there was such a range of people in the room, they had all been nominated for completely different reasons. Only a few of the other guests had a military background but she met dozens of amazing people, many of whom were devoted to charities and their local communities. Amongst the group were an actor, a musician who was being recognised for his classical work, and an adorable lady who had been selling poppies for decades in all weathers. Jess spoke to her for quite a while. The lady, who called Olive, had driven an ambulance during World War 2, and Jess had been touched by the stories she had shared. Equally, she seemed very interested in Jess's more modern stories of the front line.

Once the mingling was over, they were briefed on what was going to happen and Jess took a deep breath, preparing to go in. She felt a gentle hand on her back and she turned to find Olive right next to her, encouraging her to go forward. She stood taller, inspired by Olive's courage. It was clear to see that Olive was absolutely delighted to be receiving her award, there wasn't an ounce of nervousness about her.

A list of names was read, and the two of them were to be called through in the first group of recipients. Together with the others in the first group they were led through several rooms. Jess allowed Olive to take the lead and followed her slowly and carefully towards the Ballroom. Suddenly her nervousness was replaced with excitement and she stood with the others in a room next to the Ballroom, where they would wait until their names were called. They were told to line up in order and Jess was about half way through. Olive was at the front and she turned back and gave Jess a quick wave, then disappeared through the doorway.

Every couple of minutes another person walked through the doorway and the queue shortened. Once Jess got to the front she straightened her cap, smoothed her hands down her skirt and stood just inside the doorway, listening to the sweet tunes played by the orchestra whilst waiting for her name to be called.

"Jessica Fern!"

Jess took a deep breath and looked up at the audience of friends and family who had their eyes on the Royal Dais at the front of the room. Her mum and Liam caught her eye and she flashed them a quick smile whilst walking towards it. Suddenly another pair of eyes in the audience caught hers, and she felt her heart skip a beat. She instantly recognised them. They were deep brown and powerful, and instantly she felt that connection, the same one she had felt many times before. It was him.

***

Once the ceremony was over, Jess waited anxiously with the other recipients while they were briefed again and led to the quadrangle, where they were to be reunited with their guests. Her heart was pounding in her chest, beneath the ornate Military Cross which she now wore proudly. They passed the beautiful Christmas tree again and then walked down the grand staircase, towards the double doors which led to the quadrangle. Jess could see a relatively large crowd milling around outside and she tried to catch a glimpse of Rix through the doorway, but she couldn't see him.

As she stepped off the red carpet and into the courtyard she scanned over the crowd quickly. Almost immediately, Jane and Liam spotted her and appeared by her side. Jane wrapped her arms around Jess and squeezed her tight, then held her at arm's length to look at the cross pinned to her uniform, next to her other medals. "I am so proud of you! What was it like to speak to the Queen?"

"She was lovely," Jess smiled. "It all feels surreal, to be honest."

"I bet!" Liam said. "Well done."

As Jane fussed over her medal, Jess looked around anxiously trying to catch sight of Rix. Clearly he hadn't met her family yet - and they were completely oblivious to the fact that he was here. She felt someone come up behind her and turned around expecting it to be him, but instead she came face to face with Olive, who was smiling proudly.

"Well done, Olive," Jess praised.

Olive held the box containing her medal proudly in her hands as if she was never going to let it go. "Thank you. And well done to you too, Jess."

Jess placed her hand gently on Olive's upper arm and turned back to Jane. "Mum, this is Olive."

"Hi, Olive," Jane leant forwards to shake her hand gently.

Olive beamed, gripping Jane's hand firmly. "Hello, dear. And you must be Liam."

Liam glanced at Jess in a slightly confused manner. "I am."

"We had a chat inside," Jess quickly explained. "Olive helped keep my nerves in check while we were waiting to go in!"

Jane and Liam smiled and nodded. By now Olive was flanked by two younger men, who Jess understood were her grandsons. She turned back to address Jane. "You must be very proud of your daughter."

Jane nodded. "I am. She amazes me every day."

Jess blushed slightly and then her eyes wandered across the courtyard again. She still couldn't see him.

"Are you alright, love?" Olive asked quietly. "You look like you've seen a ghost."

Jess nodded but she couldn't keep her eyes off the crowd. She shivered and wrapped her arms around her body protectively. She was beginning to think that she was going mad. She was certain that it had been him in the ceremony, yet all the other guests were here and there was no sign of him.

One of Olive's grandsons pulled a mobile from their pocket. "Would you like me to take some photographs, Nan?"

"Oh, yes please dear. Jess, would you care to join me?"

"Sure," Jess smiled, touched by her offer. She turned away from the rest of the crowd and stood with Olive on the steps, placing her arm around her fragile waist.

She smiled for the photo and it was then that she saw him. He was walking down the steps about twenty metres from where they stood, and when he caught her eye he stopped. For a moment they both stood and stared, sharing a moment between them. It was almost as though there was nobody else in the courtyard. Olive clocked on to what Jess was staring at almost immediately, and she gave her a quick squeeze with a mischievous glint in her eye. "Is that your boyfriend?"

"Um... sort of," Jess muttered, slightly flustered.

"I can see why you like him."

"He's not really… my boyfriend."

"But you would like him to be?"

Jess said nothing but she looked back to him again, he had taken a few steps down the stairs now and was standing at the bottom, his whole body facing her. She swallowed hard.

Whilst her grandson slipped his phone into his pocket and started talking to Jane and Liam, Olive moved closer to Jess and hissed in to her ear. "Life's too short. You have to tell people how you feel, before it's too late. Love comes first, careers second. Take it from someone who knows." Suddenly she looked sad and she paused, her eyes welling with tears. "My Sebastian. I didn't tell him until it was too late. He was the love of my life. We only had one day together before he was shot down."

"But… I thought you said your husband's name was Jim?"

"It was," Olive explained. "Sebastian was the one who got away. Who knows what might have been if I'd have only been brave and told him sooner. I told him to be careful before he left, because I loved him. And he said he'd be asking my father for my hand in marriage when he got back. But he never got the chance."

Jess placed her hand on Olive's forearm and rubbed it gently. Olive's eyes were glassy with tears and she looked lost in thought for a few seconds, then she shook her head and the familiar smile crept back onto her face.

"Sorry," she wiped a tear gently from her

left eye with a handkerchief. "Look at me getting all emotional."

"Don't be. I'm sorry. That you lost him."

"It was more than sixty years ago, now!" Olive exclaimed, the smile still on her face. "And I've had a good life. I have wonderful children, and grandchildren. I learnt my lesson. Never take anything or anyone for granted. And if you love someone, tell them. As soon as you know. None of us know when we'll run out of time."

Jess looked up again and he was still there, standing and staring at her and looking a little lost himself. She looked from him to Olive and then back again.

Olive nudged her. "Go! When you're taking your last breath, you won't be thinking about work. Only about the people you love."

Jess nodded and then started to make her way down the steps, putting one shaky foot in front of the other. Jane and Liam were engrossed in conversation and for a while they didn't even notice that she was gone. When she was close enough, she saw a nervous smile play on Rix's lips, and she broke into a smile herself, throwing her arms around him. She felt his hands come to rest on the small of her back and pull her body to his tightly, as their lips met and he kissed her slowly but meaningfully. As they kissed, it felt like they were the only two people in the courtyard, and their connection ran deeper than it ever had before.

Eventually he broke away and rested his forehead on hers, his chest heaving up and down with desire as he forced himself to break away. It was only then that they began to notice a few of the people around them watching, and Jess felt her cheeks flush slightly. He took her hands in his and stroked her palms gently with his thumbs, causing butterflies to dance around in her stomach. It was the first time that they had shown any affection towards each other in public, for risk of being seen by someone they knew from the platoon. Strangely, it felt like a relief.

She was unable to keep the smile off her face. "You came!"

"I did. I'm sorry about this morning. I need to tell you something…"

"No, I need to tell you something," Jess took a deep breath, remembering Olive's words just moments ago. She could feel Olive's gaze on her back and she knew she was watching, willing her to be honest with herself and with Rix.

She took a step back but kept her hands firmly in his. The people around them looked away and resumed their conversations but Jess knew her family were watching now, confused about what was going on. But she had to tell him, she had to tell him now. Olive was right, who knew how long each of them had left. She opened her mouth to talk, but he gently let go of her hand and reached across to examine the Military Cross which was pinned to her jacket.

"What did you want to tell me?" He asked, letting go of the medal and placing his hands back in hers.

She laced her fingers with his and

squeezed them tightly, looking up into his eyes. He still looked nervous and his eyes were a little sad. She reached up with one hand and cupped it around his jaw.

"I love you."

He hesitated for a couple of seconds and then a smile lit up his face. "I love you too."

Chapter Twenty Three

Later in the afternoon they left the palace, their fingers casually entwined. Rix took a deep breath of fresh air. The damp, foggy air had now been burned off by the winter sun and his chest felt a little looser; finally, he felt as though he could breathe more easily. It suddenly occurred to him that it had been several weeks since he had felt positive about something. He finally knew where he stood; with Jess, and in life - if he put his mind to it, he could do anything. He felt as though he had made weeks of progress in just a day; that morning he could never have imagined he could get himself to Buckingham Palace alone, let alone meet her family and tell her how he felt. It had been a good day. Although he knew that he would have to get over many bad days and obstacles yet, it felt like a major win for him after all the bad days he'd had. In truth, he couldn't actually remember when his last good day had been.

Passing through the palace gates, he squeezed Jess's hand absent-mindedly. They headed towards the Victoria Memorial and then stopped as Jess said goodbye to Olive and her grandsons.

"Take care," she wrapped her arms around Olive gently.

"And you, dear. I'll be thinking of you, when I see the soldiers on the news. And remember what I said."

"I'd love to keep in touch. Shall I give my number to one of your grandsons, and you can give me a ring sometime?"

"That would be nice," Olive smiled, as the man standing closest produced his mobile and keyed in Jess's number.

Whilst he waited, Rix sat on the edge of the memorial and massaged his leg just above the socket. He had been on his feet all day, and he was starting to feel it. He was strong on his prosthetic leg now, but it took a lot more effort to walk on it than a usual leg. It was something that he would have to work on. Once he had finished, he looked up to see Liam sitting down beside him.

"Alright?" He asked.

Liam nodded. "Yeah. You?"

"Fine, thanks."

Rix felt a little awkward around Jess's family; he had only met them a couple of hours ago, and their introduction hadn't been quite what they had planned.

Liam glanced at Rix nervously out of the corner of his eye. "Why don't you come back with us? Mum's got some beef in the slow cooker. It would be nice to get to know you better?"

Rix's gut reaction was to recoil at the thought of having to spend time with Jess's family for any longer than necessary - he was growing tired of being on his best behaviour, and it was his instant reaction when he thought of family events - but he stopped himself. He had to get himself out of the hole he was in, and he knew that in order to do that, he had to stop putting up barriers and just get on with things. "Thanks. That would be good."

"Great."

They sat in awkward silence on the ledge for a few moments, watching Jess interact with Olive. She laughed at something Olive said so hard that she tipped her head back to the sky and laughed as if she didn't have a care in the world. Rix felt a small smile creep to his lips. When she was happy it was like she lit up, and that was contagious - he couldn't help but feel more positive when she was around.

"Jess thinks a lot of you, you know," Liam said.

Rix turned to him and nodded. "Likewise."

Liam smiled. "I love my sister. She was almost like a second parent to me when I was growing up. She's a good person. The best."

Rix returned his gaze to Jess who was now hugging Olive. "She is. I owe her my life."

Liam nodded. "She told me what happened out in Afghanistan. Must have been tough."

"Yeah. You could say that."

Rix felt mildly irritated, as he always did, when a civilian tried to reason with how he must have felt in a situation they clearly couldn't comprehend. But he clenched his jaw and forced himself to let go of any trace of negativity. It wasn't Liam's fault; he was only young and he was doing his best to make conversation.

"Jess said that you saved her life," Liam

announced.

It took Rix by surprise. He raised an eyebrow and looked back at Jess who was now waving as Olive walked away with her grandsons. "It was more like the other way round."

"That's not what she said. Look… I just wanted to say thanks. For what you did out there."

"But I didn't…" Rix began, but Jess and Jane interrupted.

"Right, are you ready? Let's go home."

***

As Rix stepped across the threshold of the Fern household, an unfamiliar sensation hit him. It felt different to any home that he had ever stepped foot in. It felt warm and homely, a safe little bubble. He glanced at the photographs in frames which littered the wallpapered walls, and the big pile of shoes that were casually dumped by the front door. He could smell the mouth-watering scent of roast beef cooking in the slow cooker, just as Liam had promised, and his stomach growled. He realised that he hadn't eaten anything yet that day.

Jess kicked her shoes off in the hallway behind him. "That smells delicious! I'm just going to get changed, why don't you go and sit in the living room? I'll be down in a moment."

"Ok," Rix agreed, and followed Liam through the living room doorway.

Entering the living room, his eyes fell on the collection of photo frames which sat on the fireplace; there was one of Jess, her dad and presumably Liam as a baby. Next to it was the same photograph of her parents that he had seen under her pillow, what seemed like a lifetime ago in Afghanistan. He cleared his throat, taking a seat on one of the sofas, and glanced out of the window. He imagined Jess playing soldiers in the garden when she was little.

Liam kicked his shoes off and collapsed into an arm chair by the front window. "I am exhausted!" He picked up the TV remote and began to scroll through channels, looking for something to watch.

Suddenly, Rix realised why he felt confused in this house. He had lived in a handful of houses with his parents, yet none of them had ever felt like this. This house felt lived in, it felt welcoming and forgiving. He had never set foot in it before, yet he felt comfortable sitting on the sofa in the living room as though he had been there many times. The sound of footsteps coming down the stairs jolted him from his trail of thoughts and he turned just in time to see Jess in the doorway, now wearing a pair of casual jeans and a t-shirt, her hair loose around her face.

"Smells like dinner's ready. Come on. It's just through here."

***

Jess closed the bedroom door gently behind her and stood for a few seconds, watching as Rix unbuttoned his shirt slowly. He was in a world of his own as he got to the last button and slipped the shirt down over his shoulders, exposing his toned abs. She bit her lip and smiled softly. He pulled his socks off and then stood to remove his trousers, sliding them down from his hips before sitting on the edge of the bed again in just his underwear.

She watched him unclip his leg. Then he removed the socket carefully and massaged his stump, sighing with relief at the fresh air hitting his skin. Jess unclipped the button of her jeans and pulled them off. It was then that he looked up and saw her undressing. He leant forward to take her hands and pulled her towards him.

"Hey," she whispered softly, her bare legs brushing against his skin. He smiled and reached up to lift her t-shirt over her head, kissing her belly gently.

"I'm really glad you came today," she purred.

"Me too," he replied softly, trailing kisses upwards towards her ribs. He reached behind and unclipped her bra, then watched her slowly slip it off over her arms and drop it to the floor.

Rix took a deep breath as Jess lowered herself onto his lap, placing her hands either side of his face and kissing him gently. With his hands on her hips, Jess relaxed in his grip and kissed him more fiercely. It wasn't very long until she could feel just how much he wanted her. She ran her hands though his hair as he pulled her closer. With every second that passed she wanted him more and more, but she tried her best not to get carried away. It wasn't the first time they had got this close, and she didn't want to be frustrated if it didn't happen.

Slowly, he lay back on the bed and pulled her on top of him. Her breasts skimmed his chest and she continued to kiss him, his breathing becoming more rapid. He broke out of her kiss and trailed his lips down her neck and across her chest. She had to suppress the urge to lose control as his mouth got closer to her nipples and then he carefully eased her underwear down. Her heart was thumping in her chest and her breath was heavy on his mouth as it moved back up to hers and sealed around her lips, his tongue teasing hers.

He continued to kiss her as their bodies moved together as one. They had both waited a long time for this moment. He sat up again and Jess ran her fingertips down his spine right to the bottom of his back and then back up again and he arched his back, using all the energy he had to stay in control. Then he felt her fingers dig into his buttocks as she pulled him even closer and he couldn't help but groan. He felt like his nerves were on fire - he had spent months feeling nothing and now all of a sudden he was overcome with pleasure and emotion all in one.

"I love you," He whispered against her neck and kissed her again, causing her to throw her head back with pleasure.

"I love you too."

She brought her gaze down to his so that their eyes were just centimetres apart. Her nose brushed against his and she pressed her lips to his again, parting her mouth to allow his tongue to dance with hers.

Neither of them could get enough of the other, and by the time they had finished they were exhausted. Wrapped in the bed sheets they lay together, with Jess's head on Rix's chest. She felt herself being lulled to sleep by the warmth of his body and the strong beat of his heart under her cheek. He held his arm around her firmly, and it suddenly dawned on him that this was the first time he had ever felt this way about anyone. He had slept with a lot of women, but he had never found one that he genuinely cared for this much. He couldn't remember feeling besotted with anyone before. It scared him a little to know that he had so much to lose.

Jess sighed contentedly. Within a minute or two her breathing levelled, and he knew that she was asleep. He kissed the top of her head gently and ran his fingertips down her arm, settling his hand on her hip. "I really do love you. More than you'll ever know."

She continued to breathe softly, her cheeks still flushed from their encounter, and he knew for sure that she was asleep.

"I did a really stupid thing this morning," he admitted. "But you saved me, again, like you always do." He smiled softly. "We wasted so much time, didn't we? I wish I'd just told you how I felt in the beginning."

Jess stirred slightly and moved her arm to cross his body, nuzzling her cheek against his chest. He nuzzled the top of her head with his chin and closed his eyes, breathing in the minty scent of her shampoo and the raw scent of her body. At that moment Rix knew that he would never, ever let her go. Not until the day he died.

***

Rix woke up to the sound of running water out in the hallway and he opened his eyes slowly, allowing them to get used to the light which was filling the room through a gap in the curtains. He yawned, glancing adoringly down at Jess who was still sleeping peacefully on his chest. His muscles felt stiff from lying in the same position for too long and he tried to stretch without waking her, but before he had finished he felt her stir and then she opened her eyes.

"Morning," she smiled instantly.

"Morning. Sleep well?"

"Like a log," she yawned, then she smiled. "Not surprised after last night."

Whilst they woke up properly, they lay together for a few minutes. Rix's happiness about the night before was soon replaced with apprehension as he mulled over all the things he ought to say in his head. He knew that he had to be honest with Jess about how he had been feeling. He knew that he wasn't right, and he needed to get help. He had tried burying his feelings and getting on with things, but that hadn't got him very far.

"About yesterday… I'm really sorry I let

you down."

"You didn't. You were there. That's all that matters. It's not your fault you weren't feeling well, anyway."

"No, it isn't. I should have told you the truth."

"What do you mean?"

Rix hesitated. It was really hard to put into words exactly how he had been feeling. But he knew that he had to tell her, because if he didn't then she wouldn't understand.

"I... haven't been feeling great lately. I thought I'd feel better in time, but... I've just been feeling worse."

Jess looked up at him and waited for him to go on. She knew that he had been struggling, but it was still hard to hear it from him.

"I think there's something wrong with me. I feel like I'm going mad. I'm still alive... they're not. And I don't even feel grateful. Sometimes..." he closed his eyes because it made him feel guilty just thinking it, let alone saying it out loud. "Sometimes... I feel like they're the lucky ones. At least it was over for them in an instant. But I'm still here, every day going through this, this is my life now."

Jess lifted herself up on one elbow and lay next to him, watching as his eyes filled with tears.

"And I don't understand why I feel like that because... because I still have you. And I do love you, Jess, I do *really* love you. But when I allow myself to be happy even for a moment it hits me all over again and I feel like I won't ever shake this feeling. It's always there. Like my whole life has been taken away from me and I don't know how to climb out of this hole. And I want to, I really, *really* want to. But I don't know how."

Jess felt her own eyes fill with tears and she took his hand in hers, squeezing it firmly. "Listen to me. You need to get help, we'll get you some help, ok? And you're not going mad, you're not well. But it will get better. And I'll be there for you, every step of the way."

He swallowed hard, trying to force away the lump that had grown in his throat. "I just want to close my eyes and it all be an awful nightmare. I don't know how to be me without the army. It's all I've ever known. How can I get back to being that man when I've lost all I have ever known?"

"I don't know," Jess answered, honestly. "Maybe you won't ever be that man again… but I love you as you are, do you understand? I love *you*, Rix. And since we got back, I've fallen in love with you more and more every day. That isn't because of the colour sergeant you were. It's because of the man you are now. And you just need to find a way to live with who you are now, and what you have now. And one day that will feel normal. And you'll feel happy again."

He sat up and pulled her towards him, burying his head into her neck and breathing in her smell. She held him tightly and rubbed her hands across his back soothingly.

"I almost did something stupid yesterday," he sniffed. "It was selfish and I'm sorry."

She continued to hold him close. "What?"

"I thought about ending it," he admitted, and upon feeling her tense up he added quickly, "I sat on the balcony of my apartment, and I almost jumped. But I didn't. I chose not to."

Jess's heart was thumping so hard in her chest that she felt a little dizzy. "Why would you do that? After everything you've been through, after every battle you've ever faced?"

He choked back fresh tears. "I don't know... because I'm tired... exhausted... because I feel like I'm dragging you down. Because I feel like I'm dragging everyone down. Everything that I used to do without a second thought seems so... so much effort. I just want to start living again. But it just seems so hard."

"You're not dragging anyone down. Why would you think that? Don't you ever think that, do you hear me?"

He nodded and then she pulled him close to her again, holding his face to her chest. He could feel her heart pounding in her chest and he knew that he had upset her. As he often did, he felt guilty. "I want to get better," he wiped his tears on the back of his arm. "I promise, I do. I want to have a life with you."

"I know. And that's what I want too, more than anything."

"What do I do? I want to get better, but I don't know how."

She wiped a stray tear from her cheek and held him at arm's length, gripping his arms firmly. "On Monday, you need to see your GP.

You need to be 100% honest about how you're feeling. I'll come with you, if you like?"

"You need to be back at barracks though."

"I'm sure they can cope without me for one day. Your mental health is far more important."

He shook his head. "I need to do this on my own. And I will, I promise. I'll make the appointment, and I'll go. I have to do this. I know I can't go on like this."

Jess nodded. "Ok."

Rix took a deep, shaky breath. "I just want to get better. I want to be there for you, like you are for me. I don't want you to feel like you have to stay with me because I'm some sort of... pathetic head case. It's not exactly what you signed up for, is it?"

Jess shook her head. "I don't feel like that at all. I *love* you, I want to be with you. Do you think you're the first soldier to feel like you do? Because you're not. And the support is there, you just need to ask for it. You need to be honest. If you carry on lying to yourself and other things won't get better."

He nodded. He knew that she was right. It just seemed like the most impossible task, admitting how he felt to a doctor when for his entire adult life, he had been taught to suppress his emotions and be strong. Put up and shut up. But he reminded himself, where were the army now? They had been brilliant after he had lost his leg, giving him the best medical care possible and a state of the art prosthetic leg. But now he had been discharged, where were they? He was in NHS care now, he had no access to any of the medical professionals that he had worked with for the first few months of his recovery. His mental health had barely been brushed over during the few sessions he'd had - the psychologist had pretty much taken his word for the fact that he was fine. It felt like a massive step backwards to admit that actually, he wasn't fine at all, but he knew that it was necessary because if he continued to bury his feelings he would never get over it. He owed more to himself than that.

Chapter Twenty Four
Nine months later

Jase stood by his bed, staring at the suitcases which were all packed up and ready to go by the door. This was the bed that he had slept in for the last six months since leaving hospital. This unit had put him back together. He had arrived a shell of his former self, ravaged by PTSD, drug addiction and alcohol dependency. He was clean now, and although he knew he would probably never be fully over his PTSD it was something that he had learned to cope with. He was nervous to be leaving and he knew that he still had a very long road ahead of him. But the staff said that he was ready, and his parents wanted him home. He wasn't really sure what he wanted.

Unfortunately, it had been too little too late as far as the army were concerned, and he had been discharged a couple of months previously. It had been a major setback for Jase as for the first few months in the unit, all he had focussed on was getting himself better so that he could return to the army. Finding out that he would never be returning had been a major blow to him. What was the point in anything if he couldn't do the job that he loved? But slowly, he had come around to the idea of a fresh start and he knew that he had to make the best of it - it was what Melon and the others would have wanted.

He heard approaching footsteps in the

corridor, and the voices of his parents making small talk with one of the nurses. They had remortgaged their house in order to fund his place at the unit, having been faced with the possibility of their son being sent home after he was discharged from the hospital. At the time he was still in the grips of PTSD and all he wanted to do was get home and grab the nearest bottle to blot out the living nightmare that had become his life. They had pretty much forced him inside the unit, and he had to admit that they had made the right decision. As much as it pained him to think about it, he was quite sure that he would be dead by now if he hadn't have had the unit for support.

As his parents reached the door of his room, he took a last look around, then turned his head to the doorway where they were standing.

"Are you all ready to go, son?" George asked.

"Of course he is! Just in time for his birthday," Elena opened her arms and pulled her son towards her.

Jase plastered on a fake smile through gritted teeth. He would be twenty five tomorrow and what did he have to show for it? He had not a penny to his name, having spent every pound that he had on alcohol and drugs. He had no job, and in the next couple of hours he would be back at home with his parents. He had no friends, no girlfriend and nothing to look forward to.

"It's alright son," George clapped him on the back once Elena had released him from her grip and begun to fuss around his bags. He looked at Jase knowingly, it was almost like he could read him. "Nothing will seem as bad once you're back home, you'll be back to normal before you know it."

Jase didn't even know what normal was now. He could barely even remember the person he had been before all of this. He knew that his parents wanted him to get back to normal so that they could all move on, and after all that he had done he felt like he owed it to them, but he just didn't know if he could do it. The thought of letting them down again after everything was almost too much to bear. The one thing he wanted, to go back to the family he had in the army, was out of his reach. Half of the people he longed for were dead and the others wouldn't let him back in their lives, not after the way he had behaved towards them.

Once he got to the car, Jase helped to load his suitcases into the boot and then closed it with a satisfying thump. He took one last look back at the unit, the building where he had spent his darkest moments reliving the events that had set off the monster of PTSD inside him. He had hated it at first, and counted down the days until he would be assessed and might be able to leave. But now he was here, leaving after all this time, he almost wished that he could stay longer. He just didn't feel ready for life on the outside.

***

Rix sat in his car outside the train station

expectantly, glancing at the clock on the dashboard. He had been sitting in his car for twenty minutes, and he was growing impatient. It was 13:58 and the train was supposed to arrive at the platform at 13:50. Where was she? He clenched his jaw and pulled his phone out of his pocket, scrolling through the messages that she had last sent him; maybe he had got the wrong time? But then he realised that he was right - she should be here by now.

A small crowd of people began to exit the station and he sat up straighter in his seat, examining the crowd for her familiar face. The crowd had almost dispersed by the time he saw her turn the corner, her bergen perched on her back and her cap still balanced on her head. His excitement soared as he opened the car door and stepped out, then headed in her direction. She lifted her head and saw him, and a smile spread across her face. Just like the day she had seen him at Buckingham Palace, she marched towards him as though there was nobody else around. He opened his arms and she fell into them, burying her head in his neck and savouring the smell of him that she had missed more than she ever thought possible for the past three months.

"I missed you," he muttered.

"I missed you too," she pulled out of his grip momentarily, to allow access to his lips. Then she pressed her lips to his and kissed him deeply, making up for lost time. Leaving him had been harder than she had ever imagined. For the past few weeks in particular, missing him had become almost unbearable. She had found herself counting down the days until she would see him again.

Once they broke away from each other, Rix laced his arm around her waist and secured it firmly. "Let's go home."

Jess sighed. "Yeah. I can't wait to have a long, hot shower."

Rix couldn't help but smile at the thought of that, and he glanced at her out of the corner of his eye while leaving the station car park. She glanced back at him and put her hand on his thigh, squeezing it gently.

"Oh… you've gone the wrong way," she said, as he took the second exit off the roundabout instead of the third. "Mum's is that way…"

"Oh yeah. Being with you is a little bit distracting."

"Shut up!" She grinned, and leant her head on her outstretched palm, with her elbow leant against the door of the car. "I'm exhausted."

"Long journey, huh?"

"Yeah. And I just haven't really slept properly for days with the excitement of seeing you."

"Nothing to do with the distant sound of gunfire when you were trying to get to sleep, then?" He joked.

Jess shook her head. "No, it wasn't like that really. It was just a straightforward, humanitarian mission. A world away from Afghan."

"Have a power nap. I won't take it

personally, I promise."

She yawned and nodded, then closed her eyes momentarily, intending only to rest them. But the gentle purr of the engine and the familiar smell of Rix next to her lulled her to sleep, and within a minute or two her breathing was steady. Rix smiled. Perfect timing. This made it even easier.

He continued to drive down the country lane which led out of town, brimming with excitement. He had been planning this moment for weeks. He had not expected it to all tie up together as perfectly - when he had received the call from his solicitor two weeks ago to confirm that it would all happen yesterday, he could hardly believe it. It almost felt like it was meant to be, the day before Jess returned from deployment. It had been a very busy twenty four hours, rushing around and getting the things he needed to make it just perfect. He had to admit that he had got a little carried away with the plan, and it had taken a lot longer than he had originally thought. But, just in the nick of time he had done it, and now all he had to do was get her there and surprise her.

Luck was on his side, and she slept for the rest of the short journey. As he turned down the road and up onto the driveway he grinned, glancing across at her sleeping face. He turned the car off and removed the keys, and the sound of the door opening woke her up. Momentarily groggy, she tried to work out where she was. He watched her frown, her eyes focusing on the front of the house she didn't recognise.

"Where are we? What's going on?"

"We're home. Come on."

He climbed out of the car and fumbled with his keys in the lock, his hands shaking slightly with excitement. Once the door was open he turned around to find her stood behind him, still looking confused.

"What do you mean? Whose house is this?"

"It's mine. Ours, if you want it to be."

"I... I don't understand," she replied, but the small smile which was playing on her lips gave it away that she did. She just didn't know whether to believe it or not.

Rix took her hand and pulled her through the front door with him. Everything was clean and fresh and new. The house had only been finished three weeks ago, and everything was spotless. He'd had a busy day yesterday moving furniture in with the help of Jane and Liam, and now thanks to their help in choosing some homely touches, it felt like a home.

"Are you being serious? This isn't a joke?"

"Deadly serious."

He steered her towards the kitchen at the front of the house. Catching sight of a brightly coloured oven glove and tea towel hanging from the handle of the oven, she couldn't help but smile. It was a far cry from the sparse appearance of his flat. This house actually felt like a home.

Jess smiled, looking around at the photos he had hung on the wall in frames. There were photos of them together and photos of her with her mum and Liam. "I can't believe this!"

"Come through here," he instructed, leading her back out down the hallway towards the rear of the house.

They walked through to the living room and Jess's eyes widened at the large, plush sofa which dominated the space, scattered with colourful cushions. She looked around and her eyes fell on a scattering of photo frames on shelves in the corner of the room. She studied them for a couple of seconds, picking one up and holding it close to her heart. Rix stood a few steps behind her while her eyes filled with tears and she sniffed, trying to hold them back. "You did this for me?"

He nodded. "Yeah."

She felt her bottom lip wobble and then she turned around and flung herself into his arms, the photo frame still firmly in her hand. "Just when I thought I couldn't love you anymore," she tried and failed to suppress her tears.

"I knew you'd want to feel close to him," he explained softly. "Even when you're not at your mum's."

"Thank you."

She pulled out of his arms and set the photograph carefully back on the shelf, in pride of place. It was the same photograph of the three of them that sat on the hearth at her mum's house.

"Thank you so much."

"Do you want to take a look upstairs?"

She nodded and took his hand, allowing

him to guide her back down the hallway and up the stairs. The carpet was soft and spongy under her feet and she enjoyed the freedom of not wearing her boots. Upstairs were two bedrooms and a bathroom with a large walk in shower, as well as an en-suite to the master bedroom.

"I literally can't wait to get in that shower," she raised an eyebrow, opening the bathroom door. Two towels hung on the shiny towel rail and even her favourite shampoo and shower gel were sat on the shelf next to it.

Rix leant one arm against the doorframe and looked her up and down suggestively. "I might have to join you."

Jess gravitated towards him and her eyes sparkled as she got within kissing distance. He savoured the look of pure happiness within them. She began to unbutton her uniform suggestively. "Yeah?"

He raised his arm to take the beret off her head. "You really are irresistible in uniform."

"Mmm?" She mumbled, pulling him inside the bathroom and shutting the door behind them.

Chapter Twenty Five
31st August 2011

As the bell of the nearby Church sounded over the town of Wootton Bassett, the Union flag blew slightly in the breeze one last time against the backdrop of the yellow sky, whilst the sun set over the slate roofs of the nearby buildings. The flag was surrounded by thousands of people who had, for various reasons, come to pay their respects. A sea of heads stretched across the entire high street, from the row of shops on one side of the road right to the other. Civilians, soldiers and veterans stood side by side, all of their attention focused on the Mayor and chaplain who each read a fitting tribute to the soldiers lost since the ceremonies had begun.

Whilst the sun edged down further turning the sky shades of pink and purple, the brass band began to play. With the National Anthem playing poignantly in the background, the flag was slowly lowered down the pole one last time, and Rix watched it with a lump in his throat. This wasn't just closure for the families and friends of the 345 soldiers who had died and passed through the little market town on their last journeys. It was closure for him personally, too; closure from all he had lost in the army, and all of the friends and colleagues he had lost whilst deployed. Once the flag was down the music stopped, and for a good few minutes the crowd stood in contemplation whilst the flag was blessed, silent apart from the occasional cry of an infant, remembering the soldiers it represented.

The crowd emotionally broke into applause and tears, and Rix felt Jess's hand slip through his. It had been her idea to come. When they had heard about the sunset ceremony on the radio the week before, she had asked whether he thought it might help. Coming to Wootton Bassett for the repatriation ceremony of their fallen soldiers had been a turning point for his mental health; he had revisited it many times during his counselling sessions and had come to realise that his problems hadn't just started when he lost his leg. He had been vulnerable long before then, he just hadn't realised it at the time. Coming here and closing that door in such a fitting way allowed him the chance to open another one. And that part had been his idea.

He leant down and kissed the top of Jess's head gently, holding her close to him. Although things were looking up for him, the nightmare wasn't yet over. Every time she left, he worried incessantly that the next time he saw her she might be in a hearse covered in a flag, passing down a street full of somber onlookers. He was working hard to gain more control over his feelings but he wasn't sure that the worry would ever really go away. Despite that, he knew that he had to let her go; it was what she wanted to do after all, and she was brilliant at it.

"Are you ready?" She asked softly as the crowd began to disperse around them.

"Yeah," he nodded, and they began to

342

walk back down the high street together.

To any passerby, they looked like any other couple. Rix was wearing trousers; to the naked eye it wasn't obvious that one of his legs was made from metal. He was used to it now, and he could do many of the things that he enjoyed before he had lost it. He was able to drive, cycle, and walk long distances. He could even run quite well with it. The strange thing was that his mental health had been the main barrier to him getting on with his life, even though all other people saw was the fact that he had lost a leg. That had been difficult. He had come to realise that most of the reason he had suppressed what was going on inside his head for this long was because he was afraid of what other people might think, or that they wouldn't understand. He had felt as though the fact that he had only lost one leg meant he should be grateful. There were many soldiers who had lost two, three or even four limbs and they were coping just fine. What gave him the right to mourn the loss of just one limb? He still had so much going for him and he had felt quite selfish feeling the way that he had.

The private counselling sessions with his psychiatrist, which he had paid for with a large lump of his compensation, had helped him to realise that he had just as much right to mourn what he had lost as more severely injured soldiers. He was still unable to serve - he had still lost a huge part of himself when he had been discharged. Learning to let go of that disappointment and bitterness had been one of the best things that he had gained from the sessions, together with the ability to say goodbye to the person he was before and accept that he would never be that person again. Once he stopped trying to claw that person back and simply allowed himself to be Rix - not Colour Sergeant Mellor - he had begun to heal. And now, almost a year and a half after he had lost his leg he finally felt as though he was truly looking forward to the future.

Once they reached the door, Rix swung it open and held it for Jess, just like he had last time they were here. "Are you ready?"

She nodded, trembling slightly with nerves. "Yeah. I think so."

She stepped over the large step and felt Rix's hand on the small of her back as he followed her inside the pub. She spotted them instantly, sitting in a cosy spot in a corner by one of the bay windows. They were engrossed in conversation, but Gav saw her straight away and his face broke into a smile as they approached him.

"Hi," Jess smiled, wrapping her arms around him in a strong hug. When they reached the table, Raj and Jase stood up too.

"Look at you!" Jess exclaimed, admiring Raj's elite appearance. She hadn't seen him since he had left the platoon at the end of their first tour of Afghanistan, and she barely recognised him. "You're proper special forces now!"

"Isn't he just!" Gav said. "I was just saying the same thing!"

"Thank you very much," Raj grinned, puffing up his chest comically which made them all laugh, breaking the ice perfectly.

Once the greetings were over, Jess sat down at the table as Rix went to buy a round of drinks. She slipped off her jacket and hooked it over the back of her chair, her gaze wandering back to Rix who was waiting at the bar. Her mind drifted back to the last time they were here, and she remembered how she felt when he had squeezed her shoulders, sat just metres away from the very spot she was sitting now. She remembered how vulnerable she had felt then, how guilty for losing all those soldiers. How his company had made her feel better. Suddenly she felt eyes on her and she snapped out of her day dream, back to the rest of her former section who were all looking at her intently.

"Are you alright, Jess?" Gav asked.

"Yeah. Sorry, I was miles away."

As Gav and Raj continued with their conversation around her, Jess looked up and her eyes caught Jase's. He was sat silently in the corner, his hand clamped around his empty glass. Physically he looked better than the last time she had seen him, but his eyes still looked dull and empty. She pressed her lips together and then slid along to the empty chair next to her.

"How are you doing? I'm sorry I haven't called lately. I was away for a few months, you know what comms can be like…"

Jase looked up at her. "I'm surprised you want to talk to me at all. The way I behaved

345

towards you."

Jess reached forwards to take his hand in hers. "Of course I want to talk to you. You're still my mate, Jase. You always will be. I'm just sorry I wasn't there for you when..."

"It's not your fault," he interrupted as her voice trailed off. "I wouldn't have let you in even if you tried."

Remembering the state he had been in last time she had seen him conscious, lost in his own angry world, full of resent and contempt for just about everyone around him, Jess felt sad and regretful.

"It should be me apologising. And I really am sorry. I should never have spoken to you like I did. But it wasn't me, you know. I wasn't myself..."

"I know," she squeezed his hand tightly. "How are you feeling now?"

He contemplated her question for a few moments, then shrugged gently. "I don't know how to explain it. Numb... I guess. Don't get me wrong, I feel a lot more... normal... than I did back then. But... I don't know. I just don't really *feel* anything."

"Have you spoken to your doctor about it?"

"Yeah. It's just part of being on so many anti-depressants. Eventually I should be able to try weaning off them. But for now I just have to accept it. I'm doing ok. I have a job now, at least. Things are a lot better with my family."

"That's brilliant," Jess replied, wholeheartedly. "What are you doing?"

She saw him smile then. It was a small, fleeting smile, but she still saw it.

"I'm working in the local vets. Just helping out on reception... but it's something. It gives me a reason to get out of bed. And the animals are better company than anyone I've ever worked with, so..."

He smiled properly then, and Jess nudged him playfully. "Oh, cheers! And there was me thinking you might have missed me!"

"I do. I do miss you. All of you."

"I miss you too," she said sincerely, suddenly distracted by footsteps behind her and the sound of a tray being placed on the table.

"Here we are."

Rix distributed the drinks. Jess accepted her glass of wine gratefully, and took a sip whilst the others took theirs from the tray. Then he sat down next to her and she felt his hand rest on her leg under the table reassuringly. She enjoyed the warmth of his body against hers whilst they listened to Raj talking about the beastings he had endured whilst on his special forces training.

"Anyway, what are you doing with yourself these days, Mellor?" Gav asked, changing the subject once Raj came up for air and became engrossed in his orange juice.

"I just got a new job, actually," Rix answered positively, and Jess felt her heart swell with pride just as it had when he had received the call just a couple of days previously. "There's a facility nearby which has recently been set up to

347

help veterans who have lost limbs and need something to help them move forwards... not just physically, but mentally too. They needed someone to work with the veterans, not as a psychologist but physically, setting up challenges and activities for them. That's where I come in."

"That sounds great, mate," Gav sipped his pint. "How did you hear about it?"

"Jess noticed an advert," Rix smiled at her. "She said that I should give it a go. I didn't see the point, I thought they would want someone qualified... but she said I would regret it if I didn't try. Anyway, they offered me it later that day."

"You'll be brilliant. They'll be lucky to have you."

"Thanks. It means a lot, mate."

"It's nice that you stayed in touch," Gav said, obliviously. "And I'm glad that everyone could make it. I was saying to Jess a few weeks ago on base, we should have done this before, but as usual... life got in the way."

"Yeah. It is."

Rix's fingers brushed the side of Jess's hand under the table and she felt her cheeks flush red as her heart began to pound. She knew it was time. They had to know, they had a right to know. But part of her was scared, not knowing how they would react.

"Actually, there was something that we wanted to tell you all," she began, finding the courage to speak up. It had been Rix's idea to tell them today, to finally get their relationship out in the open. Now she needed to show him her commitment too. "We um... Rix and I. We're together."

She felt three sets of eyes on her, and took a deep breath to steady her nerves. "We've been together for a few months. But I wanted to tell you all in person. Nothing happened when we were serving together, it wasn't until I got back from Afghan after he left us that we both realised how we felt. We got back in touch and... things went from there, really. Neither of us were expecting it but... it just sort of happened."

Everyone was silent for a few moments, and Jess desperately looked around, waiting for someone to say something. Eventually, Raj broke the silence. "Congratulations! That's great news."

"Yeah," Gav joined in. "It is. Sorry, I'm just surprised! But I'm pleased for you both. You deserve to be happy."

Jess smiled with relief and gratitude. "Thank you. We really are. And I'm sorry I didn't tell you before. We were just taking it slowly... and we didn't want anyone to get the wrong end of the stick. And we didn't want to say anything to anyone unless we were sure." She turned to Jase, who was sitting very quietly in the corner. "Jase? Are you ok?"

He nodded slowly. "Yeah. I'm just er... going to get some air."

She watched him slide out of his chair and march across the pub to the front door. Rix began to get out of his seat to follow him, but Jess shook her head.

"No, you stay. I'll go and speak to him."

He squeezed her hand reassuringly and then she left the table.

Jess followed Jase towards the door and then outside, where she found him standing against the wall of the pub, his back leant against it. "Jase…"

He glanced at her and she noticed that his eyes were filled with tears.

"Jase," she repeated, more softly this time. "I'm sorry, I didn't want to upset you. But we wanted to tell you the truth."

Jase shifted from one foot to the other awkwardly, his eyes firmly fixed on the floor, then he looked up at her and sniffed. "Don't be. I'm sorry. I don't know what's wrong with me. It's pathetic."

She pulled him into a hug. "You're not pathetic at all."

He relaxed in her grip for a few moments and cleared his throat, trying not to embarrass himself any further by crying. Eventually she let him go and they stood together, both of their backs leaning against the wall.

"Does he make you happy?" Jase asked eventually, turning to face her.

"Yeah. Yeah, he does."

"Do you love him?"

Jess paused for a moment, but then she nodded. "Yeah, I do. Like I've never loved anyone."

"Then I'm happy for you. You deserve to be happy. My mum said you came to visit, when I was in hospital."

"I did," Jess nodded.

She could still see him clearly in her mind, lying in the hospital bed, hooked up to machines and tubes after his accident. She had seen catastrophic injuries more times than she could count, but for some reason seeing him lying there, completely helpless and in such a state had got to her more than she would have expected. She had felt angry. Angry that he had been let down this badly, by the Army that he had given so much of himself to. He had been sent back from Afghanistan because he needed help, and everyone involved in his care from that moment on had failed him. She had later learned from his parents that he had been struggling for months and months, and instead of helping him his superiors had called the police when, out of desperation, he had deserted the army for want of an escape.

"It was hard to see you like that. Why didn't you ask for help?"

He shrugged. "I don't think I even realised how bad things had got. I was in such a state... I didn't know what day of the week it was, all I could think about was my next hit. I felt like I had lost my mind. I saw them calling me... Melon and Jay and Cal... and I just wanted to be with them. I thought it was the right thing to do. I didn't even know what I was doing."

She nodded. "And what about now? Honestly?"

"I feel... a million miles away from how I

felt then. Honestly. I can't say that I feel great every day, because I'd be lying. Some days it's a struggle to get out of bed. But I do know that I never, ever want to be in that place again."

"Good. Because there are loads of people who love you, Jase. And they want to help you. You just have to ask."

She hugged him again, straightening up with a deep breath and wiping a couple of tears that had formed in the corners of her eyes. "Right. Let's go back in. I want to hear all about this job of yours."

"Ok," he smiled weakly and with her arm around his shoulders, they began to walk back towards the pub door together.

***

The door closed behind them with a definitive bang. Rix glanced back through the window at their friends who were still sat around the table, finishing their drinks.

Jess wrapped her arms around her as the fresh night air whipped through her hair. "That went a lot better than I expected."

"Yeah," Rix turned back to her and put his arm casually around her waist with a smile. "Yeah, it did."

They began to walk down the side road together, back towards the high street where they would catch a taxi back to the station. They had, of course, made this journey before; they knew where they were going, and their minds were clearer than they had been the last time. The walk to the high street seemed to take longer than Jess remembered, but there was a small line of taxis waiting. Within a few minutes they were sat in the back of the taxi, this time hand in hand, passing out of the town and towards the station, fields flashing past the windows.

Once they got to the station they climbed out of the taxi and then made their way to platform two. It felt strange being back there again, sitting on the same bench that they had sat two years ago. Jess remembered the way her stomach had turned with nervous excitement when he had taken her hand on this very bench, during their heart to heart. She edged her hand over to his and squeezed it. He looked deep in thought too. She wondered if he was lost in the same memory.

"What are you thinking about?" She asked softly.

He smiled, and ran his thumb along the side of her hand gently. "Last time we were here, we sat on this bench, right here, together. And I wanted so much just to kiss you."

She smiled as the familiar announcement came over the speakers, just as it had the last time they were here. But this time they stood together and walked over to the platform, hand in hand. This time, they would be going home together. It felt almost symbolic, this was probably the last time they would visit Wootton Bassett, the town where it had all begun for them in so many ways. And here they were, saying goodbye to it for the last time, together.

"Two minutes," Rix mumbled.

The tracks began to hiss and the lights from the front of the train lit up the tracks. It approached the platform and then slowed to crawling pace, before coming to a standstill. The doors made their familiar bleep and Rix reached forwards to press the button.

The doors opened in front of them and they stepped onto the train. It was late and the carriage was quite empty, but neither of them made any move to head towards the empty seats. Instead, they stood just inside the double doors as the whistle blew outside on the platform, with Jess's back pressed against the wall of the train. The doors closed in front of them with a clunk but neither of them seemed to notice. Rix leant forward and brushed his fingers down her cheek, their eyes locked together. He leant into her and his lips brushed hers, then he leant his forehead against hers and closed his eyes, savouring her scent. With her hand gently cupped around his jaw, Jess tilted her head and kissed him, her lips soft against his as they danced together.

As the train began to pull away from the platform they continued to kiss, their bodies pressed together and their hearts thumping against each other rhythmically, just like the sound of the train chugging along down the tracks, taking them back home, together.

Printed in Great Britain
by Amazon

40858105R00203